Not Yet...

By D Christy Eves

To Shirley
Enjoy the book and thank you
for your support. :)

CARMEL COAST PUBLISHING ENTERPRISES
WASHINGTON, DC

NOT YET...

Published by Carmel Coast Publishing Enterprises

978-0-9829979-4-9

Cover Art by Mark J. Houston

Cover Design by CCPE Graphics

Printed in the United States of America

Not Yet...

By

D Christy Eves

Dedication

O for a muse of fire…

For Julie and Kenny

DChristy Eves

Freshman Year

1

MEMORY IS A STRANGE ANIMAL making its way through your past. It has the scent of truth on its breath, yet it also grins and lies. The first thing I remember is how green the grass was, how hot and fresh the air, and how thick the trees with leaves and grey moss.

We took I-75 south until Tifton, Georgia, about an hour north of Florida. The transition from the interstate to Highway 319 was my first clue that I was a long way from dirty, urban Detroit. The trees reached across the narrow road to tangle with each other, their canopy of moss blocking the sun. The live oaks looked like women slowly writhing, and I turned my head to see if I could catch them moving.

It was 1993 and I had just landed in the Bible Belt South on the campus of Florida Agricultural and Mechanical University. Every afternoon, without warning, the sky would open up and release a furious storm that I thought would close the town. Instead, it raged for about an hour, and then the sun would reappear with such power that you could barely tell there had even been a trickle of rain. Nature reminded you each day that its beauty had a cost.

My parents drove me down the long sixteen hour drive from Detroit to Tallahassee for school. My father was beaming and laughing that loud booming laugh that made him sound like a combination of Barry White and Santa Claus. My mom was happy, but she was holding back the sadness of letting go of her only daughter. It's the kind of hope mixed with sadness and fear that any woman in her right mind feels when she sees a young girl released into the world.

McGuinn-Diamond Hall, my dorm, looked like something out of a novel about the old South. Buildings back home looked as if they were preparing for the long, cold winter. They were stern and placid. These buildings were breathing in the hot, wet air and exhaling it through wide doors and busting through cracks in old paint.

There were people everywhere. Girls were with their parents carrying boxes and luggage, rolling in small dorm refrigerators and televisions. Some parents were already leaving their daughters on the steps of the dormitory with tears in their eyes, and young girls were clamoring to be free.

I climbed the stairs with my parents. There was a front desk with two older Black ladies sitting there. They looked up at each girl that entered checking her out and weighing how much or little trouble she might become. They whispered in agreement to each other from time to time while shuffling through papers, "Umm hummm," and nodding.

DChristy Eves

We got the key to my room and went down to the basement to find it. It was perfect. It had one large window that looked out onto the front of the building and the start of The Set—the main street of campus and the most interesting view. I learned quickly this was the major student hang out. The window was level with the ground outside; if it were open, I could touch the grass. I was close to whatever action a dorm full of girls with "No Males Allowed" could manage, which was stamped on signs affixed to each exit door.

My parents set up my television in my room. We were awkward turning it on to see if it worked. My mother hesitated to tell me that it looked like I was all set. I could see the wheels of her mind turning and searching for one more thing to tell me before she left. With nothing left to say but goodbye, we waited for my roommate.

My roommate was a girl I had agreed to bunk with from back home. Diedra arrived with her boyfriend and announced herself. Her skin was smooth and shined like dark coffee; her eyes were kind and sharply chiseled into her face. She thumped her things onto her bed and gave orders to her boyfriend where her things should go. She immediately took ownership of her half of everything in the room. She came from a large family and was accustomed to sharing and delegating authority. I came from a family of all men so I was accustomed to being the only one in the house with my own space, my own clothes and my own set of rules and regulations deemed appropriate for a girl.

My best friend had already arrived on campus a day or so before me. She was in a dorm across campus. Zondra entered college carrying her bags like an attaché case with a plan of action that would yield her a

3

degree, the perfect job and a husband at the end of four years. I entered college like the blindfold was just pulled off my eyes after my turn swinging the baton at a piñata.

We finished settling in and I walked my parents out front. When my parents' van pulled away from the dorm and left me standing there on the edge of The Set in front of my dorm, I cried. My father's eyes were wet and held on to mine as he pulled away. My mother's eyes were so filled with sadness I couldn't face them. This would be the last time that home would be home for me. In my mind, I was not away at school; I had moved out. I could not wait to be left to my own devices.

It didn't take long for our freshman class to become acclimated to the new routine of our lives. Very quickly the we-ness of groups began to boil down to cliques. I had made a core group of girls. Zondra had been my best friend for nearly ten years. I called her Z. She was short and wore glasses. She was a shade of brown like pecans, and had a disarming smile. She was a pretty girl, but had a maternal quality that prevented her from being sexy. She always seemed as though she was calculating the risks and the routes involved in our endeavors. She was so good at her job that I never wore a watch or noticed the direction we were headed because I knew she would do it for me. I was like a lost child by comparison to her. Z would nudge me and signal me back on course.

Z's roommate, Laurie, was a soft-spoken southern girl. She was very proper and had the cutest little figure that she kept well hidden. She brought her matching bags and virginity to campus unscathed. We put a

4

pair of Z's large hoop earrings on her and Laurie squealed when she saw herself in the mirror,

"I feel like a hooker!"

We all laughed and she promptly removed them.

On the first day of school, I noticed a girl with dark, brown, wavy hair that hung down past her butt; she was standing on the porch of my dorm waiting for someone. I had never seen a Black girl with such long hair. I would see her walking a few feet ahead of me every day on the way to my health class; it was impossible to miss her. She and I were in the same class and she sat in front of me. Her hair tickled my knees and gave me a jealous tingle that I dubbed irritation. But, I decided to override the feeling and I introduced myself to her one day after class.

"Hey, don't you live in my dorm?" I asked.

"Yeah, I do. I've seen you! I'm Elianna, Eli for short." She smiled very brightly. I had heard the description 'bubbly' before, but I'd never actually met anyone who fit the bill, but Eli was bubbly. So now, I definitely had to retract my jealousy and replace it with a feeling of pride knowing that a very pretty girl was going to be my friend. I subscribed to the notion that this validated my own beauty; pretty girls traveled in packs.

"I'm Billie Simone. We should walk to class together in the mornings." I said.

"Okay! We can meet right on the steps in the morning." Eli agreed.

I had noticed Eli hanging out with another girl on campus that seemed in her own stratum. She was a very polished girl. Clearly there was some money behind her look, but beyond that she was striking with a beautiful figure. I was a late bloomer and was just beginning to fill out my b-cup correctly, but she was generously donning a c-cup or maybe a d. She had tiny almond eyes that looked as if they could cut glass. She reminded me of the porcelain dolls they painted sable for Black girls. I would have never made an attempt to befriend this girl as I had with Eli. But one day while waiting in the line at the cafeteria, she walked up to me and said,

"Nice outfit."

"Thanks."

She nodded her approval and went on with her business. I quickly wiped the stupid grin off my face, just in time to appear cool. Later, Eli introduced us. Her name was Catherine, Cat for short.

Back home I used to sit behind my brothers in my house full of men and watch them and all of their friends watching videos. I knew very well the type of women that garnered their attentions. Bell Biv Devoe had a song called *"Poison"* and when the video played, a woman with high-heeled ankle boots walked slowly in front of the screen and all of the boys just died. I was pushed and shoved to the side so she could be seen more clearly.

I would never forget being insecure about my body and feeling sick inside as I watched my father and brothers ogle the thick curvy woman with a huge butt and thick thighs. They looked at her as the pinnacle of Black beauty. I was slim and light and nothing like that girl in the video. I'd cry each night praying for God to make me beautiful. I'd say, 'please God make me bigger.' I'd stuff myself with food and go immediately to sleep. And in the morning I'd still weigh a whooping 105 lbs. It was no use, I'd never be beautiful. I hated the body I looked at everyday getting dressed. I didn't even want to see myself naked, and I knew nobody else would. At school I'd hear, "Girl, you so skinny." "Do you eat?" "Damn girl, I'd probably hurt you." No one wanted me.

In my house womanhood was a secret—a shame. When I got my cycle my mother took me to the store and we didn't tell the boys or my father. I had to hide all the evidence in my room. One of my brother's friends mentioned that I was beginning to "develop." My brother responded by beating up the friend and then coming home and calling me a slut. I hadn't done anything, but becoming a woman was like an offense with a punishment.

Nevertheless, I was turning into a woman. My hips were forming underneath my over-sized clothes. And some boys, before I graduated high school, were beginning to notice me, and some men too. It took a special kind of man to spot it. He had to be more still, more quiet and patient to see it just behind the surface. The kind of man that was attracted to me was a specialized hunter.

I lost my virginity at sixteen. I waited, as instructed by my mother, to "be in love first." I had my very first boyfriend, Dale Hasbrouck; he was eighteen and had his own car. After about eight months of dating and my sixteenth birthday on the horizon, I decided that I was "in love" enough and asked him if he wanted to have sex. Dale wasn't as sure it was a good idea as he was from a religious family and he thought it better to wait. But, I was a woman on a mission. I wanted to experience what the boys were whispering about in the basement.

DChristy Eves

From neighborhood gossip, I surmised that a girl's first time would not be great and that you had to do it a few times to make it feel good. I needed to get the show on the road. After I turned what Dale felt was at least a respectable sixteen, he finally agreed. Gossip proved to be true in this case and it was sort of boring, sort of uncomfortable and sort of quick. But, I had that pesky virginity out of the way and I was sure good times would lie ahead.

I had witnessed all the guys in my neighborhood talking about sex and running through women. My brothers would tell women these beautiful stories to their faces about how much they cared, but before they were one step out of the door, another woman would be on the phone and my oldest brother would signal for me to stall her while he got rid of the other one. Men had two faces—one with the girl of the moment and another one that was real; that real one shared the stories of conquest with their friends and laughed. They all warned me,

"You see how men act. So be a good girl."

My thoughts were why be a good girl, have no fun and eventually be tricked and used?

I wanted to be a man.

2

THE CAMPUS WAS BUZZING as Homecoming approached. I woke up to the sound of music coming from somewhere outside. The metal springs that kept my bed afloat creaked as I sat up. I gathered my things and headed for the showers. When I got back to my room I checked my messages.

"Hey girl! It's me, Eli. What're you doing tonight? I want you to come out with me and this guy I just met. He's got a *friend*. Call me as soon as you get home!"

She sang, "He's got a fri-end." Eli always sounded like she just finished laughing at someone tripping in their high heels on The Set. I called her back quickly.

"Eli?"

"Hey Billie!! You got my message?"

"Yeah, you still going out?"

"Yes, and so are you. What are you doing?"

"Nothing special… Who's the guy?"

"He's *cute* and so is his friend. Seniors! There's a reggae party at The Spot. Meet me out front tonight at nine?" She sang "cu-te" this time.

"Sounds good."

That night, I met Eli out front and she was wearing a yellow, crochet knit mini-dress. Somehow Eli managed not to look slutty even thought she was scantily clad. She had her hair pulled back in the front into a high center ponytail, which made her eyes look even more slanted than usual. Her hair hung down long in the back and I wondered how all that hair would feel in the heat of the club. The guys pulled up in a silver two-door Honda Civic. Eli's guy was tall and light-skinned with short, curly hair and a pointed chin. He stood outside the car and opened the door for us, pushing forward his seat. Eli and I got in the back.

"What's up ladies?" He asked trying to impress Eli. He smiled too much. His friend was average height, brown-skinned and wore a sweater vest, which was even more puzzling than Eli's decision to wear her hair down. He was okay-looking, but there was instantly and irrevocably no spark between us. Eli sat behind her guy and occasionally tickled his ears while he drove.

When we got to the party, a crowd was waiting to get in. I could hear the music thump and whine through the walls. The club was as basic as it gets—a rectangular, tan building with no sign and a red light above the door. I adjusted my top as we got out of the car and checked my reflection to see if I looked alright.

Eli's guy took us to the door and one of his "bruhs," his fraternity brothers, let us in. The Kappas regularly threw parties that

10

drew large crowds. They were known as the pretty boys of campus because of the red and white canes they included in their step shows and the more than average amount of cute, well-dressed guys. As the doorman let us in, he eyed Eli closely as she walked by. I tended to disappear when I was next to her. This didn't bother me much because the men she attracted were never my type. They were posers and status seekers. They smelled like Obsession by Calvin Klein and they always knew the right people at the right doors; which, of course, made up for my lack of attention and made Eli a fun partner to go out with.

I slinked past the tall, muscular doorman with his baseball cap pulled low and looked for the bar. The guys were both twenty-one and got neon paper bands taped around their wrists. Eli and I got stamps marked K that glowed in the dark. We were hit immediately by the scent and feel of thick, wet air and bodies in motion. I waited for the right moment to suggest the guys buy us drinks. They told us to hang out while they bought them. I breathed a sigh of relief and watched a girl bending backwards leaving her pelvis pushed against a tall, lanky guy with short spiky dreads. Their faces were serious. I was hot and uneasy.

"There's no place to sit." I confided in Eli my growing concern. Just then the guys came back with two drinks in each hand.

"What is it?" Eli asked yelling so her guy could hear over the music.

"Sex On the Beach." He smiled and handed one to Eli. My so-called guy gave me mine, and made no attempt at the single entendre. The drink was a fruit juice mixture with cheap vodka and Peach Schnapps in it, but it was enough to loosen the mood. I danced slowly where I stood and he turned to watch me. It must have been just enough incentive for my second drink; he asked if I wanted another. This time I asked for a rum and coke.

Eventually and expectedly, Eli disappeared into the blackness with her beau and my date found some girl with a huge ass to follow into a dark corner. I stood there dancing by myself. I was bolstered with confidence by the second drink and took myself to the bar for a third. When I got to the bar, I noticed the bartender checking people's wrists for their neon bands. I turned around disappointed just in time to catch a pair of eyes cutting through the crowd to me. His stare and stillness in a room full of movement caught me off guard. His eyes were dark and sharp. He came through the crowd and grabbed my hand without saying a word. He pulled me deep into the mix with a combination of force and gentleness that sent a pulse through my body.

We landed far from the light of the doorway. The beat of the music thumped inside my chest. He put his arms around my waist and his hands landed on my hips, with his fingers grazing my behind. Everywhere his body touched, mine woke up. We moved together in rhythm and I felt his breath on my neck. He turned me around put his hands on my exposed stomach. We moved close to the speakers. The vibrations were sliding up to my throat and making it hard to breathe, especially coupled with the now sweltering heat and the closeness of this smooth-skinned man. He handled and moved me as if I already belonged to him. I couldn't get control of the flow of conversation between his body and mine. The room smelled like sweat and spilled drinks, but when I leaned my head back I could smell him. I inhaled deeply. He smelled like soap and fresh water. He danced and moved himself slowly against my butt. I could feel sweat rolling down between my shoulder blades and his hands slid from side to side on the perspiration collecting on my stomach. I couldn't breathe.

"I'm hot." I leaned my head back and whispered it in his ear. He took my hand and led me to the bar.

"You want something?" He asked me.

"Rum and coke."

He ordered two and took me outside.

Once outside in the light of the parking lot, I could see his face. He was the color of caramel. His skin was so smooth it looked painted on him. He had high cheekbones and dark, black, wavy hair. It was cut short and precise. He was tall and my eyes landed at his square jaw line. He had a muscular build. I could see the lines of veins slightly disturb the butter smooth skin of his forearms with fine, black hair dusting over them. His hands were neatly manicured. His sharp, dark eyes had long lashes that should've soften them, but they were almost cold. There was something strange behind them. I couldn't tell what he was thinking through his poker face. I had never seen such a beautiful man, and if I had, he was never attracted to me. I had to wonder what made him single me out. Any girl would have followed him onto the dance floor. He leaned against a black mustang parked out front; clearly not his car and clearly of no concern to him.

"So what's your name?" He finally spoke.

In the cool of the evening my damp shirt felt cold against my breasts. Suddenly, I felt very aware of my body.

13

"Billie Simone."

"Simone. I like that." He smiled and to add insult to injury his teeth were perfect.

"What's yours?"

"Vaughn." He moved in close to me. I could smell him again. I kept sipping my drink so I would have something to do with my hands.

"You... are very pretty." He whispered in my ear. He was very deliberate when he spoke, no extraneous words; he was like a surgeon. He knew exactly how small to make the incision to get inside. He backed away again to scan my whole body. Where his eyes landed, I felt the lightest tingle as if he were barely touching me.

"I wanna call you." He continued.

I gave my number without hesitation. He didn't write it down.

"You're not going to remember it." I said.

"Wanna bet." He liked my attitude.

"Yes."

"What will you give me when I win?"

"What do you want?"

He looked over his shoulder and saw two guys come out of The Spot and look around. He threw one hand in the air with his forefinger raised. They spotted him and waited talking to each other and giving him a nod.

"I'll tell you when I call you." He smiled. *My God, what a smile.* Checkmate. He drew his finger across my stomach in one, long, slow stroke and left me standing there.

I felt like I'd been slipped a drug. I was slightly dizzy and my heart raced. Somehow, I had been taken off course and slipped onto the set of some movie about clandestine lovers meeting in the dark. I had to decide if it all really happened. Now that he was gone, there seemed to be no trace that I had actually met him. I hoisted myself onto the hood of the black mustang and waited for the night to end. Twenty minutes later, Eli came out with the guys. She was drunk and giggling while hanging on her guy's arm.

"Let's go." I told them.

"Did you have *fun?*" Eli asked looping her arm around mine as if I was her escort and singing "fu-un."

"Meet anybody?" She whispered so my date wouldn't hear, although I'm sure he wouldn't care.

"No," I lied. "But I did have fun." I'm not sure why I didn't tell her about Vaughn. Somehow the whole experience gave me the impression of having been a secret. I never mentioned the meeting to any of my girlfriends either.

Homecoming week flew by with a flurry of events. I barely had time to notice that Vaughn never called, but I managed to check my machine every night. Deidra's boyfriend was coming up for the game. I told Deidra I'd wait with her out front for Calvin to pick her up. My mind was still floating elsewhere; since it had been almost a week, I decided that Vaughn had indeed forgotten my number or forgotten me. Deidra had spent nights on the phone with Calvin talking under the covers and trying desperately to cope with the distance between them and ignoring life as it was in front of her. Calvin went to Bethune-Cookman, which was four hours away. All of their conversations had a tone of importance and urgency. Relationships and the desire to keep them going at our age, seemed completely pointless and taxing to me. I did not understand the draw. When I got back to the room I checked the messages... nothing.

By the time Saturday arrived, campus was like one huge street party. I left my dorm and headed down the hill to Z's and Laurie's dorm. Vendors sold tee-shirts, banners, barbequed ribs, hot dogs and hamburgers, and sausages with peppers and onions. The smells wafted through the air. Soul vegetarian carts offered bean pies and curried tofu with sprouts and yellow rice. Bootleggers hawked mixed tapes of 'dirty south' music and bass and Reggae mingled with R&B as I walked along. I heard Toni Tone Tony's "Lay Your Head on My Pillow" pump from a blue jeep at the corner.

I got to Z's dorm and she was out front waiting with Laurie and a guy. Z wasted no time finding an attachment; she already had a new boyfriend. Will was a cute, southern guy that was light-skinned and tall. He talked with a light-weight southern accent and always laughed with his whole body.

"What's up Miss Billie? What cha' know?" Will sang as he greeted me with a hug.

"I know it's pointless to bring sand to the beach, but I guess Z is bringing you anyway."

"You crazy." He laughed.

The stadium was packed. We had split from Will and found our seats. We didn't care much about the game; we came to see The Marching 100. We sat excitedly checking out the crowd, spotting cuties and screaming when it seemed appropriate. Z looked back to see what Will was doing and to see if he was talking to other girls. Inevitably he was.

"You like him?" I asked Z when the crowd fell into a quieter lull.

"He's been so sweet. Yeah..." She smiled; he had been showering her with attention since the second day of school.

"Yeah, it's always nice to have the attention." I said.

"True." She smiled. "I think he's got a friend that likes you."

"Really? Who?"

"I don't know which one, but he mentioned one of his boys saw us together and was in to you." Z looked back at the guys again.

After the game, I walked Z and Laurie back to their dorms. I headed back to McGuinn by myself. I wanted to take a long drive and find the beach and lay out in the sun. I had been in Florida for two and half months now and I had yet to see the ocean. My dad had bought a car for me, but freshman were not allowed to have their cars on campus that first year or live off campus. A car meant freedom. I wanted this last piece of the puzzle to complete my freedom.

But instead I sat on my bed and the springs creaked.

3

NOVEMBER BROUGHT COOLER TEMPERATURES to Florida. It was bright and clear on The Hill. I spent the day organizing my outline for a big paper that was due in Humanities. I gathered my books and sat outside the library to write in my journal and stare across the quad at Lee Hall. The quad opened out in front of the library and served as the heart of campus with its sidewalk arteries that pumped students to the limbs of campus. And when there was wind, the quad always set the gust free in its large open space.

When I finally headed back to my dorm, the day was waning. Deidra looked up from her desk and nodded when I came in.

"How's it going?" I asked.

"It's going." She shrugged.

I sat down on my bed and started studying. I was just starting to go cross-eyed when the phone rang.

"Hello."

"Simone." My heart started to beat in chest.

"Vaughn?" It had been three weeks.

"I won."

"You won what?" I knew what he was talking about.

"You...I've been thinking about you. I wanna see you." He remembered my number. I had been so disappointed that he hadn't called that I studied the details of our meeting in my mind over and over. I had dreams of him cutting through the white lights of the parking lot outside of The Spot. I could only remember his hands and his caramel-brown forearms that flexed when he motioned with them. I didn't tell a single soul that I'd met him. Keeping him secret seemed to lock his impression on my chest. I could feel it there now when I breathed. I wanted to ask him why he'd taken so long, but I only said,

"When?"

"Now."

He was on his way and I barely had time to change clothes before he'd be out front. Deidra was curious,

"Who was that?"

"This guy I met a few weeks back. He's *cute*." I imitated Eli singing cu-ute.

I kept my answer casual, but my rushing betrayed me and she watched me through the corner of her eye. I tried to tell myself, *don't have sex with him on the first date. You'll never see him again if you do.* But, I showered anyway. I changed into my sexiest pair of jeans and black boots. I wore a brown mock turtle neck that was cropped just above my waist. When I reached up for my keys and leather jacket off the hook by the door, my stomach peaked out and I remember him touching me there. I quickly opened the door to leave and Deidra stopped me.

"Wait. I don't even know this guy or where you're going. You and I have a deal that we look out for each other. At least give me a number or something where you'll be." She was concerned and although I could imagine how this looked and what she must be thinking, I had to get outside before he pulled up. The irritation was showing on my face.

"I don't have his number." I didn't realize this until I said it out loud. She just stared at me. She was about to say something, but before she could find the words I said,

"I'll be fine" and ran out the door.

The sun had just gone down. There were a group of three girls laughing in the doorway and waiting for the pizza guy. "Close that do'!" One of the front desk ladies yelled out to them; they were locking up the office for the night. I stood on the bottom of the steps and leaned against the cold bricks of the front porch waiting for Vaughn's car to pull up. I was rethinking my shirt and wondering if it made my boobs look small. The night air smelled like wet pine needles and something sweet I couldn't identify.

A tiny, black car pulled up and I knew it was him right away. He opened his door and stood up and looked directly at me. He was wearing a clean, white polo shirt and dark jeans. My body was walking towards him before I could even form the thought.

We pulled up to his place, a townhouse connected to rows of similar houses, curving down the block and out of sight. Across the street, a tall White guy smoked a cigarette on his deck and watched the street. When we got inside, every light in the place was on. There was no music and the television was off. It was too quiet. He walked ahead of me into the kitchen. I searched the living room for signs of his personality. There were none. Not even a bad poster of a black panther or an extra large portrait of Bob Marley smoking a joint, his face laced in smoke.

"You want something to drink?" He said.

He'd gotten out two glasses and was already plunking ice in both. I sat down on the dark green sofa. It was stiff and uncomfortable. In the sliding glass door opposite I saw myself sitting there, toes pointing into each other, hands in my lap. My hair hung in sandy spurs past my shoulders and tried to reach the edge of my short sleeves. I looked like a kid waiting for my mom to pick me up from school, so I adjusted my legs and crossed them and I tried to lean to one side and appear calm and not unnerved as I was.

"I'll drink whatever you're drinking." I said.

He came back with a light orange drink. I sipped it. It was very strong.

"What is it?"

"Its vodka and orange juice."

I kept sipping until I got used to the taste. He sat next to me on the couch and turned his body to face me. He was more beautiful than I remembered. His skin glowed in the bright lights and his teeth peaked out white when he spoke. He dug into me with sharp eyes. When he sat close I forgot what to do with my hands and I was glad I had the drink to hold.

"What have you been up to?" He asked. He was staring at me.

"Nothing. I'm getting ready to go home for break."

"Where's home?"

"Detroit."

"Really, I'm from Chicago." His words were friendly and light, but his voice seemed too heavy for them. My heart had been thumping when we arrived but I was finally starting to calm down and I sipped again.

"You got a boyfriend back home?" He touched my leg when he asked and took a long sip of his drink. The blood ran up my thigh where he'd touched and sent warm trickles between my legs. This set back my efforts to calm down.

"No. I'm not the relationship type." He smiled when I said this. He sank back into the couch. His knee touched mine.

"Not the relationship type. I don't think I am either, but I find myself caught up regardless. I should be like you... honest from the start, huh?"

"Honesty is good. I like knowing what I'm getting into."

"I'm getting into you I think." He didn't say it with a sexual note, but I felt one regardless. I smiled.

"I have a girl now. We've been together a while, but... well, you know how that goes. She's from back home." The fact that he had a girlfriend was completely meaningless for me, but I liked him telling me. I liked him revealing anything about himself. He was a complete mystery.

"I prefer not to sleep alone. I guess it's my Achilles heel." He smiled.

"Are you in love?"

22

"She is. I don't know what I am. I guess I'm a bad man sitting here with you." He smiled, took another long drink and put his glass down. I tried to lean back on the sofa and relax like he had done. He was watching me closely and studied my attempt. His hand went up my thigh and traced up my hip to the top of my jeans. He took one finger and pulled the waist band gently away from my skin and let go. I felt a rush of blood down through the center of my chest and into my panties. Heat followed the blood and I had to twitch in my seat.

"Bad became good in the 80s." The joke was an anachronism to the moment. He ignored it.

"I love your waist. You're so tiny and sexy."

"Sexy?"

"Yes. Sexy." It was the first time anyone had ever called me that. "I like your style. It's funny. You kinda remind me of myself when I was a freshman." He went on.

"I can't imagine you and I being anything alike."

"You don't see yourself. But I do. I see you."

"What do you see?"

"You'll see." His eyes narrowed and his body was warming. I could smell him now, like fresh water and soap.

"Are you going to show me?" I kept sipping and emptied my drink. It was a tall glass and I had been drinking too fast. He tucked his hand under my hair and up the back of my neck. He held my head and pulled me to him. I was still holding my empty glass and it fell when I closed my eyes. He kissed me slow and deep. I was expecting a hard kiss, but he paced himself and was very controlled. My body started to

23

throb and I felt like I'd lifted off the sofa with nothing solid beneath me. He leaned his body back until my chest was on his and with his other hand, held me in place by my butt. He made circles in my hair with his index and ring finger. The circular massage added to the dizziness and I was breathing deeply. He pulled away from me and looked at my face for a long moment.

"Let's go upstairs." He said. I leaned away from him and he got up and gave me his hand. I stood up and felt awkward in my boots. He led me upstairs.

At the top of the stairs he opened a door and led me in. The lights were down very low. I was thankful for the change. I looked around his room. His bedroom was like the living room and left me very little clues. It was very neat for a guy; no shoes lying around with red dirt caked in the soles, no old drinks rotting on the nightstand; just his messenger-style leather school bag resting on a chair in the corner. I could see a chemistry book peaking out. His room smelled like him, like something clean and wooden.

He moved in front of me and sat on the bed. He lifted up my shirt and touched my stomach. He hands went up the back of my shirt and under my bra strap. He kissed my belly and lowered me down onto his lap. He kissed me harder now and used his hands to squeeze my butt and pull me close to his body. He was leaning me slightly forward and I was shaking lightly. The room was silent and off in the distance I heard a strange song playing with electric guitars and scream-singing. I felt him getting hard beneath me. I put my hands under his crisp, white, polo shirt and felt the bare skin on his back. His skin was soft like a baby's, but sheathed over taunt slim back muscles that curved as he leaned into me. I gasped for air and broke away from his kiss. He bit my neck. He lifted me to my feet and stood tall in front of me and pulled off his shirt. I leaned down to take off my boots. On the way down I saw him protruding from his jeans. He unzipped them as I went down. He looked down at me and watched me take off my shoes. When I was done and stood, he grabbed my waist and we lowered ourselves onto the bed. He removed my pants and panties in one movement. He stood up and pulled his pants down. He stood there naked and he looked like a roman statue in the dim light. He was hard, slim and smooth. He was nearly hairless expect for soft curls around his penis. He grabbed a condom from the night stand drawer and put it on. I watched and waited for him to be inside me. In a moment he was.

I was whirling inside and it felt like riding waves in a storm. His scent filled me and his body began to feel oiled and slick against me. I clutched him and moaned gasping for air. He whispered in my ear things that only made sense in bed.

"God, I've been waiting to see you." "You're mine." "I love your body." "It's mine." His neck muscles flexed and he pulled me into him until I felt like my chest was melting into his. I wasn't sure what was happening to me. Tingles began to spread to my chest and intensify. A flood of electric needles and sparks flew into the center of my body. I shook and tears eked out of the corners of my eyes. He smiled when he saw my eyes and he slowed for a moment and let me recover, then he slid his body deeply into mine and we both came. For me it was my first and second time.

He got up and went to the bathroom. I heard water running and the light framed the doorway while he washed. I nestled my head in his pillow and I could smell the faint scent of his hair. I wasn't sure what would happen next. So I started looking for my panties. When he came out he was smiling and he seemed warmer and relaxed. I was surprised. I half expected him to tell me to get dressed and get ready to leave.

"You want a tee-shirt?" He was soft and kind.

"Yeah." I said and he handed me a plain heather grey tee-shirt. It wasn't one of those awful free ones you got from filling out credit applications on The Set. It smelled like it was fresh out of the laundry. I put it on.

"Now... you look like mine." He observed me.

I got up and walked passed him to go to the bathroom. He let his hand drag across my stomach as I passed.

When I came back into the room he had straightened his bed and was not in the room. I looked around and noticed the sliding glass doors that led outside. He was on the deck. I went out and he was smoking a Black and Mild and drinking the rest of his drink from earlier.

"You want another drink?" He asked when I came out.

"Yeah. I better go back inside and put some pants on." I said noticing the chill.

"I'll get you something." He went back inside and came back with a large long sleeve blue button-up shirt. He handed me a pair of his white crew socks.

"Don't put your pants on yet. Don't worry, nobody can see up here." He assured me. He left again and I held on to his skinny cigar and took a puff. It tasted sweet and dirty. He came back with two drinks and handed me one.

"I like this on you. Are you warm?" He asked and pulled his own shirt.

"I'm warm." I wasn't, but I said it anyway. "I love that you can see the stars down here. The city's not bright enough to drown out the light."

"I'm the city type, but this is nice." He sipped this time. I could nearly see the moon in his eyes. It was high and full.

We didn't talk much. He pulled me close to him and put his hand under my shirt. My back was to him and when he lifted my shirt my panties were exposed. I worried about being seen, but said nothing. His hand rested below my bellybutton. When we finished our drinks he took me back inside. He got in bed and motioned for me to do the same. When I got in, he sucked me back into his arms and took my tee-shirt off. I was falling again and my chest ached. He was alive and instantly hard. He was behind me and quickly stuck his hands down my panties and touched me deeply. We were tangled and hot. We stayed like that all night. He would fall asleep afterwards and so would I, then he'd wake up and have me again. He woke up twice more during the night.

When morning came I was weak and dizzy. I realized I never ate dinner the previous night. I had slept hard from exhaustion. I was naked and the stiff cotton of the sheets grazed my skin. I was hoping the sun coming through his patio door would eventually creep to my side of the bed. He was completely passed out and the sun was warming his

27

back. He made no sound. I suddenly wanted to go home before he woke up, but I had no choice and lay there waiting for him to wake up.

It was about an hour before he began to stir. I was dreaming with my eyes open of water rushing the campus and surrounding the hills. It was sea water and I could smell the ocean. When he opened his eyes the moon was gone, and he stared blankly at me. He got up and I could hear him peeing in the bathroom. He made a grunting sound. He came back into the room naked, but he walked as if he was fully clothed. He checked his watch sitting on top of his pants on the chair.

"7:47 a.m. I gotta get going soon, Simone." He walked over to me. He stood close and his penis hung at eye level.

"You're a good girl." He said and rubbed my hair. "I wanna see you again." Again, his words were kinder than his demeanor.

"Me too." I said. I sounded shy and I accidentally licked my lips. The suggestion was just too strong. I tried to stare up into his face, but his penis trapped my gaze. His lips parted in a half grin, like he just found out something about me. I didn't know what.

When I got back to the dorms, it was well after ten in the morning and I'd missed algebra. Deidra was on the phone with Calvin. She looked relieved when I came in.

"Here she is now." I heard her whisper to him. "Okay….. I love you too…… Okay, bye. Well, I'm glad to see you made it back alive and nearly fifteen hours later. 'A guy I met a week ago. He's *cute*.' He betta' be. You have got to tell me who that was and what happened." Deidra quizzed. I was too tired to lie and so I came clean.

"His name is Vaughn. I met him three weeks ago out dancing with Eli." I started.

"I should've guess that girl was involved somehow." Deidra was right; trouble did seem to follow Eli.

"I don't know him that well. He's strange. He's guarded. I don't know what it is about him. There's something animal about the two of us." I said and took off my boots.

"Did you have sex with him??"

"Many, many times." I said and fell back on my bed. I tucked myself, clothes and all, in bed.

"Billie…." She started. I just pulled the covers over my head. I was in no mood to hear whatever she was going to say.

"Fine. You grown. Alright then…Miss All Night Long. I'm headed to breakfast. Did you at least get his number this time?" Deidra asked and folder her arms.

"Damn." I'd completely forgotten.

4.

BACK HOME WAS COLD for Thanksgiving. The blanket of grey clouds that put the sun to bed in Michigan was already up and would be there until May. The grey sidewalks met the grey sky and the people huddled by without making eye contact on the way to their cars.

The drive home from the airport was depressing. Hollowed out buildings and vagrants replaced the southern trees and beautiful brown college students. The fellas on the block were sitting on the fence surrounding the empty field on the corner. Nothing had changed.

My family was so happy to see me but it was strange being home. My old room was different, but still the same. It occurred to me that the paint in the room was still the same pink my mother let me pick out when I was twelve. Although things seemed pretty much undisturbed from when I packed my bags to leave, something was clearly missing. I didn't have much time to think about what because the holiday weekend was very short and rushed. Everyone in the family wanted to see me and spend time finding out "how's college?!" I had to answer it a million times and I didn't quite know what to say. I wanted to see everyone, but I felt lost at home. They were all looking for a girl that I wasn't anymore.

After Thanksgiving dinner I'd gone into the kitchen to help my mom. I found her sitting alone crying. I stopped stunned; it was a rare sight.

"Mom, what's wrong?"

She straightened up quickly; I'd surprised her. "Nothing. Your father's in a mood. The way he talks to me...the way he talks. It's nothing." She changed her tone. "I've got this new bag I wanna show you." Mom started. She peaked upstairs at her bedroom door and confirmed Dad was asleep. Then she went behind the pantry door and pulled out a large, brown paper sack. Inside it was a shopping bag. And inside the shopping bag a brown, leather, cross-body strapped handbag.

"Look at this!"

"That's beautiful." I felt the leather. "Why is it all tucked behind the door?"

"Oh, you know your father goes nuts every time I buy something. But this was on sale. I only paid forty dollars for it. Can you believe that? I couldn't leave this in the store." She tucked it back in the shopping bag and then that bag into the sack and all of the baggage behind the pantry door. It was like watching a ritual.

"What are you going to do with it?" I wondered, watching her hide it.

"Um..." She thought for a moment. "I don't know. Do you like it? You want it? You can have it if you like it."

"No, no. Mom, that's okay. You keep it. It's nice."

"Oh, I don't need it. I've got bags all over this house. I'll give it to your aunt. Christmas is coming up quicker than you'd think." She went on cleaning the kitchen and packing Daddy's lunch for the next day. "I hate packing your father's lunch."

"Why can't he pack his own lunch?" I started helping her clean up.

"Baby, never start something with a man you can't finish. I've been making his lunches so long I can't just up and stop now. I've got him spoiled. He can't find his socks if I don't tell him where they are. He act like he can't eat if I don't fix it. Oh, don't let me forget to show you the new suitcases I bought. I got 'em hidden behind the closet door in your room. You can definitely take one of those back to school with you." She smiled and patted my arm.

Even though my mother smiled and laughed, she seemed sad. I knew it was more than just my being gone. But I didn't know why and I knew she wouldn't tell me. My mother was like a sad song that played with the singer's voice low and deep so that you could barely make out the words. Her café au lait colored skin and auburn hair made her look like the warm glow of a lamp in the evening. She was so pretty with her kind eyes and guarded smile that never revealed teeth. We talked for hours cleaning up the Thanksgiving dishes and putting away the food. I could almost feel my pink baby's blanket that I carried for much too long after childhood. Home.

The trip was fast and before I knew it, I was getting off the plane in Florida. The grey cover was far behind me and the open blue sky was shameless. My thoughts traveled from time to time on Vaughn. The whole affair seemed sordid and unreal. When I thought of him I couldn't get a picture of his face in my mind. I could only picture his forearms flexing when he lifted me high. I tried to quickly put it out of my mind.

It was Finals week and the semester would be over soon. My first journalism course was a disappointment. I was doing well in the course, but the subject could not have been more boring. My mother chose my major for me after having a discussion with a recruiter from FAMU that was in Detroit at Cobo Hall for a college fair. They both discussed me as if I was a child at the pediatrician's office.

"My daughter writes very well." My mother beamed.

"Does she?! And she's very pretty too. She should be on television." The recruiter chimed in.

"Oh, she would be great on television! She competes in oratorical contests at school. She's very confident on stage. She competes in pageants, too."

"Broadcast Journalism would be perfect for her." The recruiter said.

They both nodded and the tall woman in the cream suit wrote it down somewhere. They had decided my future and it didn't even occur to them to ask me what I thought. I don't think it would have mattered much, because I had no idea. I let her write it down and that became my major in college. I liked writing it better than admitting 'undecided.' I never even watched the news.

DChristy Eves

It was a stressful week. I had a different final everyday and they were each like sand bags on a hot air balloon; I'd get lighter after I finished each one. By Friday I was high.

Z, Laurie, and I all met up at my dorm room that evening and compared war stories. Z knew some guys from one of her classes. She popped with Detroit attitude when she spoke to the guys on the phone saying,

"If you want us to come, you need to pick us up *and* buy us drinks. Otherwise we're staying here." She used the phone in my room and made silent laughing faces to us while she snapped directions to him. They were freshmen, but somehow one of them had an apartment.

They came to pick us in a huge rusty old 1978 Buick Skylark. They thought it was a classic. All three of us girls fit in the back seat. They blasted "Passing Me By" by Pharcyde. When we got to their apartment I could smell a familiar smoke in the air. It smelled like my parents basement after they had gone out and left my second oldest brother in charge.

Scrap, the captain of the Buick Skylark, knocked on the door and another guy, Tre, opened the door. We all piled in and A Tribe Called Quest announced, "Check the Rhime." It was a cheaply assembled, classic guy's apartment. It had a basic futon, a couple of mismatched chairs and a found or passed down, old, wooden coffee table partially broken and rigged with electric tape. But, the room was energetic and the music was nice. Z, Laurie and I pilled onto the futon together like backup singers.

Scrap was skinny, lanky and he reminded me of a puppy when he moved or spoke. He was infatuated with Z and watched her move with an unbroken smile on his face. Tre was tall, dark and quiet. He didn't say much, and he appeared to be joining us via satellite from an alternate universe. Occasionally he'd laugh at something one of us said and it'd remind me he was in the room. Mike was the coolest guy in the bunch; he was just to the left of fat and he laughed loud and hard.

Mike was the bartender of the group as well and poured us all Hawaiian Punch with rum in it. We were laughing and competing to see who knew the most lyrics to raps from the 80s, when Tre butted in from nowhere and said,

"Blaze one up, man."

"Y'all smoke?" Mike asked The Supremes. We were fidgeting.

"I never have." I said.

"Me neither." Z turned her nose up.

Laurie was already tipsy and laughing a little.

"I'll try it." Her voice was high pitched and excited. Both me and Z snapped our heads to Laurie. I couldn't believe she wanted to try it.

"Okay me too." I felt nervous waiting to see how it'd feel.

"Zondra, you in?" Scrap asked.

"No. You guys go ahead. Don't let me stop you." Z shook her head and made a disapproving face.

Mike was already emptying the tobacco from a blunt into the trash can. He came back to the table with a baggie and the empty cigar paper. He sat next to me. He meticulously stuffed the brown paper and picked out the sceds. Then he rolled it and licked it to close. I was immediately turned off by the sight of his tongue; but then he took out his lighter and ran the flame back and forth across the blunt. Mike lit it and started the cipher. He hit it twice and passed it. I quickly deduced that these were the rules; two slow hits and then pass it to your right. Mike passed it to Tre, Tre passed it to Scrap. Scrap bypassed Z as requested and Laurie held it in her hand like a single chop stick.

"Okay, now, how do you smoke this thang?" Laurie's accent was perky. She made me relax the minute I heard her speak. I had been watching the blunt circulate closely and trying to see if I could figure out what they were doing with it.

"Take a hit... Go ahead." Scrap said. Laurie breathed in deeply like she'd seen them.

"Now hold it." Mike was giving instructions like a swim coach at a meet. Laurie looked like one of those plastic cat clocks whose eyes moved while the second hand/tail swung, right left, right left. Mike continued,

"Okay, now breathe in and then exhale."
Laurie started coughing and everybody laughed and clapped. She sipped her drink to clear her throat and said,

"Okay now you do it!" while passing it to me.
I remembered the instructions, but Mike talked me through it anyway. When I breathed in, the smoke tasted bitter and dry. I wasn't sure if I could hold it in, and then I got confused on when to breathe and I started coughing and choking. My chest felt terrible and my eyes were watering.

"Take it slow, girl…you got it." Mike said and patted me on the back.

They continued around and both Laurie and I gave it one more try and then we waited to see if anything would happen to us. The guys went around until the blunt was the size of a black eyed pea. Tre burned his fingers when it got that small.

"Do you feel anything?" Laurie whispered to me.

"I don't think so." I said and blinked.

"I don't know. Do you think we're high yet?" Laurie asked.

"If you have to ask," Scrap chimed in, "then you probably are." He laughed out loud and went to the kitchen to grab a bag of chips.

I studied the room to look for changes. Everything looked the same. I checked myself to see if I was thinking clearly. I was pretty sure I was. But then I noticed the room seemed brighter and the air puffed out the space and made the ceiling seem further away. The music on the stereo was crisp. Mary J. Blige was singing, and she reminded me of home. I suddenly wanted potato chips.

"Billie's high." Scrap announced and laughed. Mike put his arm around me.

"Congratulations and welcome to the club." Mike said and grinned. I laughed way too hard and Laurie was nearly in tears laughing; I had no clue why this was so funny.

The next day I was sitting on the library steps. I was working on a poem about the dreams I'd been having about the ocean when I noticed someone behind me looking over my shoulder. I looked back and there was a neat looking guy with glasses, a heavy, brown, leather coat and a plaid scarf. He hung his body back and to the side like he was studying a painting in a gallery.

"Can I help you?" I asked, covering my work.

"I was just wondering what someone like you was out here writing about." He said.

"Someone like me?"

"Yeah," He invited himself to sit down next to me on the steps. "Someone so young, who looks so serious; you're too pretty to have any problems."

"Nice intro. Do you do an encore?"

"Seriously," he smiled and laughed a little. His smile was kind, and his eyes were gentle. "What are you writing about? You just looked so involved; I couldn't help but be curious."

"Well, I don't know really. I've been writing since I was nine. I don't know what I write. It's just thoughts that come into my head and it's my way of staying on the ground and not floating away. Do you write?"

"Yeah, sometimes." He said and cocked his head back.

"What do you write?"

"Bad poetry."

"How do you know it's bad?"

"Oh, it's bad. Trust me. But, it just makes me feel good to do it anyway. I feel like I'm a part of something." He said looking closely at my face. It made me blush.

"That's strange that you feel a part of something because to me, poetry is so lonely. It's something you tune out the world to do."

"Not the way I do it. That's probably why it's 'bad' poetry. I hang out with this group of poets that meet up every week and read their poetry and give each other critiques. It's cool."

I thought about the idea of meeting a group of people that wrote. None of my friends did and the only person that would listen to my work was my mom. I was getting thoughts in my head lately that I didn't want to share with her, so that left most of my work locked safely in my notebook.

"So, can I read what you're working on?" He continued.

"I think I should know your name before you start looking into my pages." I said.

"Grant."

"Billie."

"Billie?"

"Yeah, my mother likes sad songs and Billie Simone couldn't get any sadder."

We talked for a long while on the steps of the library. It was really easy like talking to someone I already knew. He was from Michigan too, but not Detroit. He was a senior in the School of Business and Industry, SBI. We exchanged numbers and I told him my girls and I were heading to a club that night. He asked to meet me there. I wondered if such a neatly packaged guy could dance.

Later that night at the club we danced and joked all night. When Grant bought my second drink, he told me I was a lightweight and he wanted to look out for me, so he cut me off. I couldn't help but like the tone of protection from him. He was like solid earth. I wondered how it would feel to lean on him. When we danced slowly, he held me close, but he was careful with me. His body didn't talk to mine, like Vaughn's, but his eyes did.

The trip home was good. Z and I made the rounds with friends and family and stayed up late to talk. Grant called while we were in Michigan. He wanted to drive over from Grand Rapids, where he lived. When he got to the house he came in and met my parents. He was easy in front of my parents and I could tell that my dad liked him. Dad nudged me on my way out of the door,

"He seems like a good solid guy." We went downtown and although it was cold, we walked along the riverfront at the Renaissance Center. He told me about himself and his dreams. I watched him laugh when I made dumb jokes. We talked about poetry and life. He was right; there was no verse or beauty in his expression. He didn't think in pictures or see the world in some odd metaphor. He saw life as it was, real in front of him. He had a five year plan. He had an internship scheduled for the summer that could lead to a "good job." I had a spiral notebook that swept up my past and speculated on my present and didn't give a damn about tomorrow. I had napkins shoved inside the margins and poems on the backs of receipts from Publix. I didn't even think about the next moment. But despite our differences, I let him hold me. I let him wrap his plan around me and shield me from the strange motions that made me drift. He gave me his fuzzy scarf when I shivered and brought me back to my parents before it was too late or too cold. He kissed me lightly in the door.

5

THE NEW SEMESTER CRACKED the seal of the boundaries of campus. We ventured out and met more people and went to parties off campus. I had been seeing Grant for weeks and he had become a part of my routine. I woke up, I went to class, I came home, he came to pick me up and I stayed at his apartment. I did my homework there and used his computer. I ate take-out Guthrie's chicken dinners with buttered toast and crinkle fries. I took shower-shoe-less showers and he had a warm cozy bed with a fluffy comforter that I pulled up to my chin when I slept. We made love nice and neat under the covers and I made sure to moan. The price of all this comfort was the infamous word "boyfriend." I could hear my mother in my head calling daddy her boyfriend. I could see her up late making his lunches and hiding her freedom from him behind closet doors. Now I had to say it when I introduced him in public. I had to say it when someone asked me. I had to carry it with me into the poetry meetings he'd begun taking me to. The word wrapped around my torso like a corset. I'm not sure how it caught me, but comfort somehow made me ignore my gut. I adored Grant, but I was antsy.

DChristy Eves

It was January and the winter was colder than I expected it to be. Grant had to pull out his heavy winter coat to head to the meeting. I grabbed my book bag and reminded him I needed to go home that night.

"You're not staying with me tonight?"

"No, I have a meeting with my algebra professor before class at 8:30 a.m. Since I got a D last semester and had to retake it, Hickman wants me to meet with him to discuss my ignorance on the subject." I was lying and I wasn't even sure why.

"Okay, I'll drop you off tonight. You know I can help you study." Grant said.

"I know. You're the logical one." I patted his head. Grant grabbed his bag and two 2-liter bottles of orange pop from the cabinet. He walked with his head pulled back like he was looking for a spider on the ceiling. I could tell he was calculating the evening in his head. 'Okay, it should take about eleven minutes to drive there. We need to be there at six. It usually takes Billie five minutes longer to get ready than she says'....and on and on.

It was a strange poetry group meeting for me and I held back. Grant kept putting his hand on my knee or flopping a heavy arm around my shoulders. His touch was irksome and he sat too close. Last week Grant couldn't come and I got to come on my own. Rasheed, one of the other poets, picked me up and brought me. It was so liberating being there without Grant. I was there as a poet, a real poet, not Grant's little freshman girlfriend. Afterwards, I hung out at Rasheed's talking about the poetry set and drinking orange pop. He read me some of his new work he was thinking of reading the next week. Rasheed was really talented, super cool and so much fun to hang out with. I felt like it was *my* poetry group and these were *my* friends, not borrowed friends of Grants. But with Grant back, I didn't have much to say.

When I got back to the dorms, it was just after eight. Deidra was surprised to see me.

"You've been gone a while. How's Grant?" She was eating cup-o-noodles over a pile of open books.

"He's good. I just needed to be home tonight. I'm over there too much. I feel like I'm married or something."

"Not quite your bag is it? Well, Grant's a good guy. Hey, I'm headed out soon. Some of the other girls from the first floor are all going over to Jackie's sister's apartment to watch a movie. You wanna come?" Deidra s said closing up her books.

"Sure. Why not?" I shrugged.

"Okay, we're meeting upstairs in five minutes. I almost forgot. You got a message. I'll be right back." Deidra stepped out to go to the bathroom.

I checked the messages.

"Simone. I've been looking for you. Call me back. 555-7343." I hadn't even been thinking of Vaughn since I came back from Christmas. I figured we were over and that was that. I guessed we exhausted our possibilities.

"Looking for me?" I said out loud. My pulse quickened and I picked up the phone.

"Yeah." He answered.

"It's Billie."

"Simone. Where have you been hiding?"

"I've been right here."

"No you haven't. I called you several times."

"When? I never got any messages. Did you talk to my roommate or leave a message?" I asked.

"No. I called one night late. Your girl answered the phone and said you weren't home. I told her don't worry about it and hung up."

"Oh, *that* was you?"

"I called another night, she answered. You were not home." He had a 'you're caught' tone in his voice.

"Why didn't you leave a message?"

"Where do you go so late at night?"

I smiled; I didn't think he gave a shit where I was or what I did. I sat down on the bed.

"Not with you, because you don't want me." I pouted.

"I don't huh?"

"No. And if you do, I can't tell."

"You can't tell how bad I want you after last time?"

"Last time was a long time ago." There was a long pause.

"I'm on my way."

"I'll be out front."

I ditched Deidra and the girls and waited for him on the porch. He got there fast. I went to him before his car even stopped. I got inside and he looked at me for a moment and then pulled off. I had forgotten how beautiful he was; his skin, his forearms flexing on the wheel. We were halfway down the hill and he pulled off onto a small, dark, side street and stopped the car. He reached over and grabbed me by my neck and hair and started kissing me. He undid my pants and put his hands inside the back of my panties to touch my ass and grab me towards him.

"Take your pants off." He said in my ear. I took them off. He threw his seat back and I was on top of him in the front seat. I opened his pants and felt how hard he was. He was ridged and tight. It was happening again, I was falling into the sea. He was wild and aggressive. I beat my hands on the roof of the car; I was so dizzy I had to close my eyes and bury my face in his chest. He held my hips and rocked me against him. We were like waves crashing into the docks during a storm when the surge was high. I could almost taste the salt air. When I came, I threw my head back and my back landed on the horn; it screamed.

He pulled me back and looked at my face.

"You're mine. You know that?" I knew it. There was perspiration on his face and he stared without blinking. I knew there was something horribly wrong with me; he had complete control of me. We went back to his house of secrets and we fucked all night. He was tender then and stared at my face. While he was inside me, he watched me closely to see my reactions. He was driving his image into me. He was tattooing me from the inside. I woke up in the middle of the night naked and cold and thirsty. The black night glared at me through the window. The stars lied and told me how beautiful the night was. I lay back down quietly and tried not to wake him.

The morning came and I woke up to his arm clamping down on me, his hand landed on my belly.

"So, you've got a boyfriend now?" He said in my ear.

"Yes."

"You lied to me."

"When did I lie?"

"You told me you weren't the relationship type."

"I guess things change, things happen." I said.

"I get it. You didn't lie to me. You lied to him." I didn't say anything. "You can't be his girl. You belong to me." He was sleepy but his voice sounded matter-of-fact. He was jealous. I turned toward him. He kissed me. He got up and led me to the shower and he washed my body in hot soapy water that smelled like him—like something clean and wooden. He made love to me while I faced the tiles like a suspect. My skin was electric and he made the tears eke out of my eyes.

The next few weeks were strange. I had fallen into an altered routine and Grant was beginning to notice the difference. I still spent nights at his place, but my mind would wander off and he'd ask me,

"What are you thinking?" and I'd always answer

"Nothing."

I was replaying the look on Vaughn's face in the car. He looked almost vulnerable when he was inside me. I could smell him when he entered my mind. I would only stay at Grant's two nights a week and never after poetry group on Thursday. Vaughn began to call me every Thursday night and I would spend it in his intensive care. It was the combination of the sordid secret-ness of it, the feel of his skin on mine, the sense of urgency, the darkness and dim room; it was his scent and the way he sounded when he called me. The foreplay began when my phone rang

47

with him on the other end. He made me feel like I was living in a movie; some unreal affair played out in the 1700s between a nobleman and his concubine. I released myself to the experience and let him take over my life when I was with him. I was high.

It was another Thursday at poetry group and we were snacking on cut-up bits of raw vegetables and dipping them into ranch dressing. The poetry meetings were held at Sam's place. He had a townhouse in a wooded area near campus. Sam had simple furniture and cool African sculptures on his end tables next to dim lamps that looked like oil cans. There was a great framed poster of John Coltrane on the wall. I loved this place. It smelled like the woods and it felt like a cabin tucked away from the world.

When we got to Sam's, everyone was just starting to pile in. Sam was medium build with light hazel eyes and a soft face. His eyes vacillated between friendly and hesitant; he looked as though he was weighing judgments behind them. I found myself checking his eyes throughout the night to see what he approved and what he admonished. Sam had guacamole out and chips. Sumiyah, a tall girl with short hair twisted into tiny knots, brought a black bean vegetarian soup with flecks of green cilantro in a large crock pot. She always came with her boyfriend Omar, who preferred to be called O. Rasheed lived two doors down and had big, bushy hair that seemed to enter the door before he did. He was quiet, but when he spoke it was always something good and usually clever and funny.

DChristy Eves

The poets were a gathering of diverse sisters and brothers that came in carrying leather bound journals with attached hemp string bookmarks, papyrus laced, hard covered, blank books with hieroglyphics decorating the front and spine, hand-woven orange and red recycled cloth with a string of natural grass to wrap around like a present, embossed designs of Chinese symbols on leather, and soft pale white journals with feathers decoupaged onto the front. They were armed for poetry and were coming for the floor. I held on to my messy spiral notebook and tucked the loose papers back inside. We arranged ourselves in a circle on the floor. Each poet took a turn reading circled up on Sam's floor.

One minute there was a poem about changing the world, the next a poem that discussed the beauty of black skin, and then there was the musings of the food at somebody's mama's house—a whole diatribe on greens and cornbread. They were different than the average campus clique. They were intentional outcasts forming their own niche of conscious brothas and sistas. Some had natural hair (not popular back home where long straight hair reigned supreme), some were vegetarians, some were Muslim and a few guys claimed to be Five Percenters, and I had no idea what that meant. As a matter of fact, I didn't know anyone back home like them; I didn't know there was a different type of Black people. I always felt out of place back home. The girls with long painted nails layered in designs and pierced with nail charms were nothing like me. They dated "rollers" and cut their hair into sharp asymmetrics with touches of color for highlights. They popped gum loudly and could cuss out a seven foot man until he felt like seven inches.

49

DChristy Eves

I was often accused by my brother Chris of wanting to be White; in his mind anything not Black, like him, meant White. But, here was a whole world of beautiful Black people that were interested in the things that made me tick. They listened when I spoke. I listened when they spoke.

Tonight, Sam read a poem about Black male responsibility that sparked a heated discussion. Kellis, a tall girl with red, spiky hair was responding. She had just broken up with her boyfriend after a very obvious affair had come to the light.

"A man's first responsibility is to his woman. Now, y'all quick to say 'treat sistas right,' but I don't see any of you brothas trying to make a commitment and really stand by a woman. You are too busy out trying to load as many women into your little black books as possible. Like the number of women equal the inches of your penis. It doesn't! And what the hell does a woman want with a massive penis pushing all up in her stuff anyway?! You brothas haven't got a clue." Kellis said banging her fist on the floor.

"Okay, okay… now you're getting personal." Trent tried to calm her.

"Don't trip. You know it's true. Maybe Kellis is a little emotional, but it is personal. The way men rip through women is personal. Don't act like you ain't never been a so called player." Another girl said and put her hand up. "Cause I've known you for a lotta years buddy."

"Every man out there is not a player. I hate when y'all throw us all in one category. I'm a good man. Right baby?" Grant asked with his arm around me. I nodded confirmation.

"Yeah, dog, me too. Tell 'em Sumiyah." Omar backed Grant up.

"That's right baby." Sumiyah said petting his head like a puppy.

"Well, what's the woman's responsibility in all this?" Trent continued. "You all will willingly participate in some shady ass stuff and know what's up when you get there. But, all of a sudden your feelings get involved and you start showing out. All of a sudden... 'Where you been?' 'Who was dat?' 'Why you ain't call me last week?' Then y'all start keying cars and putting sugar in the tank." Trent finished his speech with a big flourish of his hands and sat back down.

"He ain't lyin'. Women are too emotional. It's 'cause y'all let a man inside you and let him take it from you. Then you stuck holding the bag. It's nature. It's how y'all built. Y'all stuck with that shit too." Sam chimed in.

"Yeah and showin' up at night unannounced. What's that shit about?" Rasheed's voice was slow and melodic and he sounded like he was rapping.

"What's the problem with showing up at night if you ain't got nothing to hide Rasheed?" Kellis persisted.

"It's bad manners." Rasheed broke the tension with his disarming smile. Everybody laughed.

"Okay, alright, alright. Somebody else read, and please, change the subject. Billie Simone. What cha' got kid?" Sam moderated the meeting back to the readings. I was the only freshman, and he always let me know it didn't go unnoticed.

"I'm not sure if it'll change the subject or not. Men and women seem to be on everybody's mind tonight. But I'll read it anyway…

I think of you
When I don't need to…
And life passes by my window
I move and go through motions
That remind me of you
I am infected
By your sting
Tattooed by your touch
I laugh at mental tickles
And arch my back for invisible touches
And climax for intangible intimacies
I remember every thing we've said
And…
Sometimes I go on like
We never kissed
Then up from behind
Your arms reach for my waist
And suddenly in the middle of a lecture
I'm in your arms
And carried away by your scent
And even the air serves you up unplanned"

When I finished, Kellis sighed,

"'Even the air serves you up.' I know exactly what you mean."
She took a long breath and Trent put his hand on her knee and gave her a little bump with his shoulder. She shrugged and we went on to the next poet. Sam stared at me a moment and narrowed his eyes. Grant grabbed another broccoli floret and dipped it in the ranch.

"Hey, Sumiyah. Damn, bring some meat next time. Everybody ain't vegetarians you know. Some people enjoy poetry and some hot wings. That was good baby." He patted my hand.

"Yeah, bring some rib tips next time." Rasheed finished.

"Bring your own damn dead animals." Sumiyah barked.

"I've got one." Fatima read the next poem and my poem disappeared into the air as quickly as it came. Except in Sam's eyes, from then on he watched me with suspicion and stopped calling me kid.

6

I SPENT THE MORNING trying to convince myself that time was not standing still; that the second hand was moving therefore time could not possibly be stagnant. But, it was an uphill battle against the long drawn out colloquium that all journalism students had to sit through on Thursday mornings. There was a guest speaker from WCTV. She was a stunning tall woman with honey-colored skin, long fluffy hair and bright grey eyes like Vanessa Williams. During the question and answer period a girl raised her hand and asked,

"Do you find it hard working in a male-dominated field when you're such an attractive woman?" Miss Obviously Stunning replied,

"I never really considered myself that attractive." *What a load of bullshit.* Here she was, a candidate for Miss America, and she still felt the need to be coy. She went on to say that working as a woman, you needed to work twice as hard to be taken seriously, especially a Black woman. She was wrong. The problem with being a woman in a male-dominated world wasn't working twice as hard; it was pretending to be whatever men thought you should be—some sedate version of yourself with no power. I lost respect for her instantly and I got out my notebook to write. When I checked the time again, only one minute had passed.

Everyday seemed to pass slowly and I kept my eyes on the clock waiting each week for Thursdays. This Thursday crawled by and I was anxious and irritated all day. When the meeting ended I went home and waited for the phone to ring. I was growing desperate to see Vaughn and he waited so late to call last Thursday. It was midnight when he finally did. The moments of his sweetness that tucked themselves between his coldness came fewer and fewer. I could only see sweetness on his face right before he came. Then his eyes would soften and he'd start the whispering in my ear. He would tell me I was beautiful, he told me I was the best, and he told me I belonged to him. It sounded so true when he said it. He told me he loved my body and couldn't get enough. But, the coldness returned and its heaviness increased each night. It was like he built up a supply of human-ness during the week, and after ejaculation it spilled out and that was that until next week. But, I needed that sweetness. I needed to see it in his face.

I sat up in bed awake and pretended not to watch the clock move. Deidra was already asleep and I watched her back swaddled in her comforter. She fell asleep after having a long conversation with Calvin. They exchanged 'I love you's' and she slept like a baby. I lay awake like a fool waiting for Vaughn to call. The high of being with him had an asking price of a very low feeling in the pit of my stomach. It was after midnight. No call.

By Wednesday the following week I hadn't heard a word from Vaughn and I tried not to call him, but I'd lost the battle. There was no answer and I left an attempt at nonchalance on his machine. Nothing. I was sick. Maybe he found another girl to possess. The girlfriend never bothered me, but another mistress was unbearable. The more I thought of it the angrier I got. When Z called me that evening I was sketching dark lines in my notebook with my pen so that the paper ripped underneath.

"Hey Bill. Whatcha doing?" Her voice was sweet. I thought about telling her what happened and how I was feeling, but I knew she wouldn't understand. She would just tell me cut it off with Vaughn. I still hadn't told her about him. I never even discussed it any further with Deidra.

"Nothin'. Sitting here looking stupid."

"What's wrong? I can hear it in your voice."

"I'm just sick of Grant that's all. I'm bored as hell." I said.

"I thought you really liked him. What happened?"

"I do. I think I'm not cut out to be in a relationship. There's too much responsibility. 'Where are you going?' 'Who with?' 'Gimme a call when you get back, so I know you made it home safe.' 'Don't have more than one drink; you know you're a lightweight.' All that crap makes me crazy."

"Bill, he's supposed to say that stuff. He cares about you, that's all. Maybe you just don't love him and that's what's really wrong." Z's tone was motherly.

"Yeah. Maybe. I do care about him. I said it and all when he did. It felt like maybe I meant it when I said it, but how the hell do I know? I never say 'I love you.' Pronouncing the words feels awkward to me. Mom never says it. But, it doesn't matter because I know it. She doesn't have to say it, it's obvious. I don't know why people feel like they have to say it to each other. It could be a lie all day long; the real proof is in what you do." I countered.

"I have to hear it. Men have to say it out loud to remind themselves they're committed to you. Otherwise, they'll forget and be out and some girl with a big booty will be flirting with them and they won't have any 'I love you' to stop them." She laughed. "I'm kidding, but for real, you're just comfortable with Grant, but you don't *love* him, that's why you can't really say it. When you really love a man, you won't be able to stop yourself."

"Yeah, I guess you're right. You tell Will?" I asked and raised an eyebrow.

"I tell him. He's a fool, but I tell him and he tells me. But I know what will make you feel better." She changed tones and sang a little.

"What do you want?"

"Come out tonight with Laurie and me to Wicked Wednesday."

"Wicked Wednesday?" I asked. I was already intrigued.

"Yeah, it's this party the Q's are throwing at Metropolis. It's supposed to be fun."

"How are we getting there?"

"Some guy Laurie knows agreed to drop us off there if we're ready at ten. He's not coming 'though. It's free for ladies if we get there before ten-thirty, so it's perfect." Z was smiling through the phone.

DChristy Eves

"Okay, yeah. Now for the important question of the evening… What are you wearing?"

It was a mob scene when we arrived. The club was on the main strip of restaurants and bars on Tennessee Street. The entire parking lot was filled with a swarm of brown faces and a mélange of music bursting from every car. It was hard to tell if the party was inside or out. The line of people led up to the doorway which was guarded by a big, muscle-bound guy in an army cap, purple Q-dog tee-shirt, camouflage pants and those notorious horrible gold-painted combat boots for which the Q's were famous. If the Kappas were known as the pretty boys of campus, then the Q's were their polar opposites. They were known as the dirty dogs of campus. They were rough, unpolished and unapologetically male. It was just past ten when we arrived.

"Oh my God!!! Look at that line." Z was amazed.

"I hope y'all brought some money. Y'all not getting in free." The guy giving us a ride laughed.

"Yeah, I brought money. Did you guys bring enough? How much is the cover?" I asked cupping my hands in my lap and looking as nervous as I felt.

"I think it's only five dollars. Let's just get out of here and walk up." Z took over; she was fearless.

"I have ten dollars. That's probably enough to get in and get one drink." Laurie added.

"I'm gonna need that drink right away." I admitted.

DChristy Eves

We jumped out of the car and made our way through the crowd to the line. When we finally reached the front, Z asked the bouncer,

"Did we make it?"

"Yeah cutie, you got it." He said. He stamped each one of our hands in an invisible stamp that could only be seen under a black light and inside we went.

We were hit immediately by the wall of warm air. There were red, blue and green stage lights over the dance floor and they moved and changed with the music. I looked for the bar. "Freak Me Baby" by Silk was blasting. *I hope to God they aren't carding.* We made our way to the bar and I immediately ordered a drink.

"Rum and coke please."

"Fuzzy Navel." Z ordered.

"Me too." Laurie followed.

The bartender seemed to not care or not notice we didn't have bands. I got my first drink and drank it as quickly as possible. I was waiting for my click like Brick in *Cat on a Hot Tin Roof.* The first drink was not helping. Z, Laurie and I huddled near a group of bar tables overlooking the dance floor. We were hawking a table hoping to get a seat. Dr. Dre's "Nothin' But a G Thang" came to the rescue. Three girls screamed and abandoned their table to dance. We were close to the bar and had a perfect perch to watch the dance floor. I immediately decided I would stay there all night. I wished I was fearless and free like Z, but I needed something to help release me.

"I'm getting another drink. I've got enough money for three and I will be drinking all three." I told the girls.

59

"Wow, you're done already?" Laurie was just starting to sip hers. I got another rum and coke and scuttled back to the table. On my way back, a tall guy with bad breath and a gold tooth in the front grabbed my arm by the back of the bicep.

"Wassup Red?" I pulled my arm sharply away and ran back to the table. "Bitch." He called as I went.

I drank my second drink and was beginning to relax a bit. Z and Laurie both accepted dance invitations from guys and I promised to guard the table. The first set of music was mainstream Hip Hop and R&B. Next they segued into a short Reggae set, and then played an aggressive, high energy dance music called Bass, which was popular in Florida but hadn't yet made its way into Detroit. It was hard hitting, sexually explicit and chauvinistic—basically candy for college students. The dancing changed and girls were throwing their butts against guys' pelvises and gyrating to the music. Girls were coming off the dance floor drenched in sweat and with their hair frizzed and disheveled. Z stepped off the floor without a hair out of place and came back to the table.

"What's wrong? You don't wanna dance?" Z asked adjusting her top.

"No, I do. I'm just holding the table."

"I can hold it while you go dance."

"I'm cool for right now." I said scanning the room.

"Ok. Guess who's here?" Z's voice picked up.

"Will." I said. It wasn't hard to guess.

"Yup. Checking up on me. He knew I was coming and he just wanted to roll up on me and surprise me."

"Where is he?"

"Look." She pointed to the other side of the room where more tables were. He was sitting with a group of guys. "So, I'm dancing with Patrick from econ... you know Patrick right?"

"Yeah."

"Right. He's nobody I'm interested in; we were just dancing. Anyway, Will comes up from behind and taps me on the shoulder. Then he basically tells Patrick to beat it. Can you believe him?" Her smile during the story told her secret; she loved it.

"Was he mad?" I played along.

"Not really, but he is really showing his ass. I think he's already drunk."

"Well, make him come over here and buy us another drink."

"Oh he will. His friend that wants to meet you is over there." She pointed.

I couldn't really make him out, but I told her I'd meet him provided two things.

"Is he cute and will he buy me a drink?"

"I'll go ask." She said and headed over to them.

While I was waiting, Laurie came back and was sweating lightly.

"Did you see me?! I was dancing with that guy in the baseball cap. He kept tryin' to grab my butt, so I left him there." Laurie said and pointed him out.

"Will is here." I told her.

61

DChristy Eves

"He doesn't like the idea of her dancing with other men, so I knew he'd show up." Laurie said letting out a sigh. They were making their way over; Will had his arm around Z. There were two guys with him. One of the guys was slightly heavy set and was dancing a little as he walked. The other guy was slim, had dark eyes and he snaked through the crowd as if he'd parted the Red Sea. I was sure this one was coming for me.

He had a deep, slow voice like he was a DJ for an after-hours radio show that only played slow jams and make-out music. He was a soft, light brown color and had dark, piercing eyes. He was slender but moved his body with great confidence. He had an understated gold necklace around his neck that held a coin shaped medallion that looked as if it were an important accolade of some sort. He wasn't flashy or garish; just relaxed and very sure of himself.

"Billie, this is my boy Derrick." Will introduced him. There was something very sexy about him, but I couldn't quite figure out why. He was cute, not gorgeous like Vaughn, but he was cool personified. We spent the rest of the evening talking in the group and they did indeed buy us another round. By my fourth drink, I was loose and Derrick asked me to dance. It was the slow jam set. We danced close, but he was very respectful, which actually surprised me.

When the night was over Will asked,

"How were y'all planning to get home?" None of us had any idea. The thought never occurred to us, not even Z. Will was tipsy and laughing, but tried to affect a father's tone,

62

"See, I don't know what the hell you women be thinking 'bout, comin up here with no damn way home. We'll take y'all."

Although Derrick and his brother Rod were both freshmen, they had a car and an off-campus apartment. On the way home I noticed that we were not headed up the hill and back to campus.

"Where are we going?" I asked.

"We're getting drinks." Derrick explained. "Don't worry about anything, we've got it covered." I looked at Z and she looked at me and shrugged. They pulled up to a liquor store and went inside while we stayed in the car. They came back and Rod was carrying a two liter of Coke and a big bottle of orange juice.

"Let's ride." Derrick said.

I had a slight uneasy feeling about going to their apartment without even being asked if I wanted to go, but Z and Laurie didn't seem to mind so I went along with it. The sound of the radio and the laughter gave me permission to block my disappointment about Vaughn. But, I couldn't help but wonder if tomorrow would produce his call. Was it really over? No conversation, no 'hey I think we should stop seeing each other,' nothing. Just gone. I couldn't accept that. How can you spend weeks making love to someone and then just disappear without a trace? Maybe his girlfriend found out and he couldn't call anymore. Maybe his need for control extended to him deciding when and how we would end, and there was nothing I could do about it.

By the time we arrived at their apartment my unsuccessful attempt at clearing my mind had fueled an underlying anger. Derrick and Rod had a simple apartment in a complex not far from campus. They had a nice couch that did not appear to have come from a resale shop or a hand-me-down from Grandma. There was an aquarium against the back wall with no water in it, but rocks and thick broken branches. It was lit by a florescent light and two large snakes lay coiled under the lights.

"Are those real snakes?" I had to ask.

"Yeah, those are my girls. Don't look so freaked out. They're not poisonous." Derrick smiled a little and continued, "Let me fix you ladies a drink." Derrick and Rod went into the kitchen. Will took a large handled gallon bottle of Tanqueray out of his jacket and set it on the table. Zondra's eyes widened. Derrick also removed another one from his jacket; he picked up the remote to a very elaborate stereo system. It was the kind someone's parents would own, not a college student. Derrick left little to the imagination and played Snoop Dogg's "Gin and Juice" while pouring drinks.

"Did you steal that?!" Z's tone was sharp.

"Z, don't worry about it. It's ours now. Here have a drink." Will tried to calm her down.

"This is too strong, put some more juice in it. I can still taste the gin." Z ordered.

Will added more juice to her mixture and Rod brought drinks for Laurie and me. We spent the evening listening to the music, talking loud, laughing and comparing funny moments from the club. After a while Laurie and I were sitting on the floor laughing. We were smoking cigarettes and Laurie's ankle-length demur dress was hiked up to her thighs as she smoked and cursed and then laughed at herself. Her cocoa legs stretched out in front of her. I stretched out on the floor next to her

64

and propped my head against the couch and tried to see if I could make smoke circles. I was just drunk enough to think I could. Z had started to nod off on the couch and Rod was getting bored with us and started making his way back to his bedroom.

Derrick made his way over to the floor where I was lying and tapped my knee lightly. He was a contradiction to himself—he stole gallon-sized bottles of liquor like a thug but made sure all of the ladies had a properly mixed cocktail; he played jazz on his trumpet and gangsta rap on his stereo; he was trying to make sure I was comfortable while also trying to assess when I was drunk enough for him to make his move.

"What's this on your back?" He could see the tip of my tattoo. I leaned away from him so he could see it better. My bodysuit had a racer back and he pulled it further away so he could see it all.

"I got that when I was sixteen." I explained, "A rose on an ankh." He fingered the lines of my tattoo. I'd seen *Poison Ivy* with Drew Barrymore when I was sixteen and this, in combination with an interest in Egyptology and my mother's permission behind my father's back, resulted in my first tattoo. His finger tips were cool from his glass on my shoulder blade.

"It's sexy. Do you have any more?"

"Not so far."

"You want another one?

"Yeah, I guess I love the pain." I said and looked him in the eye. By then Laurie had leaned back against the couch and was starting to lose fuel. Will was holding Z and Rod was passed out on his bed with the door open. I could see his feet hanging off the bed.

"Would you like to sleep in my room?" Derrick offered.

"Yes." I accepted.

He stood up and put out his hand like Rett Butler to Scarlet O'Hara. I took it in matched fashion and off we went. *The best way to get over a man is to get under another. Fuck Vaughn.*

We went back into his bedroom and I could barely make out his bed against the wall in the dark. There were some clothes in a chair and a few books piled neatly in the corner. His trumpet case stood up right and rested in the corner. I was not quite as drunk as Derrick thought. I stumbled a little and giggled to watch his reaction. He liked it. He wanted to believe he'd trapped an unsuspecting innocent wide-eyed freshman girl back to his cool off-campus apartment, plied her with stolen Tanqueray and got her into bed. I played along.

I got into bed and pretended to be vulnerable. He slid in next to me. When he was close he smelled like fresh cotton and powder. I liked the combination. He spooned me and started kissing the back of my neck. He lifted my hair and stroked it. I made soft moans to let him know he should keep going. He explored my body with his hands and moved me very gently in rhythm. The stereo was still playing in the living room, but so faintly I couldn't tell what the song was, but I could feel the gentle beat of something familiar. He rolled me over on my back and then eased his way on top of me. He kissed me very deeply and I closed my eyes and let myself drift away. He reached down into my pants and unsnapped my bodysuit; it was tight and I felt the pressure release. He undressed me slowly as I watched him look at my body. I felt beautiful, the way he stared at my hips. He put on a condom and pretty soon we were rolling in time with each other and I shut out the world and let him have me. I buried my face in his neck and took in his scent.

Powder and fresh cotton.

7

"WHAT ARE YOU OVER THERE THINKING ABOUT?"

"Nothing."

"Don't lie."

"I'm just thinking, that's all. Some thoughts are private."

"Private. Okay, well at least private is honest. I can accept private. I hate when women say 'nothing' or 'fine.' It always means something is up." Grant said and finished off his bowl of Frosted Flakes and got up to put the bowl in the sink.

"Well, nothing *is* up and I *am* fine. I just keep turning some things over in my head. Like why do you eat cereal at night and pizza in the morning?" I asked changing the subject off me and onto him.

"Don't be cute. I'm serious." Grant said trying to regain his line of questions.

"I'm not cute?"

"Stop it." Grant came back and sat next to me on the couch. I grabbed a pillow and put it in his lap and lay down and curled up. He stroked my hair.

DChristy Eves

"You know I love you right?" He said. I smiled and tucked my hands under his knees to get warmer and I closed my eyes. It was warm and comfortable at Grant's place. I could tuck myself away from my world and forget myself in his cozy brown apartment.

It was getting harder to be two people. One life invariably bled into the other. Grant was getting so close to me. I was getting closer to him too. I could talk to him; tell him what I was feeling. He listened to me and held my hand. We talked about our childhoods, our futures, our lives. He made me laugh. He took care of me and watched me when I walked away from him. He made sure I made it to the door before he pulled off. He never sped off not caring whether or not I was abducted on the way up the steps. I did love him. I loved his voice and the way he laughed and told jokes. I loved the way he missed me when I was gone; and I mean missed *me*, not having sex with me, but me. He asked me questions about myself and hung on my every word. We went places together and people called us Grant and Billie. But, regardless of love, Vaughn was a thread in my mind; he weaved in and out of my days without rhyme or reason. He hadn't called in weeks. One missing Thursday turned into four. I promised myself right then that I'd leave other men alone. Grant was a good man. I did love him.

Spring was early in Florida and by March it was already getting warm and the sun was shining. The Wednesday before Spring Break we decided to go to Wicked Wednesday again to celebrate. By this time we had a routine established. We left by nine-thirty to ensure getting in free and arriving before the parking lot madness had set in; we figured out

DChristy Eves

that it was at precisely 10 p.m. the parking lot exploded into the Black Woodstock. We got in early with no hassle and I was able to get in at least one drink, sometimes two, before the crowd set in. This supplied me with just enough anti-anxiety medicine to be warm and friendly when the people arrived. We had no problems securing a table and we alternated who stayed behind to guard it. I still stayed at the table more than Z and Laurie, but I made my way to the dance floor when either the song or the man seemed good enough. Will usually showed up at some random moment in the night and Z managed to be surprised each time. Laurie always seemed slightly disappointed. Derrick and Rod hadn't been back since that first time.

I was particularly fueled with liquid courage tonight and was dancing more than usual. It looked like I might actually pass algebra this semester, a celebration was in order. I was dancing with some guy I'd met earlier that was kind enough to buy me drink number four. We were pressed close and I was dancing with my butt against him and making him hard. He pressed his face close to my neck. I enjoyed the thought that he had a crush on me and I was fulfilling some fantasy of his. I was in my own world with the music when I heard my name squealed from the railings above the dance floor.

"Billie!!!" It was Sumiyah, from poetry group.
What in the hell was she doing here? Seniors rarely came to this party; even if they did it was only senior guys fishing for drunk freshmen to take home. I was so startled to see her that I stopped dancing for a moment, but with nothing to say or do, I just turned to face my partner

and we kept on dancing. Grant was sure to hear about this one. But it didn't stop me.

By the end of the night we were tired, tipsy and ready to go. The Q's had begun their step parade around the floor to "Nothing But the Dog in Me" and that was our cue to leave. We still never planned a ride home. We would just stand around outside and wait to see a guy we knew and then he would offer us a ride. If we didn't like that guy, we'd just wait for another one. When we got outside the familiar sight of Derrick's turquoise Eclipse caught my eye. He had come for me. We had a couple of short conversations in passing on The Set. He asked when we were going to hang out again, but I told him I couldn't, that I had a boyfriend. I knew this would not deter him, but only make him more anxious. I was wondering when he would just come to take me away again. I knew it wouldn't take long, and here he was.

"Ladies." He said perfecting his southern way and opening the door. I hesitated, but not for long. How else was I getting home? I wondered if Sumiyah was outside and saw us leaving with them. We got in and crammed in the back seat. The three of us shared the back seat with Will. Rod and Derrick posted up front. Z sat in Will's lap and Laurie pressed in the middle. I sat on the passenger side and had a diagonal view of Derrick. He had a long peak in the back of his hair trailing down the nap of his neck to a point. His pale, gold necklace rolled and glinted a little when he moved. *Powder and fresh cotton.*

We got back to their place and the events of the other evening pretty much repeated themselves. We drank gin and juice, listened to

71

music; we laughed about the club and we all got drunk and started winding down the evening. Derrick rarely took his eyes off me. He knew and so did I. This time Rod decided to go for Laurie and asked her if she wanted to sleep in his room. She wobbled a little and sang Hall and Oates,

"I can't go for that, no-oo. No can do."

Rod laughed and went to bed. I had never seen Laurie so drunk; she stayed in the living room with Will and Z. They pulled out the sofabed. Z and Laurie shared the sofabed while Will stayed on the floor. Derrick and I went back to his room and started kissing immediately. There was no pretense this time and no pretending to be drunk and him trying to be gentle and not rouse me from a compliant state. He knew I wanted him too. He was strong and sure with me and I was falling down the rabbit hole.

"Is it good to you girl?" *Powder and fresh cotton.*

"Yes."

Afterwards, he was still a gentleman and held me close. He tucked himself in bed against the wall and then opened his arms for me when I came back from the bathroom. He pulled me close to him and turned me to face him and kissed my forehead. I fell asleep with my head on his chest breathing in his scent and playing with his medallion.

A while later I woke up alone in Derrick's bed and it was still very late; I heard the door open and he was coming back with a glass of water.

"Are you thirsty?" He offered. I nodded still hazy. I drank a bit and gave it back to him. He finished the glass and set it down on the nightstand and got back into bed. He grabbed me close to snuggle.

"Are Z and Laurie alright?" I whispered.

"They look more than alright to me." He laughed a little and squeezed me close.

"What do you mean?"

"Nothing. Go back to sleep."

I turned back into his chest, nuzzled his neck and went back to sleep.

Thursday was another poetry group, the last one before Spring Break, and this seemed to bring out the militant in some of the writers. Sam read a poem about Blackness being perceived as subjective. He read it as a separate personality ala Bigger Thomas, but in this case 'Blacker' was the persona non grata. It sparked a discussion.

"Who determines how Black you are? Black people are always checking each other. They check you if your speech is too proper. They check what you're eating... 'Ain't Black enough, where's the pork?' They check the music you listen to, 'Ain't Black enough, what...you wanna be White?' 'Black people only listen to Rap and R&B.' " Sam said. He sat on the floor with his legs crossed and was getting fired up. I knew what he meant about being accused of not being Black enough. Back home I never fit the mold of what was expected of me as a Black girl. I didn't eat the right foods, I was nearly vegetarian, and I didn't speak the way I should either; not enough of the right kind of slang. I "talked White" they joked on the block, and now I was the wrong kind of

73

woman to boot. I didn't wait to have sex until I was in love and I didn't make a man deserve it either. I just fucked when and where I pleased. I had to hide what kind of woman I was back home. I wasn't sure what kind of woman I actually was. What did my desire make me?

"Try the double stamp of being a woman and Black." I said deciding to join the forum.

"Yeah, it's true." Kellis backed me up.

"We don't just have the voice of internal racism, but sexism as well. We are pushed down by brothers trying to make us into this mother/whore image. There's no wiggle room for a woman. It's like there's some standard of Blackness that we are all expected to meet, and if you're a woman, then there's a different standard to meet. You have to be sweet, smart and wait 'til you're married and if you don't you're a different type of girl. What about shades of Blackness and shades of a woman? We're all just people. Human. Why do men get the freedom to just be?" I asked.

I looked over at Grant. He seemed the same. *I don't think he knows,* I thought. I kept thinking about last night, the club, Derrick. *What the fuck is wrong with me?* I put my head in my hands and shook it from side to side. Sumiyah wasn't there and I wasn't sure if she had talked to anyone there ahead of time or even talked to Grant. But he seemed normal, munching on the chips and salsa and patting my leg every so often.

Sam ended the evening with some Marvin Gaye to lighten the mood as people packed up their notebooks to leave. Grant was really tired and in a hurry and told me he would wait for me in the car while I went to the bathroom. When I came out, everybody was gone and Sam was cleaning up the kitchen.

"Goodnight Sam."

"Wait a minute."

"What's up?"

"Grant is my boy, you know that right?" He said and I nodded. "Grant and I go back a long way, since freshman year. He really cares about you…. And I think you are a shady little… You just watch yourself. You look all sweet and innocent, but I can see through all your shit." Sam's eyes were straight as arrows and he stared at me. My heart started to pound in my chest. *Sumiyah.*

"Sam, I don't know what you are talking about."

"All your sexual poems and the way you look at me across the room. Look, I'm not stupid and I see what I see. I feel like I'm watching my boy make a huge mistake. You don't know how much he loves you." Sam said and his inflection went up.

"I know. And I think you should mind your own business. Grant is a grown man." I said and held my ground. I grabbed my bag and headed for the door.

There was nothing else to say. I went out of the door stung by what Sam said and not just what he said, but what it meant. He was half right, I was shady. But, I did not have my sights set on him. I admired him and his work; he was clearly one of the best poets in the group. The reality was whatever I felt about him, I loved the group and now I wouldn't feel comfortable to come back here and hear the poems and sit in the incense filled room brimming with people that found a place to

75

belong. Between Sumiyah and Sam, I wouldn't be welcomed and I couldn't be free with my poems anymore. I tucked my head down and ran out to Grant waiting in the car.

"What took you so long?" Grant said watching me enter the car.

"I just wanted to help Sam straighten up a little."

It was now officially time for me to break up with Grant. I decided then I would tell him when we got back to his place. But not long after we got back the phone rang and he answered.

"Hello……. Hey what's up?………Yeah, she's here….no, don't worry about it. That's okay, I don't mind at all." Grant handed the phone to me. "It's Z."

"Z? What's wrong?" I knew immediately something was up.

"Something happened between Laurie and Will." Z started.

"What?!" I shot up on the couch. Grant looked over at me and I got up and went into his bedroom. "What….. what happened?"

"Last night at Derrick and Rod's… after you and Derrick went into his room, Will pulled out the sof bed. Laurie was pretty drunk at that point and was sitting up in bed and still drinking. I was tired and laid down on the sofabed next to her and I guess I passed out. At some point during the night Will got into bed in between us. That's when it happened."

"Wait, what happened?" I said.

"Laurie said she's not sure, but she thinks Will may have been touching her."

"Touching her? Where?"

"Fingering her." Z said with bitterness affecting her tone.

76

"Wait, wait, wait. So Laurie told you all this?"

"Yeah."

"When?"

"Just now. Laurie was acting strange and not looking at me all day. I didn't pay her much attention because we were both a little hung over. But then she told me she had something bad to tell me. She said she wasn't sure what had happened but she thought something went on between them. So, you know me, I said let's call Will. We did and I listened on the extension while she talked to him. She asked, 'Will, did something happen between us last night?' He told her 'Look, it didn't mean anything and we should never tell Z. You don't mean anything to me and I wanna be with Z.' That's when it got real. I'm sitting here looking at Laurie, and I know she had to be hurt the way he was talking to her, and listening to Will admit that 'something happened.' Now, I'm not sure what exactly happened, but I'm going over there to find out. Can you get Grant to take us? Will is still over at Derrick and Rod's?" Z asked, but it hardly sounded like a question.

"Yeah. I'll be right there."

I hung up the phone and told Grant Z really needed a ride to go see her boyfriend. Grant was hesitant, but I persisted. We drove to the dorms to get Z. When we got there, Z was standing out front like a soldier waiting to engage and Laurie was sitting on the steps behind her with her head down. When they got in the car Z took over. I got in the back with Laurie and let Z sit up front with Grant to give directions. Laurie was stone silent and I stared at her through the corner of my eye.

77

But, I was more concerned about Z who now had a steely focus on her face.

Grant pulled up in front of the apartment and we all got out. Grant grabbed my hand,

"What's going on Billie? I think I should come up there with you."

"No. Z's just really mad at her boyfriend. It'll be fine." I said. I was anxious and pulled my hand away and hurried up after Z who was already at the door knocking.

When Rod opened the door I told Grant, "Go. We're fine." I waved him away.

"Hey ladies." Rod opened the door and smiled surprised. Z put on a pleasant smile and said, "Hey" and walked inside. She was calm now, causal even. Laurie was still quiet. Derrick was on the couch watching television and some guy we sort of knew was in the kitchen drinking a beer. Will came out from Derrick's room and met us at the door. He smiled and gave Z a hello hug.

"Hey baby." Will said.

She hugged him back and said, "Hey sweetheart."

Laurie and I looked at each other for the first time. Everybody was kind holding their breath a little. I sat down next to Derrick. It was awkward to say the least, sitting next to Derrick, rethinking my decision last night with him and sitting there waiting for something to blow up with Z, Will and Laurie. But, Z just continued the evening like nothing was wrong. Will was happy and joking around. Then out of nowhere Z said,

"Something ain't right." Everybody paused.

Will asked, "What do you mean?"

"I can feel it. I don't know what, but something ain't right."

Will got nervous and a chink in his armor showed.

"I'm sure it's nothing." Will said.

Z got up and went to the kitchen with Rod and asked for something to drink. When he handed her the glass it slipped out of her hand and shattered on the floor. It seemed louder than it should.

"See.... something ain't right." Z proclaimed again. Will shifted in his seat. Rod picked up the big pieces and set them on the counter and got a broom to sweep up the rest. Z came back and sat down next to Will.

"There's something wrong with Laurie." Z whispered to Will. "I don't know what it is, but she's been acting strange all day. Now, I can tell.... something ain't right."

"I'm sure it's fine. Don't worry. She's fine." Will tried to reassure Z.

"No. I think I should talk to her myself." Z got up and Will started a motion to stop her then just sank back into the couch. Will looked sick. Z went into the room with Laurie and a few moments later she stood in the door.

"Will," the Z from the car ride over was back. "I need to talk to you in here, right now." Will went over to her in the doorway. "Is there something you want to tell me?" Z continued.

"No." Will said, defiant.

"Did something happen between you and Laurie last night?"

He looked right at Laurie and said, "No."

"Laurie said it did." Z said.

"Well, she's a fucking liar." Will's voice was dry and flat.

"I don't think so." Z was quick to retort. We all watched them go back and forth like a tennis match. Nobody moved.

"Look somebody better tell me what the hell happened last night."

"Nothing happened!!" Will yelled.

"Yes it did! You're the fucking liar!!" Z matched his volume.

"Z dammit…"

"Tell me what happened!!!!"

"WE FUCKED!"

Silence.

"We fucked, and it didn't mean anything! It's no big deal. We were drunk and it didn't mean a damn thing. I want to be with you, not her. Now just quit overreacting!" Will left Z standing there in the doorway and went back and sat down and started watching the rerun of The Jefferson's that was on. Z headed towards the kitchen to lean on the counter. It looked like she was going to faint. Rod was still in the kitchen and he looked over at me for some guidance. Before I could get up, Z picked up a big piece of the broken glass that was shaped like a knife from the counter and charged Will screaming,

"I HATE YOU!!!!"

Rod grabbed Z from behind and Derrick leapt up from the couch and got her from the front. Z's arm was fully extended with the broken glass and she was swinging.

I shot up. "Oh my God!!!"

"Overreacting?!!! You fucked my roommate while I was in the bed you piece of shit!!!" She was screaming and crying at the same time.

Will was hiding behind Derrick and looked stunned. The guys got the broken glass from her hand, and not easily, and I took Z by the arm to the bathroom. We passed Laurie sitting on the floor crying.

I sat her down on the lid of the toilet and put my arms around her. She cried hard and for a long time. Then suddenly she stopped, got up and went to the mirror. She wiped her face, smoothed her hair and looked at me. The business Z was back.

She said, "We need to leave here. Right now."

"Let's go." I said and stood up.

We left the bathroom and Z stopped and looked at Laurie who was still crying.

"Come on." Z said.

All three of us walked past everyone and out the front door without saying a word. We walked to the gas station just outside the complex and used a pay phone to call Grant. On the ride home we said nothing.

I asked Grant to take me back to the dorms. I knew I couldn't talk to him now and I wanted to be close in case Z needed me. I told her to come with me, but she said no. *Laurie might want to sleep with one eye open*, I thought. I got home and crawled into bed heavy with my thoughts. I couldn't imagine how anything would be the same after what happened. Worst of all, there was nothing I could do for Z. When the phone rang I picked it up without a thought.

"Simone."

Before I knew it, I was in another world. Vaughn took my hand and led me into the kitchen.

He asked me, "What's up with you?" in a very sweet and low tone of voice.

I said, "Nothing."

He leaned back against the counter and pulled me close to him by my waist. He lowered his hands to my butt and nudged my face with his. He leaned in and kissed me soft.

He said, "I missed your lips."

I replied, "Did you really?"

Dizzy. I was dizzy. All the promising and swearing I'd be faithful meant nothing. My relationship with this man kissing me was simple, no complications. I wanted to have sex with him, over and over; and he wanted to have sex with me, over and over. I did not want to spend my days with him and nor did he want to spend his days with me, but damn if we didn't want to spend our nights together.

He sat up on the counter and asked me to "kiss it," and he pulled it out. His voice was somewhere between a plea and a command. I kissed his lips a minute and then lowered my head, tasting the instrument that would soon stir my desire. After a while we went into the dining room. He sat down in a chair and I fell to my knees kissing and caressing him. Soon we'd be locked together in lustful clutches. Soon

I'd feel him rise inside of me and fill me up, and satisfy my urge for him. I sucked him until my mouth ached, then he asked,

"You want some of this dick?"

I nodded yes.

Then he told me to take off my pants. And I did. I sat on top of him and rocked back and forth and up and down as he watched... carefully.

"Where did you learn how to do this?" ..... "Did you learn from your boyfriend?" ..... "Where did you learn this?"

I responded, "I know what you like."

We rocked and swayed and rolled. It felt so good. Then he picked me up and put me on his dining room table. He watched my face so he could see how he was making me feel. Occasionally, he'd lean his head back and moan and say my name and tell me how good I felt.

"Simone....Simone."

When we finished we went upstairs to his room and got in bed. He fell asleep. And not cuddling close, but on opposite ends leaving me cold. I felt like if I had my car I would've driven home. But I was there for the night. I started kissing his ears and woke him up. I listened to him laugh. I ran my hands through his soft, brown hair catching each curl with my nails. I felt his silky skin and touched his hard legs. I loved his body. Not an ounce of fat, just smooth, caramel colored silk on muscle. I have never felt a man with such smooth skin. It was absolutely intoxicating. I wanted him over and over until my head was spinning and I was too weak to move. And as I wanted him, he wanted me.

"YOU OKAY?"

"I'm alright. Laurie and I finally talked. The strange thing is I'm not really mad at her." Z said and exhaled lightly. We were in the backseat on our way to Daytona Beach for the weekend. Deidra and one of her girlfriends were up front humming along with her Brian McKnight tape. Deidra was going to see her boyfriend and asked if we wanted to tag along. With nothing better to do and a desire to see the beach, off we went.

"Why not?" I asked.

"Because at least she told me. She was honest and I know she didn't have to be. I feel like Will took advantage of the situation. He was not that drunk." Z said.

"Well, whatever you say. I'm gon' keep my eye on her, I know that."

"I know you are." Z looked at me and her eyes softened to know I had her back.

"I'm surprised you still wanted to go on this trip."

84

"Well, I may have forgiven her, but I didn't want to look at her all weekend. The timing of this trip couldn't have been better. Will started calling me as soon as I got home. He was begging to talk to me and pleading. I was like, 'you didn't have shit to say in front of your boys.' I told him it's over. I'm done." Z said and pushed her glasses back on the bridge of her nose.

"Did you tell him 'something ain't right'?" I bumped her.

She laughed, "Okay, did I fuck with him a little or what?"

"That was hilarious. I didn't know what you were doing."

"I just wanted to see if he would come clean on his own. Well, fuck him." Z crossed her arms and turned to look out the window.

"Well," I said and reached in my purse and grabbed my suntan oil. "Here's to a weekend full of denial and fun." She grabbed her sunblock and toasted.

I looked out the window and tried not to think of Vaughn, but the more I resisted the stronger the images. I could see his car when he picked me up. I could see his eyes. I could feel his hands underneath me. I could hear him whispering close to my ear. "You're beautiful," "You're the best," "You will always belong to me." He claimed he'd missed me terribly while he couldn't call. He said his girlfriend got wind of our affair and he had no choice but to cool things down. I wasn't sure if that was true or just something to tell me just to make me relax. It didn't matter. I'd missed him so much I wasn't sure I cared why he was gone, just that he was back. His room was dark and familiar. He was strong and persistent. He enveloped the whole night, like he did that first time. When I returned home Friday, I was so tired I slept through the last day of classes before the break. I almost changed my mind about going to Daytona, but then I knew I would just end up at home waiting for the phone to ring.

I was starting to hate myself. I hated being a liar. I hated being a fool. Sam's comments really got underneath my skin. Did he think I was after him? I think he could tell that I wasn't talking about Grant in my poems. The sense of urgency and touch of roughness definitely didn't point to Grant. Why didn't Grant notice? I was almost telling on myself. He wasn't even listening. He was just waiting for the talking to swell up again so he could munch and complain about the food. I had to let Grant go. I was more like my brothers than I'd thought. I had no interest in committing and I loved the game.

Our first trip to the beach was surreal. The crowd made me crazy; I hated all those people sticking together in the heat. The music was too loud and you could barely see the ocean for the people. It was disappointing. Men cat called at us as we walked by. Strange hands groped for our upper arms. I was disgusted and decided then that I hated being grabbed on my upper arm by a man. It was the modern day equivalent of being clubbed and dragged back to the cave. Women were walking down the beach in crazy outfits. Girls with huge asses wore thongs and net shirts and small bikini tops. Every so often a woman would stop the line and bend over exposing herself and letting swarms of guys video her. It was like watching hyenas attack leftover meat.

We managed to stay safe and together the whole trip and I vowed never to return to such an event ever in life. I couldn't wait for the weekend to end and go home and check my machine.

9

WHEN I GOT BACK I checked my machine straight away. The light was blinking and I couldn't wait to hear it. "Billie. We need to talk." It was Grant. *Uh, oh. Famous last words.* I unpacked slowly then called him. He answered quickly like he was waiting on me. He wouldn't say anything on the phone and told me he was on his way up to campus to see me. I went outside and met him out front about a half hour later. We started walking down the Spring Break abandon Set towards the center of campus.

"Grant what's on your mind?

"What I really want to know is what's on yours?"

"What do you mean?"

"I mean do you want this relationship? You're always distant now. We hardly ever make love anymore; you don't spend the same kind of time with me. You're always rushing off. If you want something different you need to tell me." Grant said.

"Maybe…. Maybe I do. Maybe I'm not cut out to be in a relationship." I answered.

"Have you been with someone else?"

"Why would you ask me that?"

"Why don't you answer me?"

"Where is this coming from? That's all I'm asking?"

"That's not important. What's important is your answer….. So have you?" Grant persisted.

"Yes." I said. There was a long silence and Grant stopped walking.

"So what happened?"

"I was drunk, that's all."

"So that's when you met him? Drunk and out at some club?" Grant shook his head. The day fought against itself; it was sunny and warm but chilly when the wind blew and the trees hissed. Grant sat down on the concrete wall flanking the walk down hill. I sat next to him and tucked my hands in my lap.

"Yes. I was out, I had too much to drink and that's when it happened. But I think the point is that I'm not ready for a relationship. I just got here and I'm trying to figure some things out still. You're established and getting ready to graduate and leave…" I tried to explain.

"Why would you wait to tell me all this now? You could have said that when I met you."

"I really liked you and I wanted to keep seeing you. I didn't know…"

"What didn't you know…. that you'd drink too much and want to go home with a strange guy from the club?"

"Grant…"

"Did you fuck him?"

"Grant..."

"You did. I can tell. Some strange guy from the club.......Did you at least know him from class or something?........." Grant stared.

I said nothing. There was another long pause. Grant put his head in his hands. I touched his shoulder; he shot a look at me that I'd never seen on his face before, so I let go.

"I think I should go. I'm sorry." I didn't know what else to say. My throat felt tight and I was starting to cry. I walked very fast back up the hill and tried not to run. The tears starting rolling down my face and then I couldn't stop myself from running. I had never seen him get upset before. He was always so cool. Grant always told me if a girl ever cheated on him it would be over. It was over.

A few hours later the sun set and it was just cool enough to need a sweater in the dorms. I was wearing a grey cardigan over my tee-shirt and sitting cross-legged on the bed writing about my conversation with Grant. *I wonder if he's okay.* There would be no more nights at Grants snuggling under the covers, no one to pat my leg at poetry group, no poetry group, and then I realized it...there would be no more friendship. Grant was my friend. He was my friend and I hurt him and I destroyed our friendship. I took a deep breath and lay down on the bed and pulled my knees into my chest.

Deidra was typing at her desk.

"I'm getting so tired now. This last push to end the year is driving me nuts." Deidra said getting up and stretching. "I'm getting some popcorn. You want some…..?" Deidra's voice trailed off. "What the hell?" She stared out the window behind me.

"What?" I turned around and there was Grant kneeling on the ground in front of our window and knocking on the glass. He had a crazed look on his face.

"Oh my God!" I said.

"Go out there and get him away from that window! What the hell is wrong with him? Is he drunk??" Deidra asked pointing. Grant kept tapping.

"Come out here I want to talk to you!" He was yelling at the window and the small crowd outside was beginning to stare.

I found my shoes and went outside. Grant met me on the steps and grabbed my upper arm and escorted me down to the sidewalk. Some of the girls outside were staring. It was hard not to trip down the stairs with him leading me so hard. I could see Deidra inside the window peaking through the blinds.

"I wanna talk to you." He was drunk. I could smell it on his breath. Grant almost never drank.

"Okay." I said. He was still holding me by my arm and leading me down The Set to the darker part of the street where there weren't any people.

"I want us to stay together. I don't care about that guy. You made a mistake and I can forgive you. Alright?!" He was squeezing now.

"Why are you squeezing my arm? Just let go of my arm."

"I said I forgive you. Okay?" Grant said.

"Okay, but Grant… I think we should still, you know, break up. I just…"

"What is wrong with you?!" He stared at me.

"You told me you could never forgive someone who cheated on you."

"I changed my mind." His face softened. I knew this was a big step for him, but I also knew it was already too late. I was never his; I always belonged to someone else. I was frozen.

"You made a mistake. It happens. You're right…. you're younger than me and you don't know how to drink. It's college. You made a mistake. I forgive you. Come back to the apartment with me. You can spend the night like before and we'll talk about it in the morning. I love you. Okay?" Grant was pleading.

I started crying… I wanted so bad to say yes and go back with him and lie in his bed and snuggle and get up in the morning and watch him reheat pizza, but I couldn't.

I struggled with the words, "I'm sorry. I don't think we should get back together. I'm just not ready. Okay? Please… let me go." Grant's face twisted until I didn't recognize him. His eyes were different.

"What the fuck is wrong with you? Huh?!!! So you want that fucked up guy that fucked you when you were drunk?! Huh?!! You think someone like that cares about you? Huh? What the fuck?!" He was pressing into my bicep and we were too far down the street for people to hear. Every time he said "fuck" the spit flew in my face.

"Grant please. You're hurting me. Please, let me go."

DChristy Eves

"I don't wanna let you go!!!" He grabbed both arms and pushed me against the cement pillars of the bus pavilion on The Sct. My head hit the pillar. He held me there and was close to my face and I started sobbing uncontrollably. My head was throbbing and my throat was closing. I felt like I was choking. The whole scene seemed unreal. Was this really happening? I stared in Grant's eyes looking for my friend. He was gone. The evening set in and the street lights above clicked and you could hear the electricity surging them on. Suddenly the spell broke and Grant let me go. He took a deep breath and looked at me sobbing and trying to catch my breath.

"Look I'm sorry…. I didn't mean to hurt you. I didn't mean to scare you." He backed up and sank down on the brick wall that framed the bus stop. A stiff breeze picked up someone's lost ID and blew it across the street. Tomorrow someone would be searching the campus for it and never find it. There was nothing left to say, but I tried anyway.

"Grant…." He wouldn't look at me.

"Leave me alone." He sat staring at the ground. I stood for a moment frozen to the ground. I took a deep breath and turned away and walked quickly back to the dorms.

When I got back Deidra was waiting.

"Are you okay?" Deidra asked and touched my arm.

"Yeah. I'm fine."

"You don't look fine."

I didn't say anything. I looked at my face in the mirror and saw my puffy eyes.

"You got a call while you were out there. That guy that never leaves his name."

I grabbed the phone and dialed.

10

VAUGHN TOLD ME HE WANTED to see me. I had just seen him the Thursday before break and it was only Monday. I was surprised and thrilled that he missed me so quickly. I was exhausted but I had to see him. I wanted to erase Grant from my mind completely. I put a cold cloth on my puffy eyes, showered, changed clothes and ran out the door.

It was a soft night. Even Vaughn's eyes were soft. He seemed more romantic than usual. He hugged me when I got in the car and I could smell the faintest suggestion of sweat on his neck, really a mixture of moisture in the air and his natural fresh scent. It made me feel relaxed and sleepy, like I'd smoked his air.

When we got back to his place I sat back on his couch and took my shoes off. I was curled on the sofa waiting for him to come back with a drink. We had rum and coke, which he never has.

"This is my favorite."

"I know what *you* like." He smiled.

We talked for a while and I was surprised at how open he was with me, telling me about getting ready to graduate and his plans for the future. I told him about breaking up with Grant earlier and his grabbing my arm. His eyes narrowed,

"He grabbed you?"

"Yeah, I was really scared."

"What did you do?"

"I just started crying and begged him to let me go."

Vaughn didn't say much about it but he listened closely. I couldn't figure out if he was disturbed by my reaction to the physical display or Grant's impulse to do so. But his eyes never left me.

"So, you're single again?"

"Yes. That's it for me. I know for sure now that I'm in no space for a relationship."

"You've got this one…. Take this off." He motioned for my sweater. I was wearing a short sleeve top underneath and a pair of my standard uniform—jeans. He was looking at my arms.

"Are you cold?" He said. I felt a little chill on my arms, but I shook my head no.

"C'mere." He was sitting next to me on the sofa with a new look on his face.

"You know this really means you belong to me now. All mine." When I moved close to him he kissed me with his whole body; his hands went around me so tightly it felt like they wrapped around me more than once. He pulled me very close and leaned me forward. When he let me go, he looked directly in my eyes and didn't blink. He finally stood up and said,

"You.... are a serious encounter. Let's go upstairs."

We headed up and he held my hand and led the way. When we got inside the door he turned me towards him and kissed me hard while sliding his hands down the back of my pants. I was slipping over the edge and falling into the rhythm of my quickening heartbeat. My breath was short.

"Take these off."

He meant my pants without motioning for them. He leaned flat against me with his whole body as he ran his hands up my thighs. He pulled away from me and then headed towards the sliding glass door. He opened it and went out; the blinds made a shuffling sound as he passed. I watched him go and I stayed against the door, although I knew he expected me to follow him. He leaned against the side railing and said nothing. The silence was loud and clear and eventually I pushed myself off the door and followed. I stood in front of him with a couple of feet in between us. He stared at me.

"C'mere." He said finally; his voice was soft and low.

He was laying out a challenge for me; he knew I didn't like being on the balcony uncovered. He had tried several times to suggest that no one could see us, but I always asked for a sweater or a long shirt. I never lingered long and we always moved our affections to his room.

I didn't move.

He sucked his teeth.

He moved quickly grabbing my arms and pulling me towards him. There was an instant momentum that felt like flying. He was taking my panties down and unzipping his pants.

"Wait, wait." I said.

He was putting on a condom from his pocket in a quick motion. My shirt was only cut to my waist; without my panties I felt cold and exposed.

"I'm not wet."

He continued rolling the condom down his very erect penis. He made no change in his motion. He finished and with both hands on my hips moved me towards him. I tried to break his rhythm. I pushed against him but he was unfazed.

"It's gonna hurt." I told him.

He stopped for a moment and looked directly in my eyes. His face was soft but matter-of-fact.

"It's gonna have to hurt."

The words hung in my head like a road sign. BRIDGE MAY BE ICY. It was just a part of winter; there may be ice on some bridges. It's just a fact of life. If it's cold... there will be ice. Sorry. Just the way it is.

My body went stiff. We said something to each other, but I was hyperconscious of being outside and watched for his neighbor across the street that would have the best vantage point if he came outside. I looked downed the curving street to see if any cars were coming or anyone was out laughing with friends. It was dead quiet. Nothing moved.

ITS GONNA HAVE TO HURT. I turned the phrase over in my head. He was right, the bridge was icy, and it did hurt. It took a long time. I was drier by the end and each motion caused my vagina to pinch and tear. I tried to let my body go limp, but it wouldn't. I thought to pull free, but I didn't move. He dug his fingers into my hips.

When he finally finished, he went inside and headed for the bathroom leaving me on the balcony. I bent down and picked up my panties and went inside. *What just happened?* I stood by the bathroom door. He came out and walked passed me like I wasn't there. I went in and shut the door. When I sat down to pee it stung. I wiped and there was blood. ITS GONNA HAVE TO HURT. *Maybe I should just stay in here.* I got a cold wash cloth and put it between my legs. I held it there and the cold water ran down the insides of my legs. I turned my back to the sink and the mirror and made no attempt to check my face. I stood still and time left me there.

"Simone. What are you doing in there? Come to bed, it's late."

His voice woke me up and I didn't know how long I'd been standing there with the damp cloth pressed between my legs. I folded it and put it by the sink. I put my panties back on and peaked out of the door. Vaughn was in bed with his shirt off.

"Come here to me." His voice was soft again.
I came out and went to him on his side of the bed. He grabbed me close to him.

"Take this off." He said and didn't wait for me and he pulled off my shirt, unhooked my bra and pulled off my panties. He tucked me under the covers and spooned me. He was naked and I got cold chills down my spine when I felt his penis touch my behind.

"You alright?" He asked. I said nothing. "Simone?"

He checked my face and I just stared blankly at him. He gave up and rubbed my hair and found my hands and held them. He was light and soft and I could feel his breath on my neck. My body involuntarily relaxed.

"That's my girl."
He kissed me softly and then shut his eyes. He held me like that all night.

It was the blackest sky that peered through the window and showed me the stars; they were a bright witness to the night. I stared out of the half cracked blinds, as my eyes without warning closed and my mind wandered off.

My eyes burst open. The most convincing sunlight pierced through the window onto the bed. It was quiet, completely still and silent. I stared at the man lying next to me. I reached out to touch him. He groaned and pushed my hand away.

"You gotta go." He grumbled.

I could hardly sit up my lower body ached with pain. ITS GONNA HAVE TO HURT repeated in my head following the now vivid memory of him intruding upon my body. He'd gotten up, gotten dressed and stared at me.

"I gotta go. Get ready."
He left the room and the thought of getting out of bed stumped me. My body ached. I covered myself with his tee-shirt and searched for my clothes. He came back into the room.

"Where are my clothes?" I whispered.

He rifled through his bed, found my clothes and threw them at me. I thought of all the time we'd spent together, and how it all meant nothing. This couldn't be the same man who I'd given myself to willingly so many times. The night replayed itself in my head.

"I'm not wet, it's gonna hurt."

"It's gonna have to hurt. Stop crying... Why are you crying??"

"I don't want to... No."

"C'mon now." He held my waist firmly. "You like this. Doesn't this feel good?"

Silence.

I dragged into my clothes and he took me home. He pulled into the driveway next to the dorm.

"I'll never see you again will I?" I said beginning to cry. I couldn't even imagine why. Everything was fine before this happened. What happened? I would miss him. *Look how beautiful he is.*

"You'll see me again. I promise you that. You'll see me again." He said staring at me.

I got out of the car and pushed the door close, and watched him whiz away in his tiny, black car. And if my legs could make it, I'd walk to my room and forget everything.

"You'll see me again."

11

"ONE MINUTE LEFT."

It was cold in the room with the air conditioners cranked way up. April was already heating up.. *I'm doing good. I'm doing fine this semester. Back on track.* I finished my exam and laid the paper faced down on Professor Hammel's desk. I wasn't sure what I had to look forward to, but I made an attempt at it on my way out of the door. I made an attempt to feel excited about being done; but there was only the sad realization that the year had ended, I was alone and I had to turn my pumpkin in and go back home. I couldn't imagine going home and squeezing all I'd become this year into that pink room. How could I wake up, eat in the kitchen and later watch mommy clean the stove while fantasizing over the Young and the Restless. What would I have to say to my brothers? How could I answer the question, 'how's college?' *Next summer, I'm staying here.*

I walked very slowly across campus and the energy had changed. There were already girls leaving the dorm. I tried to push my thoughts forward to next year, getting an apartment and finally having my car; but now I had a room to pack and I had a tiny bed to sleep in that creaked and No Males Allowed. There would be even less freedom at home. *Definitely No Males Allowed at home with Daddy. I won't even be able to spend a night out.*

I loved spending the night out. I loved waking up in someone else's world, checking out their stereo to see who's playing, smelling the scent of the fabric softener they used on their sheets, and looking at how they situated their dishes in the cabinet. Grant's kitchen was always a little messy. The beige dishes had a dull, brown trim that wrapped around the edge like a bad ring mark left by a plate-sized coffee cup. Derrick had lots of different drinking glasses; ones for martinis, ones for margaritas, ones for a highball, and some with a glass handle for beer. Vaughn never let me look in his cupboard, but he always used these tall plain water glasses that had a blunt edge and a little glass bubble in the base. His sheets always smelled like Snuggle and he always smelled like something clean and wooden. This was one thing Derrick and Vaughn had in common—the uncanny ability to always smell freshly bathed. The scent of soap drove me wild and the combination of a neat and orderly room sent me over the edge. Grant's room always looked like he'd just stuck all of his dirty clothes in the closet to hide them or stuffed some under the bed. His bedspread was always lumpy from not having pulled the sheets tight underneath. You could see the reality in his room. *I guess I'm not a fan of reality.*

Instead of heading home and facing my own reality, I decided to stop by Z's and see how her packing was going. I took the elevator up to her floor and turned down the hall to find her door. Her door was open and she was silently putting her things in a large black trunk. Laurie wasn't there.

"Hey. Getting ready to get outta here?" I came in and plopped on her bed. She sat down next to me and was quiet for a minute.

"What's wrong?" I asked.

"I called you. Where were you?"

"Finals, why?"

"Oh, yeah...I forgot you still had one left."

"Z what's wrong?"

"We can't talk in here. Let's go."

Z got up and I followed her and we went back down the hall and down the elevator without her telling me what was the matter. Once we got outside she started talking.

"I think I'm pregnant." She walked and whispered.

"Zondra. What makes you think that?" I asked and stopped her.

"I'm late and my boobs are all tender and getting big."

"Jesus. Alright let's go."

"Where are we going?"

"To get a test." I said and pulled her hand.

We headed down the hill to the drugstore. Z looked completely lost but I led the way. I picked out a Fact Plus, paid for it and marched us back up the hill to her dorm. When we got back Laurie was there. She looked at me like a deer lost in the woods. I forgave her in that moment and I somehow knew what she felt. I could relate to being in bed with a very bad man. We didn't talk about it. I turned my attention back to Z. I handed her the bag.

"What?" Z asked me.

"What do you mean 'what?' Take the test." I took over.

"You're probably not pregnant. Just take the test and it'll be all over." Laurie said, she already knew what was happening and offered her support.

"How does this thing work?" Z took out the test and stared at the back of the box.

"Just pee on the stick and wait." I ushered Z out to the bathroom.

She came back a few moments later hiding the test under her sweater. She put it on her desk and we all sat there waiting for two minutes to pass.

"How was your final?" Z said tapping her foot.

"Fine. It's all done now. Come what may….. I told you to get on the pill."

"Billie, how is that helping??" Z snapped.

"I'm just saying after this… pills."

I had been on the pill since I was sixteen years old. My cycle was always irregular and once it actually skipped a month. I was worried I might be pregnant and I went to the drugstore alone and picked up a test. Dale, my then-boyfriend, and I had only done it twice and we'd used condoms but I was sure I was pregnant. The whole time buying the test and avoiding the eyes of the cashier, walking home with it in my pocket and then waiting for the results, I thought I would be ready to commit suicide when the little window gave a plus sign; but when I looked at the test and saw the negative sign my heart sank. I stood there staring at it and starting crying. I was actually disappointed. I caught myself in mid-emotion and said, "Wait a minute." I shook myself off and threw everything away. I stuffed some toilet paper over the test in the garbage and closed the lid. I knew two things right then; one, I would *never* be able to have an abortion and two, I was getting on the pill immediately. The next day I told my mom how bad my irregular cycle bothered me, she made an appointment and the next month I was on the pill. I don't know if she bought my story or if she just didn't want to dig any further and figured if a teen-aged girl asks to be on the pill, you put her on the pill.

Laurie was keeping the time and said,

"Time's up."

Z didn't move.

"Z. Go ahead...look." I told her.

"You look." She told me.

I looked. Laurie looked. Z looked at us.

"Z, look at it." I said.

Z looked at the test and sat back down. We were all quiet for a minute.

"What should I do?"

"I think you need to call Will." I said.

Sophomore Year

12

IT WAS A NEW YEAR and a new start. I loved being in school. The year was only eight months long and then you got four months to reflect and cast your thoughts to the sea. I needed all four months to process my first year in college. Now, I was saying 'Happy New Year' in August and the sun was bright welcoming me back to life. The sun burned away all of my mistakes and erased all of the marks on my record from the previous year. I had my own place and best of all, my own little red car. *I'm free!*

It was a two-story town house in Worthington Park. It sounded much more impressive than it actually was. But we didn't care. It was our ticket to adulthood; our first apartment and our first chance to pretend that we knew how to manage our lives. The first order of business was to plan my birthday party. This year, my birthday fell on a Thursday and it was the first week of classes. Just enough time to reconnect with our friends from last year but not enough time to amass any significant homework.

Cat and Eli had taken an apartment in the same complex right across the grassy knoll behind our townhouse. Eli frequently came by and knocked on the glass peaking in through the windows smiling and waving. She was like the funny neighbor on our very own sitcom. I'd told the girls about having a birthday party at our apartment and we also told Rod and Derrick about it. They were back sans their partner in crime Will who had dropped out and stayed in Montgomery, Alabama. The guys promised they'd come by and I looked forward to seeing Derrick again. It'd been a long dry summer in Detroit under the supervision of the Hazard family men. I wondered what it'd feel like to see him again. I wondered what it'd feel like to feel him again; I'd been four months sober of men.

"Are Eli and Cat coming?" Z asked.

"Yeah, I talked to Eli this morning and she said they would stop by." I said.

"Great. It'll be fun to see everybody again."

We were sitting on the floor in Z's room playing in her jewelry box. I was in retro bell bottomed jeans and had gotten my belly button pierced over the summer. I was experimenting with wearing a waist chain and my growing selection of mid-drift tops.

"So, is it weird being back down here for you?" I asked her.

"No. I guess not. It was a hell of a summer. Being home was so strange. I'm glad to be back. I feel like I can be real again." Z said.

"I know what you mean. Back home we're daughters, here... we're ourselves."

"Right."

"I can't believe Will dropped out." I said.

"I know. When I went down there this summer he told me he was staying. He said he wanted to work at his parent's store. I told him, 'don't drop out because of me.'" Z said and folded her arms.

"It's over. There's no point in ruining your life over it."

"Exactly. But he told me that's what he wanted to do; he said college wasn't for him......He was really hurt 'though. But I had to do it. I could not have it. He begged me to, but I couldn't. He tried to get his parents to talk me out of it. They actually sat me down and told me not to kill their grandchild. Can you imagine how that felt??"

"No. I'm surprised Will wanted a kid."

"He wanted me to have it, finish school, still be with him, and just have it all. I'm not stupid; no way that was gonna work. I went down there because he begged me to do it down there so he could be with me. I really didn't want my mom finding out so I thought that was better too. But, when I got down there I realized he wanted to 'show me the town,' show me how great it was and how we could have a life together; how we could make it work. It was like a whole set up. I didn't even know his parents knew, and there I was with Jimmy Dean and Pearly Mae telling me how they would help me raise my child.

"I thought about it. At every turn they want you to stop and think about it. At the place where they did it, before they call you in there, they make you sit in a room and think about it for an hour. They

108

give you all this literature about your options. You're sitting there with all these other girls in a room, all of them just like you—young, in trouble and sitting there with a stupid-looking boyfriend or a girlfriend with a 'thank-God-it's-not-me' look on her face. There were like eight or nine girls in the room with me. Before time was up a few girls starting crying and left. I just sat there waiting; waiting for them to call me; waiting to see if something would happen to my mind about it.... but my mind was made up. That just could not be my life, stuck with Will, living in Montgomery, raising his kid while he worked at the general store.... I have plans for my life. That was not the plan. Eventually they called my name. After that, it was over pretty quick. Will looked like he was gonna cry. I was fine until they said it was all over, then out of nowhere I just started balling, right there on the table. Will was holding me and everybody just left the room like it was perfectly routine. And that was that." Z finished and sighed.

There was a long pause and neither one of us spoke.

"I think you did what was right for you." I said finally.

"I had a lot of time to think about it on the way down and then again on the way back. That ride back home, after it was all said and done, was so long. Here I am riding home from Montgomery, Alabama, twenty something hours on the bus, with all of that on my mind. And I had to get home and pretend everything was normal. Being back home is stressful. At least here, I don't have to pretend to be.... perfect." Z said.

"I know. Come what may. We are figuring it out. Isn't that what we're supposed to do?........ I'm not sure how good we are at it yet." I laughed.

"Not very…..." Z said.

"Not yet.."

The night of my birthday came and the girls had gotten me a cake. We were playing some old school R&B, Frankie Beverly and Maze. We had a light-colored couch that came from my mom who reasoned it would be a good way for her to go shopping for a new one if she gave us her old one.

"Well, Billie's got to have something to sit on." She told my dad.

You could still see the depressions left in the sofa on opposite ends from my parents sitting in the same spot every night watching the news and being afraid to go out into the world.

"Billie! Did you hear what happened last night over there by Six Mile and Greenfield??" My dad would start. Our neighborhood used to be a nice place to raise a family. Kids playing in the street, old oaks lining the block, nosey neighbors planting tulips and telling on kids caught kissing behind a bush. But, the downswing of the auto industry left the sons of the Big Three hurting. Good neighborhoods began to go bad. Blocks were switching from mostly home owners to renters. You could see the change and hear the crime rate rising nightly on the news. Daddy still held his spot at Chrysler and Mommy her job as a nurse, but all around us people were losing faith.

"Nooooo, that's right down the street!" My mom would shake her head.

"Be careful." They'd say together and look at me.

DChristy Eves

Laurie, Z and I sat in the living room munching on chips and waiting for anyone to arrive and I was beginning to feel stupid. Finally Eli knocked on the patio door and slid it open and poked her head in with her bright ear to ear smile.

"Hey!" Eli sang.

"Where's Cat?" I didn't see her behind Eli.

"She had a thing to go to with her man. She might be by later." Eli said bouncing in and joining our threesome.

It was officially the deadest party in the world. An hour later when the doorbell rang, I didn't care who it was; anything was better than the four of us trying to pretend this wasn't pitiful. Z got the door. I could hear male voices and quickly recognized the deep hum of Derrick's voice. I smiled. He glided into the room ahead of his brother and another guy.

"Hey birthday girl." Derrick said.

He was holding a bag. He came up to me and I stood up from the couch and gave him a hug. *Powder and fresh cotton.*

"What's in the bag?" I asked.

"Just for you." It was a huge bottle of vodka.

"Perfect. Just my size." He kissed my check and winked.

For the next few hours Derrick flirted with me *and* Eli, Rod poured us shots and their friend made an unsuccessful play for Laurie. This time Laurie put a hand up and sang, "Stop in the Name of Love." We were all sufficiently loose and moved from the ugly green table that marked our dinning room, to the couch with matching butt depressions. We were sitting around the coffee table playing truth or dare.

DChristy Eves

"Truth." Laurie exhaled. "I don't know y'all well enough to risk dare; I'm not chugging a drink or taking anything off."

"Okay, when did you lose your virginity?" Rod asked Laurie.

"Please God. This isn't a story I know too well is it?" I said and looked over at Laurie.

"No, no." Z tapped me.

"Well…" Laurie started. "It was late one night on the campus of seven hills." Derrick threw a toss pillow at Laurie; he was sprawled out on the floor in front of the couch.

"Get to the good part." He grinned.

"Like I said…. Ahem. It was late one night on the campus of seven hills. Me and my boyfriend, who shall remain nameless to protect the satisfied, were walking around campus. He told me he knew how to get into Tucker Hall through a door that never properly locked." Laurie continued her story.

"You mean Tucker Hotel." The guys laughed.

"Tru dat." Rod said and high-fived the guys.

"Anyway, we were up on the third floor in one of the classrooms. We were having a very private moment on the teacher's desk when I saw a bright light flash over my head. I looked up and a security guard was flashing a light on my boyfriend's butt. Needless to say, it was a memorable night and my virginity and dignity became casualties of The Hotel Tucker Hall." Laurie finished and gave a bow for drama.

"I cannot believe you guys used to have sex in Tucker Hall." I was giggling and spilled my orange juice and vodka a little.

112

Eli came back into the room from the kitchen getting another drink and handed me a napkin.

"That's where you had to do it. Everybody lived on campus. Where did they expect you to go?" Z defended.

"Oh my God… you too?? To an older man's apartment, that's where." I said.

I was proud of never having dated a freshman except Derrick, who had his own apartment. I loved escaping the dorms.

"Yeah you had a real man like me baby." Derrick said rubbing his chest like it was massive and covered in grown-man chest hair.

"Yeah, right." I threw a toss pillow back at him.

He tucked it under his head.

"It's your turn Billie. What's your pleasure, truth or dare?" Derrick challenged.

"Dare."

"Okay, brave girl. I dare you to show everybody your too-good for Tucker Hall moves." Derrick said trying to call my bluff.

"OOOoooh!" Eli said in proper junior high fashion. "Show him how it's done!" She laughed and pinched my arm.

All of us girls were sitting on the couch and Eli had plopped herself onto my lap. She was affectionate with her girlfriends, not like any girl from Detroit would be. I could tell that Derrick liked seeing us sitting like that. It gave me a charge.

"Okay, you have to give some kind of a time limit." Z ordered.

"Five seconds." Derrick obliged.

"Alright." Z let it go.

When I was drinking I felt like there was nothing I couldn't do. Eli laughed and I stood up walked over to him straddled his lap and grinded my hips on top of his lap. I looked him dead in the eyes.

"Okay, you're drunk." Laurie laughed. She was right.

We winded up the evening and Eli went home. The guys were headed out and I grabbed Derrick's hand and asked if he would stay longer. He kissed me and said,

"My girlfriend's having a party tonight, too. Gotta swing by there."

"Can you come by after?" I put my arms around his neck.

"I wish I could," He kissed me again but longer. "I came to see you first; do I get any points for that?"

"No."

"Be good, now." He squeezed my butt and then kissed me once more and tried to let me go. I grabbed his arm,

"Well I won't let you leave then." I smiled and pulled him from the front door.

Z had already gone to bed and Laurie was in the kitchen throwing away paper cups and cleaning up. Rod and Jeff were already in the car waiting outside. He laughed and pulled back. I pulled him again towards me and he pulled back again. We were laughing and falling a little. I pulled him once more but too hard to be silly, and I meant it too much to hide. I surprised myself and he looked stunned.

"I really have to go. I'm sorry." He kissed my cheek and left me standing there.

13

AT THE APARTMENT the Lady's of Q6 were getting into a routine. We all met after class carrying in fast food from campus and eating at the ugly green table. On Friday's we'd pile up in one of our rooms and try to figure out what to wear and where to go. Eli had decided to cut her long hair. Cat was ultra cool and had her shoulder-length black hair cut into a sharp angled bob. I thought she looked older with it cut. It wasn't long before we all started thinking on cutting our hair.

No beauty salon Eli went to would cut her hair. They all tried to talk her out of it.

"Nobody will cut my hair!" She complained.

Cat was quick to cut in. "I will."
We were all in my room and we all looked around and surprised.

"No, Eli. Don't do that. Keep it long. It's so pretty." Laurie said sitting behind her on my bed and playing with the ends. We were all sitting on my bed in front of my dresser mirror.

"That's what my father always says. 'Keep your hair long; Get some of those boys in love with you to buy you things; Long hair keeps the boys interested; You can have anything you want like that.' But I'm tired of all this hair." Eli said. She stared at herself in the mirror.

"Wow. Did your Dad really say all that?" Cat said. She was rifling through my bathroom drawers.

"My hair was that long when I was younger, and it was a lot of work. My mom used to pull me out of school just to get me to the hair salon sometimes." I said. I studied my hair in the mirror. I was trying to force it to snap into a banana clip. "I can never make these damn things work."

"My mom doesn't care what I do with my hair as long as she's not involved. I've pretty much been on my own with my hair since I was old enough to do it myself." Z said flipping through a magazine lying across the bed.

"Oh yeah, I remember you did your *own* hair for homecoming." I gave up the banana clip and moved on to bobby pins.

"Yup. I think it looked nice." Z was proud.

"I've been going to the salon as long as I can remember. I have no clue how to do my own hair." I said.

"Me either. And if I did, I'd still go to the salon." Cat said still searching.

"I would never cut my hair." Laurie cut in.

"Found them." Cat got out a large pair of scissors, tied Eli's hair in a ponytail and hacked it all off with three strong pulses. Poof. Eli was just like the rest of us with shoulder-length hair. Her chopped ponytail

116

was shiny and smooth, she took a picture holding it and grinning her trademark ear to ear grin.

Visiting Eli's apartment one night, Cat came into Eli's room.

"Hey Cat." I said. She was staring at my face strangely. "What?"

"Your eyebrows." She said.

"My eyebrows?"

"Yes, your eyebrows." Cat's voice lowered. "You don't pluck them?"

"No. Pluck them? Am I supposed to?"

"Girl," she laughed. "Yes, they are so wild."

"I don't know how." I said looking at them in the mirror. She went back in her room and took out her little black kit.

"Let me show you. We gotta handle this."

She left the room and came back with it and unzipped it in one sharp motion. She took out her tweezers and started shaping my eyebrows. It really hurt but I was excited. She didn't have plans that evening and I became a project.

She was not gentle, but she was right. When I looked in the mirror afterwards I looked much better. Older. I smiled.

"That does look good." I said.

"Told you."

She looked pleased with her work. She sat down and we spent the evening talking, looking at pictures and snacking on chips.

DChristy Eves

I became a regular fixture at Cat and Eli's. I'd come over and hang out and Cat would fix me up. She looked at my legs another time and asked me,

"Why do girls from Detroit not shave their legs?"

"I don't know. I never thought about it." I told her.

She was laughing at the absurdity.

"You should shave your legs." Cat said raising an eyebrow.

I did. Cat was always well dressed, poised and smooth. I was still on the fringes of awkward and trying to outrun uncool, so if she suggested it, I did it... period. I'd leave Z and Laurie and head over. I wouldn't invite them to come.

Cat began spending more time with me and less with Eli. Eli had a new boyfriend and she started locking herself in the room with him and not coming out for hours. One night I was over with Cat complaining about leg hair stubble.

"Look how fast it grows back. This is a lot of maintenance." I complained.

"Yeah it is. I bought some Nair but I've never tried it. It's supposed to work for weeks." Cat was reading the back of the pink bottle.

"What is it?" I said looking over her shoulder.

"I don't know. Here, let's try it."

She opened the bottle and per the instructions we spread it all over our legs and waited for the magic.

"Where's Eli?" I asked her.

"Eli and Shawn have been locked in that room for *days*. I had to knock on the door to make sure she was still alive in there! I'm serious. They only come out to get food and use the bathroom. They just stay in there fucking all day. " She was totally disgusted.

"Jesus."

"I know."

"I haven't met him yet. Is he cute?" I asked.

"No." Cat said and started laughing.

"Really?"

"Nope. And you *know* she's the finest girl he's ever been lucky enough to get. He won't let her catch a breath alone."

"Hey, are your legs starting to tingle?" I said noticing my legs.

"Yeah…. they are."

"Mine are starting to burn."

"Oh shit!! Mine too!" Cat screeched.

"AAAaaaaa!!!" We screamed.

We shot up, ran into the bathroom and jumped into the tub and turned on the water. We were splashing and laughing so hard we were in tears. Eli came into the bathroom to see what the commotion was. She looked at us both in the tub together.

"What's going on?" Eli asked.

"Nothing." Cat's voice was dry and dull; she sat down on the edge of the tub.

"We were trying to remove leg hair." I was still laughing.

"Oh." Eli just turned her head and went back to her room. Her eyes were different. They'd lost their spark.

DChristy Eves

"What'd I tell you?" Cat said and nudged me.

14

ON CAMPUS THE HUM of activity was steady. It was October and the weather was still mild. I was cutting through The Set on my way to the post office. The marching band was practicing and I could hear the faint sound of horns. Today the crowd was swarming and I was glad I had on something cute and fitted to show off my hips. When I made my way through the crowd to see the draw, I saw Derrick, Rod and a few of their friends all standing together and holding snakes.

"Oh my God! Is that a real snake??" A girl yelled.

They loved the attention and the girls were crowding around asking questions. Derrick saw me peaking through and smiled.

"What's up girl?" He said.

"What are you doing up here with that snake?" I loved being picked out of the crowd by him but hid my pleasure.

"Taking my baby for a walk." He was grinning that devious grin.

"Yeah right." It was ridiculous, but clearly effective.

"Come over here." He pulled my hand. I stepped away from the gawkers and stood next to him.

"I'm still mad at you." I pulled my hand away.

"Don't be mad."

"I hate you and I'm pissed."

"I had to leave B..... That was a month ago.....I've been trying to get up with you for weeks now." I turned my head. He turned it back.

"Billie, come on... you know you love me. Can't resist me. Want to kiss me." He sang it in my ear and I laughed a little. His albino snake was about a foot or so in length and was curling around his wrist. He leaned against the side of the bench.

"Come by and see me tonight. I wanna make it up to you." That grin... I had been avoiding him for awhile, but actually seeing him made it impossible.

"What time?"

Later that night I drove to his place. Derrick was good at distracting me. Vaughn would not leave my mind and every time things slowed down, he was in my thoughts. I still couldn't process what had happened between us. That Night. That night haunted me and I tried to erase it. Every thing but that night was perfect. *I should have just said yes, I bet no one could see up there. It wouldn't have happened if I'd just said yes and gotten into it. If I say yes, **I'm** in control of the situation.*

I shook off the thoughts of Vaughn and went up to the door and knocked. Rod answered.

DChristy Eves

"Hey beautiful!" Rod hugged me hard and tried for a little grab of my butt. I grabbed his hand

"Nice try." I smacked him lightly. "What are you doing here? I thought you had a date."

"A date with you." Rod flirted. He looked over at Derrick. "Yeah, I did. Some foolishness was up, so I'm back."
I looked over at Derrick and he grinned.

"What's up B?"

I went over to him and he took me upstairs to his room, they had a townhouse like us. I rolled a joint while he left the room to do something. I had spent the summer perfecting my roll; my secret weapon was a roller I'd gotten from a gas station downtown. His room was so... him.... Derrick. Very Derrick. He had a huge black and white photo matted and framed of a naked woman from her clavicles to her knees. She was all curves and softness; a lot of taste, not at all vulgar. He had a sculptural relief of an old sax player and a very large framed print of a vertical fish. His secret love, he'd told me, was fishing. Derrick played the trumpet and loved music; he always had something interesting playing on the stereo. There was organized clutter, like my room. He had a stereo system with small surround sound speakers placed on diagonal corners of the room. Most people let the wires scale up the wall any kind of way, but he had nails in precise position to look neat and make ninety degree angles. Simple bedding. Burgundy on one side, green on the other. His sheets were stripped burgundy and green. Very neat and concise. On top of his desk was his phone/fax machine.

Okay, what did he need that for? I tried to imagine a scenario, but to no avail.

I was sitting at his desk and taking in the room. Soon he came back and the joint was rolled, like a cigarette. He liked that, and smiled at me.

"Very good." He said.

I should be his girl, I thought. *I match his room. I'm unique and interesting.* He sat down and I stroked his ego lightly by telling him his room was so…. Derrick. He smiled. He liked to hear about himself. Men are simple creatures. Soon we were talking about his hometown. He told me about the "adventures" he had as a kid. The stereo whined in the background something slow and deep and the smoke lifted around us as we puffed and passed. He knew how to set a mood, or maybe I was setting myself up. I was feeling high. He told me he wanted to travel but eventually end up in Montgomery. I quickly thought, *I can't marry him and move to Montgomery, Alabama. Alabama? You can have Alabama, Derrick.* I tried to imagine Derrick at thirty… *I'd like to see that. I hope we keep in touch.* Pretty soon it was happening. We were making love, or rather having sex. It was nice. Very nice.

My eyes were closed and I was listening to the whine of the trumpet. It sounded like a man crying and moaning at the same time. The music cut into my chest and pierced my thoughts with something true I didn't understand. It felt open with no crevices to hide in. It was deep and painful and Derrick was too close. His face was over mine in the fading light of the evening. I opened my eyes and saw Vaughn's eyes staring at me; I jerked pushing him off.

"What?? What happened?" Derrick was surprised. I blinked hard. Derrick's face.

"I'm sorry... I think I just got lost for a second." I tried to explain.

"You okay?" Derrick was tender and looked worried.

"I'm okay. I'm sorry." I said. He came back to my arms and kissed me.

"You're alright?"

"I'm fine... What are we listening to?"

"Miles Davis." There was a still pause... the trumpet sliced through the air.

"Kiss me." I pulled him into me.

We went on and I kept my eyes opened and fixed on his face. That night we listened quietly to the most beautiful music I'd ever heard and Derrick held me all night long and never let go.

15

"HI BABY, HOW ARE YOU?"

"I'm fine."

"No you're not. What's wrong?"

"Nothing. I'm just tired that's all."

"That's not true, but you just tell me what's wrong when you're ready."

"Mom…. I'm fine."

I changed the subject and asked how my brother Jay was doing. Mom accepted the change and answered but the subtext was clear. "You just tell me when you're ready." It was pointless to hide anything from my mom she could always tell when something was wrong. But I couldn't tell her what was wrong when I couldn't piece it together myself. I couldn't get Vaughn out my head. There was something dark now clouding my mind about his face and at the same time the rush of excitement when he'd call was missing. The tide ebbed and took him away from me as quickly as he'd come. "You'll see me again." He sounded so sure. I couldn't figure out if that scared me or gave me something to hang on to. Where was he? Why didn't I hate him?

I hung up the phone and lay in bed staring at the ceiling. Boredom and the desire to chase away an unsettled feeling filled my chest. I picked up the phone and dialed.

"Derrick?"

"Billie, what's up girl?"

"What are you up to?" I asked.

"Chillin'. You want to see me?" I could hear him grinning.

"Yeah. Come over."

"You can't come over here?" He said.

"You can't come over *here*?"

"Nah, Billie. Rod's got the car out with some girl. Come through B."

"……..Alright."

It was a Thursday night and nothing was up and nothing was due. We had a peppered routine that sprinkled itself throughout the semester. He would call mostly. I always tried to remain aloof, but every so often the sound of lying in bed alone was too much and I called him. Derrick was very proud of being a southern gentleman, but he made no secret of other women and would flat out tell me if he had another date or another girl over. He told me I was the only woman he had that didn't care and he could be honest with; that made me his friend and lover. Somehow this position felt honorable to me. It was a better option than falling in love.

DChristy Eves

Love had completely dismantled Eli's world. She and her boyfriend were now completely oblivious to the world around them. Eli was missing classes and ignoring life. She didn't knock on our patio door with her bubble gum smile and wave, she didn't go to parties and she stopped coming over to do hair and gossip on Friday nights. More confusing, was the guy himself. Eli liked really cute guys with nice cars, money to spend on her and access to the front of the line. But this guy was so plain, broke, and had access to nothing but her bedroom.

The thought of love conjured up images of my mother and father. She did everything for him, ironed his shirts, packed his lunch, and fixed his dinner plate just so. And he would yell at her, call her stupid and demand that she stop doing this or start doing that. Fuck love. Love looked like a prison to me.

I headed out the door and off to Derrick's. I felt safe there; safe from my thoughts, safe from love and safe from reality. When I got there he played Phil Collins "In the Air Tonight." *We think alike... I was hoping he'd play that song. He never disappoints me.* We smoked a joint, made love and laid there in each others arms. The drums rolled over my head and the sensation of being high and in Derrick's arms sent me flying. Afterwards he kissed me softly, put his arms around me tightly. He lifted the hair up from my neck gently with his fingers, kissed me lightly there and settled himself with me in his arms. That was all I needed.

16

THE SEMESTER PULLED UP TO THE BUMPER of the
holiday season. Thanksgiving had come and gone. It was the last week
before break, finals week. I was trying to focus on my classes but that
was hard when I felt so out of place with the other journalism students.
But I tied myself to the only option I knew and did my best. I was
pulling mostly A's and B's. I was in good shape.

Our second year was getting more serious academically. But, I
still made my way to the club most Wednesdays and danced to find my
peace. Usually Cat and Z went with me. It was an addictive feeling
dancing there with someone close to you. Derrick would show up
occasionally, but not too often. When he came, there was energy in the
room and he filled me with a sense of eagerness. I loved the way he held
me and I wanted to get to that part of the evening quickly. He always
paced himself and never rushed. We'd dance, hang out with friends,
drink and talk. He loved talking to me. I always sat quietly listening and
offering encouragement for him to continue. He wanted to know about

me, but I didn't want to share too much. I would answer and turn the conversation back to him.

It was Thursday night and a middle of December chill was working its way down my spine. My phone rang and I rolled over on the bed and got it.

"Hello."

"Billie."

"Hey Derrick. What's up?"

"Come through sweetheart. I wanna see you."

"You're lucky I just finished studying."

"Then I have perfect timing. I wanna see you before you leave for break."

"Be careful Derrick, I'm gonna mistake you for sweet."

"I am sweet. You know how sweet."

"I can hear you grinning."

"Don't hear it, see it."

"I'll be over in a little bit."

I headed out and got to his place pretty quickly. He opened the door for me and kissed me.

"Hey, thanks for coming." He said.

"Sure."

The living room was crowded with guys. I was the only girl there and I had no clue why he wanted me to hang out with his friends.

"Everybody, this is Billie Simone." He introduced me like I was a guest on The Aresnio Hall show. I smiled. There were four other guys there including his brother Rod.

"Hey beautiful." Rod winked at me.

I sat down on the couch and Derrick went to the kitchen to get me a drink. The guys were all seated in a circle around the coffee table. Rod was on the couch and the other three guys were in chairs semi-circling the coffee table; A, B and C. They were smoking and leaned in close. When Derrick came back with a drink for me, he sat down next to me and put his arm around me. It was all very strange. He was really affectionate with me. Not that he wasn't usually, but he wasn't so public about it before.

Guy B sitting across from me continued talking like my entering had interrupted him in the middle of a story.

"Anyway, like I was saying. She cut up a niggas tires with her nail file. She fucked my shit all up. I had to buy two new tires behind that shit."

"Man, bitches are crazy." Guy C responded.

"You gotta keep your woman in check." Derrick offered.

"This nigga can't keep shit in check." Rod laughed.

"Fuck you nigga. I keep my women in check. They just get crazy when I give 'em all this good dick." Guy B went on.

"Nigga please." Guy A laughed.

What the hell am I doing here? I was dumbstruck as to what was going on. The blunt got to me and Derrick handed it to me.

I said, "No thank you."

"Come on sweetheart." He handed it to me again.

I stared a minute at him. He put it in backwards in his mouth and gave me a shot gun kiss. I took the smoke from his lips.

"That's my girl." The phrase stung me with its familiarity.

The guys kept talking around me and the smoke and Derrick's voice floated me out of the room. I could feel the vibration of his chest when he spoke with his deep radio voice. I put my head on his chest to feel it more closely. I held on to my drink and sipped. Bacardi and pineapple juice. Whenever it looked low Derrick would refill it for me.

The guys kept talking and laughing and I ignored them and smoked again on my turn. I wasn't sure how much time passed, but I dropped back into consciousness and the conversation when I heard them land on the subject of sex.

"I was with that bitch from accounting. You know who I mean right?" Guy A went on.

"Yeah, dog. She's fine." Guy B.

"Anyway, we in my room 'bout to get into it and she licking all over the dick. I was like suck it bitch. It's not a lollipop!" Guy A was laughing hard and I noticed he was kinda fat and kinda ugly. He should have been thanking God some girl wanted to suck his dick not complaining about her technique. *Fucking men.*

"She was probably lubricating it so she could, you idiot." I heard myself say. The room stopped and everyone stared. I realized I'd just broken an unspoken rule. I was supposed to be seen and not heard. No one spoke for a moment and the guys looked confused like they didn't know if they should look at me or not. Derrick was cool.

"Listen, Billie knows what she talking about." He turned to me and asked, "You don't mind do you honey?" I nodded no. "She's excellent in that department." The guys stared at me and in awe.

Derrick patted my arm and kissed my forehead. 'Good job, honey,' was implied.

Pretty soon the guys filed out and left. Rod headed off to his room with one last smile at me before he did. Derrick took me back to his room to spend the night.

"Get in here girl." He got in bed and motioned for me. I was still uneasy but too high to think clearly. I got in bed with him and he swallowed me in kisses and caresses. I closed my eyes and floated off again. The holding me all night part was just around the corner.

17

WINTER BREAK ARRIVED promptly the next day after my final was over. I had a plane to catch that Saturday morning and I could still smell Derrick's cologne on my sweater as I stared out of the tiny window. I had a strange dream about that last night with Derrick, but I shook it off and got myself mentally prepared to be home. It seemed only a heartbeat and I was back at home watching the snow fall from the grey sky. Every time I went home I felt more and more lost, like I was floating on a raft out at sea. When I'd go home I noticed how far I'd drifted from the beach. I was right there with my family but they were the size of tiny ants way far away. I spoke and felt like I should raise my voice so they could hear me.

I finally figured out how to answer 'how's college.' I'd simply tell everybody my grades. If you had good grades, nothing else mattered. They all smiled and were more than satisfied, they were proud. I spent the break eating, talking with family and hanging out with my friends. Detroit looked pretty at night with the Christmas lights circling the trees downtown. They looked like twinkling statues of dancers lining the streets.

But regardless of grades by the end of the break, I still managed to run into trouble with the King of the Hazard men. My dad was furious with me over a snow storm and a man. I'd met this PhD student from Wayne State University. Z and I were having drinks at Floodz when he came by and introduced himself. He was nice and he took me out a couple times while I was home. I recognized his type right away—good for taking you out and paying for things. He was the kind of guy you could introduce to your parents. I knew better than to get too involved with him. After Grant, I felt that kind of man was dangerous. Besides, I'd be gone in a couple of weeks. He was cool and threw a really great New Year's party. The next day he wanted me to come over and watch movies with him. I agreed and he picked me up in his Explorer. It was snowing, but not too hard. But by the time I'd gotten to his place a full winter storm had blown in. We sat in the window of his apartment and watched foot after foot of snow pile up outside. The dirty city was hiding beneath the new blanket of white and you couldn't see a trace of street.

"You better tell your parents you're not coming home tonight." He said. I thought about it a second and called home. My dad was livid.

"He's got a truck with four wheel drive! He can drive you home!!"

"Dad, there's blizzard outside. He doesn't want to have an accident."

135

"If you stay over there with that man, don't ever come home!!"
He handed the phone to my mom.

"Billie. It's alright. Just do what you need to. It is really bad outside."

"Mom, why is dad so mad? It's storming outside. We're not doing anything over here."

"I'll talk to him Billie. Don't worry about it." I could hear my dad still yelling in the background.

"She wanna stay out all night like some tramp!! Get yo' ass home!"

I spent the night at his apartment watching the snow fall. The snowflakes were big and fluffy and sparkled under the moon. Snow storms are silent and rage without a sound. It was beautiful. But I could feel my father across town not sleeping and waiting for me to come home. My date thought that was his moment. He put his hand on my back and tried for a kiss. He was wrong. I turned over in his bed and went to sleep. In the morning, he took me home and didn't hang around to come in and say hi. He watched me to the door and pulled off quickly. I laughed. My dad was a big man and I knew even this grown PhD student was scared of him. I thought maybe dad would be over it by the time I got home, but he wasn't. He didn't look at me the rest of the break. When I left he barely said goodbye. I tried not to cry when my mom took me to the airport without him. But saying goodbye to her sent me over the edge and when I left her at the gate we were both sobbing. I was still crying when the plane took off. By then I didn't know why I was crying anymore.

It was clear dad had no clue how to protect me anymore. He was worrying about me in all the wrong places. If he really knew me, would he even love me anymore? If he was that mad at that small night in the snow, what would he think of the weeks in the sun I'd spent with the men at FAMU. Men. Not man. Men. Was I a tramp? I was too far gone to turn back to the dock and pull myself in. I was already floating somewhere too far to reach.

18

THE NEW SEMESTER KICKED OFF and we settled back into our routines. Cat and I had become thick as thieves now, Eli was gone with the wind, Laurie was stressed about school and Z was at work all the time trying to pay for things that came easy to me and Cat. She was saving up for a car. I had a massive oak bed set, the matching armoire, dresser-mirror combo and my pretty red Sundance out front. I had Derrick and no love and I felt really good.

It was a Tuesday, early March and I could smell the scent of the curry, spices and beans from the Soul Vegetarian food cart near the parking lot at the bottom of the hill. A short line of conscious brothas and sistas chatted patiently in line. I made my way across Wahnish Way and passed Paddyfote on my way up the hill to the library to do some research for an English Lit paper. There was music trailing from every car and the sound of laughter and chatter mixed a pleasant cocktail.

Sometimes the beauty of the campus with its pretty brown faces, rhythmic speech patterns and the sweet, southern air were too much for me. I had to stop and thank God for being in this place. We all had our futures ahead of us. When would we all be in one spot again, thousands of young, bright, Black brothas and sistas, all with future goals and no stamp of our old neighborhoods or urban decay framing our lives? I stood still and breathed deep.

When I got to the quad there were red tee-shirts everywhere. The Kappas were circulating something new. A tall, lanky guy from my American History II class made his way over to me and handed me a small, red, square flyer.

"Wassup girl? Come out if you can." I took the flyer and he zoomed on past stamping every girl with red squares. I read the flyer: *Kappa Luau Saturday, March 7th. Barbeque, Drinks, Music... Come out, Get leid.* The Kappa Luau was a huge event and a sure sign of spring. The weather was turning warm and girls were peeling off their winter skins and letting their arms and bellies show. Guys were slowing their pace on the set and parking themselves strategically to watch us all go by. I tucked the flyer in my backpack and headed in the library.

When I got home later that day Zondra was getting dressed to go to the Stars Café for work.

"You working tonight?" I peaked my head in.

"Yeah. I'm not staying late, though. I'll be back around eight or nine."

"Where's Laurie?"

"She left a minute ago with Pride." Laurie had a new boyfriend named James Proudfoot. We called him Pride.

"What are you getting into tonight?" Z could tell I was bored.

DChristy Eves

"Nothing. I've got some work to finish on this Lit paper. Maybe I'll get some of it done tonight."

"Alright, just don't call that shady friend of yours."

"Why do you say that??" Z's comment seemed out of the blue to me.

"I just mean Derrick is shady and I have no idea why you keep spending your time with him."

"I don't see him that often. Why don't you like him? It's not like he's my boyfriend. We just hang out, that's all."

"'That's all'….He has a girlfriend. I met her the other day; she's actually nice. Now, she's gotta be stupid if she actually believes he's really her man, but it's not only that. It's the way he talks."

"What are talking about?"

"I just remember him talking about you to Will and Rod while I was over there last year telling all of them that only five hours after he met you, he was all up in you. He's got that gentleman talk and smile when he's in your face and the second you're gone, he's one of the guys talking shit. He's different than you think."

"Well, five hours after I met him, I wanted him. It's as simple as that. And believe me I am very familiar with how guys talk. I'm not in love with him. He's just fun. Haven't you ever had a really good… I mean really good time with someone? Ever had an orgasm?"

"Billie… that is not the point."

"It's my point."

"I don't know. I guess."

"No guessing. If you had one you'd know."

140

DChristy Eves

"Whatever." She was giving me her trademark stare; a mixture of granny and attitude that only Z could produce.

"Look, I just wanna have fun. I'm in control of it... He's just the right mix of wrong."

"Alright. I guess you know what you're doing.'"

"I do. I feel like I get the best of both worlds. I love being with a man, being held. Derrick holds me all night long."

"That's to keep you locked down so you don't wake up and realize what he's up to."

"Stop," I laughed. "All of the drama and the bullshit of a real relationship, no thank you. I'm free. I have my own mind, my own time. With Derrick, there's no guess work. We both know what's up."

"I'm just saying don't be played and disrespected."

"Why do men feel like they need to disrespect you anyway? It's like they want to punish you for making it too easy or something. Why can't two people just meet, want the same things and not play games? Derrick should love our hook up and not have a word to say in complaint."

"Well, 'should' is bullshit. That's what I know for sure."

"Can't argue with the truth. I 'should' leave Derrick alone but I'm not."

"I gotta head out. I know you; you look like you're thinking up trouble. Stay home and do some work." Z smiled patted my arm and headed out.

I went into my room checked my caller ID and no trouble appeared. It'd been a couple of weeks since I'd heard from Derrick. I

141

was starting to get mad again. I did NOT want to play that same game with him as I had with Vaughn; being tortured for weeks waiting for him to call. I refused to beg for Derrick. Things just worked better between us when he was looking for me. The only problem with that was that he was looking for me less and less now. We were getting to the inevitable fading phase.

"Don't worry Z; I couldn't get into trouble if I wanted to." I said out loud to myself. I picked up the phone and dialed.

"Cat?....... What's that girl's name that cut your hair?"

In the space of a couple of hours I was staring in the mirror at my first short hair cut. I had a very short bob, cut very high in the back, like Josephine Baker. I felt the back, it was soft. There was barely enough hair to run my fingers through. For just a second I could imagine what my brother Dex would say. I don't think he'd approve. I could imagine my Dad's reaction; he still was not over my mother letting me get a belly ring over the summer. But I liked it. My head felt light and I had a defined look. I looked styled and sharp, not so nice-girl-from-strict-parents anymore. My neck looked long and my face lost a little of its round shape in favor of more angles. I was wearing a spaghetti strap, cream tank top and jeans, and immediately my shoulders looked bare. I felt sexy.

"This is good." I said.

Later that night, with an empty caller ID next to my bed, I decided to go to a Q party. Cat went with me. Ladies were always free

142

before a certain hour at Q parties. Before they let the guys in, they treated us with a strip show. Horatio Miller, a newly crossed Q with medium, brown skin and dark, curly hair was there. He was cute, but so annoying it was difficult to let the 'cute' sink in. Everyday in class I watched the way he eyed every girl that walked in the room and the way he picked at his fresh brands. He had no concern for the people around him. He just did his thing. But, he was like an occasional thorn in my side, whose pain began to intrigue me.

Horatio came out on stage and started dancing for the crowd. The girls went wild and screamed. He had a nice body. I noticed as he got down to his shorts. He danced over in front of me and gave me personal attention. Cat laughed at him. I just gave him attitude. When he was done and dressed again, he came from backstage and found me in the crowd.

"I'm glad you came." He smiled brightly.

"I can see that."

"Let me call you sometime."

"I don't think so."

"Come on."

"I gotta go. Thanks for the show." I winked. Cat and I left early. The party was pretty lame. When I got home the phone rang as soon as I got in the door.

"Hello."

"It's me, Horatio."

"How did you get my number?"

"I have my ways."

"You got it from the Class List."

"Yeah. Anyway, let me come see you?"

"No."

"Please."

"I don't know."

"Billie...come on. I'll be good to you I promise."

".....Alright. Worthington Park. Q6."

Within thirty minutes I could hear him knocking on the door downstairs. It was like ordering pizza. It was around midnight but Laurie was up and let him in.

"Billie, someone's here to see you."

"Send him up." I yelled.

He opened my bedroom door and smiled that ridiculous grin. He bounded like a puppy to my bed and flopped down on it and stared at me. I was reading a book and barely budged. He slid next to me and put his hand on my book.

"I'm here now." He was proud of himself....

There would be no kneeling in his honor.

I let him do the kneeling.

It was nice. He wasn't so goofy without clothes. He was so happy to be with me and eager to please. *This must be how Derrick feels ordering me off the menu and my showing up at his door all excited to see him.* I looked over at him lying in my bed afterwards and having pulled the fitted sheet off his side. He was still staring at me with that goofy grin. I said,

DChristy Eves

"You need to go now. Tomorrow's Thursday and I have an early class."

"Really?" He looked disappointed. But I was firm. *I'm no Derrick and no Vaughn. I'm not holding him all night long.* He pouted a bit, dressed and left. I laughed to myself and slept like a cat.

Saturday night—I'd learned a new word. Blackout. I was at Derrick's for a party. His girlfriend was there too. We were all there at their apartment piled in and drinking rum and coke, or gin and juice or any combination the guys felt like mixing you. Derrick spent a little too much time smiling at Cat. He actually had the nerve to tell me how pretty he thought she was. His girlfriend was a pretty girl too with light pecan skin and blondish hair. She had hazel eyes and really filled out her jeans. I refilled my rum and cokes quickly and tried not to sulk openly. Derrick's attention had definitely waned and I was not in the mood for waning; I wanted waxing.

My night with Horatio only made me miss Derrick more. I thought I caught him giving me the eye at one point in the evening so I made my way over to the bathroom and went inside and shut the door. I was hoping he would follow me in. I stood in front of the sink pretending to wash my hands when I saw the door open and a man's hand slide in and turn off the light. I turned around and in the dark I felt Derrick's presence in front of me. He leaned in and kissed me and I put my hands on his butt. That's when I noticed his pants were cloth like jogging pants, not jeans like I'd seen Derrick in. I reached for the light. Rod.

"What the hell are you doing?"

"Giving my girl a kiss."

I punched him in the head. "Rod!"

"Come on. I won't tell Derrick. It can be between me and you." He held me close to him and looked into my eyes. He almost looked sincere. He almost looked like he was begging. I almost considered it…

"Derrick would never speak to me again. You have to know, I would never burn that bridge."

"Okay. Alright. You can't blame a guy for trying." He let me go and leaned on the sink next to me.

"Why does Derrick treat me like this? Flirting with my girl all night and inviting me when he knows his girl is here. Why is he doing that?"

"A better question is why do you let him?"

"I don't know."

"There's your answer. He does what you let him do. I wouldn't treat you like that." He bumped my arm with his.

"I know." I bumped him back. "You gotta get out of here before someone realizes we're in here together."

He kissed my check, very sweetly, and left me. I stayed for a moment wishing Derrick was Rod. Then I left and went straight to the kitchen for another drink. One more drink turned to three or four more drinks.

The next thing I remember is waking up on the bathroom floor at home in my room. It was pitch black and I was still dressed but missing a shoe. When I sat up the room was spinning. I was sick. Very sick. I was sick until late in the afternoon the next day. I asked Laurie in the morning when she came to check on me what'd happened.

"You were so drunk girl. You kept dancing with this guy who was a friend of Derrick's. You cursed out some girl for spilling your drink and then Pride said, 'we gotta take her home before she starts fighting.' He had to carry you out. You passed out in the car."

"Oh God. Did Derrick see me? I mean, did I look like a fool?"

"Well, everybody was drunk. I don't think it was a big deal. You were funny."

"Where's Z?"

"At work."

"Do we have any Excedrin?" I put my head back on my pillow and Laurie got me Excedrin and hot tea. Later she brought up crackers and soup. But, it really bothered me that I'd lost so much time. The last thing I remember was watching Derrick's girlfriend sit in his lap while he smiled like a cat. I wondered who else at the party he was fucking. I tucked myself under the covers and went back to sleep.

19

THE KAPPA LUAU was the biggest event all year long. It was more than warm that day, it was turning hot. I was already sweating and regretting the decision to wear a skirt. My legs were sticking together.

We parked, got out and made our way through the mud and red clay to the grassy field that was completely packed with people. *Where the hell is the bar in this place?* Z was the first to head into the gate passed the Kappa handing out plastic colored leis. Cat was excited and was already getting her fair share of attention. Some skinny kid with lofty goals zeroed in on Cat and tried his luck.

"What's up girl?! You lookin' good."

She kept walking.

"Well, fuck you then you fake Halle Berry." She turned and checked him.

"Halle Berry is fine and if you are trying to insult me by comparing me to her, you missed." And she dismissed him and kept stepping.

DChristy Eves

Notorious B.I.G's "Big Papa" was bumping through the speakers. The hunch punch, a mixture that was rumored to contain grain alcohol and red kool-aid, was $2 a cup. We had no clue what was in it, but made sure to get some. Laurie pointed out a spot on the fence where we could sit and we all parked ourselves.

"It's packed in here. Pride said he would be up here, but I don't know how I'm gonna find him in all these Black folks." Laurie searched the crowd.

"Give it up. Chain links and boyfriends." I waved the air away and downed my drink. "Too heavy and totally unnecessary."

"Girl, you are crazy. You betta hope Pride is here in case we need to carry you outta here like last weekend." Laurie laughed.

"Good point. God, I think my head is still hurting from that shit." I admitted.

"I'm ready to make my rounds." Z hopped off the fence and adjusted her carefully coordinated outfit. She made sure to get the red lei from the Kappa at the gate to match.

"Come on. There's no real seat to hold here Billie. This fence'll be here when we get back. Let see who's here." Z pulled me off the fence and led the way. Cat walked next to me and checked out my new do.

"You look so cute like that." Cat smiled.

"Thanks." Her bob from earlier in the year was already growing out and her hair was almost shoulder length again.

"You make me wanna cut mine again." She nodded. I waxed a strut.

149

DChristy Eves

I was relaxed by my second drink and noticed a few extra stares in my direction. They weren't just staring at Cat, they were looking at me. Cutting through the grass in my white tank top, ethnic print skirt and new cut that freed my neck and shoulders to the sun, I felt something new... confidence.

The day just got better and better. We danced and drank, ate hot dogs from the barbeque and snapped a few pictures of the group of us girls in Charlie's Angels poses. I was checking my purse to see if I had any more money for another drink and Cat pulled my arm.

"Hey, come over here with me." She whispered pulling me away from Z. Laurie had already found Pride and was dancing with him.

"I'll be right back." I told Z, she was occupied with some guy that was flirting with her.

"What's up?"

"You wanna smoke?"

"Let's go." Cat led the way and we headed to the parking lot where these guys she knew were leaning against a burgundy sedan. One was tall and lanky and the other was short and wore a baseball cap pulled low. Cat and I got into the back seat and they got into the front.

"Let's get it rolling." The taller one said. His voice was squeaky for a guy. We sat there for a short while smoking and watching people come and go in the parking lot. I only hit a couple of times to keep the paranoia at bay. I liked the action of smoking, but the result of being high needed a little work. I found having a drink counteracted the hyper-aware-of-the-size-of-my-head feeling.

"So, did Laurie say what she's doing this summer?" Cat asked.

"She said she's going home for the summer to work."

"Work?" Cat puffed.

"Yeah, work and save up for a car."

"Why can't she work here like Z?"

"No clue." I puffed. "But she's going home and her room will be empty, so if you wanna stay with us you can."

"Okay. I'm staying for the summer, so that'll work. Eli is just totally gone now. I don't even think she's coming back let alone staying for the summer. She's on academic probation now. She's failing all her classes."

"God. You gotta be kidding. What is she doing?"

"Fucking up, that's what. And over him…"

"I know! Whatever. I wish I would let a guy ruin my life."

"Right. Please, my boyfriend was too involved in my life as it was. I had to let him go."

"Oh, so you're single now?" Mr. Low Baseball cap cut in; I'd completely forgotten they were there.

"Let's go back to the party." I told Cat.

"Yeah, I'm ready."   We got out and took a big puff of fresh air and dismissed the guys to their own devices.

"Call me later Cat." Cat's friend called out from under his cap as we headed off.

I was hoping we didn't smell like weed and that no one would be able to tell we'd smoked…. When I saw him.   The back of his head. That stance. No mistaking it, it was him. Vaughn was leaning against the fence talking to a guy and holding a drink. My heart jumped and my feet felt like bricks trudging through the dirt. My hands suddenly had no place to go and hung like dead weights from my arms. I walked Cat back to Z and Laurie who were both talking with Pride. I told them I'd be right back and I headed off.

Walking up to him, I didn't know what I would say or how my voice would sound. His eyes were grazing the crowd and as I approached, they landed on me and locked. He smiled. As soon as I got in arms reach he grabbed my hand and pulled me to him. He hugged me tight.

"Told you you'd see me again." He ran his hand up my bare neck; his fingers combed up my short hair.

"You look good." He said. I smiled and my chest thumped. I couldn't speak. He was so close to me and I was searching his eyes for a sign. *Does he remember? Why am I still attracted to him? God, I had forgotten how smooth his skin was and that scent...clean.*

He pushed me back and held my shoulders and took a long stare at me like a painting.

"Yeah, you look real good."

"What are doing back here?"

"Internship with the television station here in town. I'll be here about two months." He paused. "You look different...... Did you miss me?"

"Did *you* miss me?"

He laughed, "That's my girl. Simone." My name slid down his tongue. "You missed me. I can tell."

20

"SO HOW DOES ALL OF THIS MAKE YOU FEEL?" Dr. Pinter jotted some notes down on her pad then looked at me. I had been seeing Dr. Pinter now for about a month. I began going after starting up with Vaughn again. I hadn't been able to confront him about that night. We spent the month of March together not talking, not sleeping, and not letting each other go. My mind would go blank as soon as the phone rang and I heard him call my name. I would feel myself running to meet him without even the slightest pause. The whole affair was confusing me and I didn't have anyone to turn to about it. Counseling services were free for students, so I decided to put my tuition money to some good use. I could sit in a room for a whole hour and talk and not worry anyone would judge me. I liked it.

"It makes me feel stupid. Stupid and exciting." I started.

"Exciting?"

"Yes. He's exciting. Being with him is the most exciting thing I've ever done."

"How so?"

"Well, it just is. Now that he's back everybody else is just an after thought. He… I don't know… makes me feel so good."

"How does he make you feel good? You've said all you do is have sex, is that it then?"

"That's not all we do… we talk."

"Is the talking exciting?"

"No."

"What then?"

"I don't know."

"Did you ask him yet?"

"No."

"Are you still planning to ask him about the rape?"

"Don't say that."

"Say what, rape?"

"Yeah, don't say that."

"Why?"

"I don't like that word."

"Why not?"

"It's too harsh."

"Didn't he force you to have sex with him?"

"He didn't mean to."

"What do you think he meant to do?"

"He meant to have sex with me and for me to be into it as usual."

"So then what would you call what happened?"

"Unfortunate."

"Do you always use humor to mask your feelings?"

"I'm not that funny."

"If you could change that night, what would you change?"

"I would say yes."

"Would that fix everything?"

"Yes. A lot of women say yes just to get their man to shut up. That's what women do. That's what married women do."

"According to whom?"

"According to married women."

"What married woman told you this?"

"My mom said that it's not always fun, sometimes when you're married you just do it for them."

"But, you're not married."

"I know that……. There's no way to say it out loud and make it make sense. I'm all these things when he's not around, a girl with some sense, an intelligent person, but when he wants me, it's like nothing else matters. I don't know what's wrong with me. I need him. I keep thinking I'll be this strong girl that walks away from him, but I can't. I cannot. When he calls me…."

"Yes."

"I just should have said yes and I wouldn't be sitting here looking stupid."

"I think you should think about saying the word. Rape. Let's talk more about that next week."

I grabbed my backpack and headed out to the lobby. I wondered if the work-study girls at the front desk ever listened in. They were ignoring me and reading a magazine. I would never, never say that word. Never.

I just kept trudging across campus to the parking lot. I found my little red car, opened the door and sat inside. I listened to the radio for a minute. SWV was singing "Rain Down on Me." I headed to Tennessee Street. My mind was racing and everything was a blur. I couldn't stop a stream of tears from running down my face. *What the fuck am I doing?* I thought to myself. I wanted to punch myself. I wanted to scream. I wanted to make sense of everything. I wanted to hate myself. I wanted to hate him. I wanted to be with him. I wanted him to wake up one morning and call me and tell me he was sorry and erase that night and kiss me and be with me. At a red light I closed my eyes tight. I could see his eyes, they way he looked at me. When it turned green a woman with a car full of kids behind me wailed on her horn. I tried to drive and stop crying, but I could feel him in the car with me. I could hear his voice in my ear. Whispering, telling me the things I loved to hear.

"Be with me?" I said out loud. "Why? What the hell could I do with a man like that in real life?" I shook my head and decided to stop thinking.

I rode down until I saw KARMA TATTOO. I got out and went inside. A scraggly, little, white guy came out from the back. He looked like Kurt Cobain. I liked him instantly.

"Can I help you?" He spoke really slow and stretched out his words.

"Yeah. I want a tattoo."

"Cool. You know what you want or you wanna pick from the wall?"

"I know what I want."

"Okay. Fire when ready."

I explained to him an image that had been in my mind of a woman with wings, not an angel. He knew exactly what I meant. I felt like we clicked and he understood me. He seemed like better therapy than Dr. Pinter. Plus, I liked the way he smelled like patchouli and cigarettes. While he tattooed a large Native American woman on my thigh with wings that sailed into the air, I sat back and listened to his music.

"What is this?" I asked.

"Fleetwood Mac, ' Landslide.'"

> Oh, mirror in the sky- What is love?
>
> Can the child within my heart rise above?
>
> Can I sail through the changin' ocean tide?
>
> Can I handle the seasons of my life?
>
> I don't know, I don't know

The song swirled around me and the buzz of the tattoo needle and the pain of a woman with wings being cut into my skin calmed me. Everything seemed smaller than it had a moment before. Getting a tattoo actually made me think of my mom, she always told me that,

"Being a woman involves a certain amount of blood and pain." Razz, the tattoo guy, wiped the last of the blood from my thigh and sat back to look at it.

"It's done."

I took a look. "Perfect. She'll go with me all my days."

Afterwards, I went out back with Razz and bummed a cig and sat on the hood of his car smoking and talking about music. I loved hanging out with men. I loved the way they thought in matter-of-fact terms, not emotions and randomness like women. It was the perfect day… except for that word.

21

"TURN AROUND." He bit the back of my neck and sucked. There would be a mark—a visible mark. "I love your neck."

Something new was happening to me at Vaughn's. I couldn't speak. When I'd see him, a cement block would pour into my chest and stiffen, under the weight of which I couldn't manage to loose my words. It took awhile for him to notice.

"You not speaking to me?" I was nervous and turned back to him and kissed him to reassure him.

He laughed a little, "I can make you speak."

When he made love to me, he was like a very slow moving jackhammer breaking away the cement. My voice was under arrest until he freed it. Then he'd talk to me and I'd answer.

"You're still mine."

"Yes."

"That's my girl."

"All yours Vaughn."

I was completely addicted to him.

22

Saturday morning Cat and I hit the mall to find outfits for a party later. Cat was a morning person and loved getting started early. I wasn't, but what the hell. I also wasn't sleeping well lately, so I went.

"I'm going in the dressing room." I flapped the pile of clothes and hangers over my arm and headed to the back of the department store. Cat looked up from the rack of sundresses and nodded.

"I'll come with you." She pulled a pretty, black dress with skinny straps off the rack. I went into a small dressing area. There was no attendant so I just picked a room and went inside. Cat took the room next to mine.

When I shut the door I took a long look at myself. I was filling out more this year and I liked the look of my hips. I put on a few skirts, tried on a few dresses and studied my curves. When I got to a one shoulder, pale, lavender dress and slipped into it I knew that was the dress I wanted. I checked the tag,

DChristy Eves

"$56?!" I put it down on the chair in the room. "I don't like it $56 much." I tried the other dresses again and none seemed to compare. I put the lavender dress back on. *He's never seen me in a dress,* I thought. I thought a minute and then put my clothes on top of it. The dress was so slinky that you couldn't see it with my jeans over top and my tee-shirt. I walked out of my dressing room and stood in front of Cat's stall.

"How'd you make out?"

"I like this black dress, but I don't think so."

"You ready to head out?"

"Yeah."

She gathered her things and we headed for the door. I wondered if anyone would say anything. I could see the sunlight through the double doors and my heart was beating. But no one noticed. The sales girl smiled as we walked by. In a second we were outside and headed for my car. Simple as that. She didn't know and I didn't say, but the lavender dress went with me.

Later that day we all met up to look at a house for rent. The apartment at Worthington had worn out its charm. The house was in the woods near a park and had hardwood floors and a deck out back. The master was a converted garage and it was almost separate from the rest of the house. It made it feel private. I was in love. Laurie, Z, and Cat all loved the house too. We signed the lease and were set to move in May 1st. I couldn't help but think that by that point Vaughn would be gone. *Thank God. I can't leave him. He's got to leave me.*

DChristy Eves

I was tired of my own self. I didn't want to want him anymore.
I hated the feeling of thinking that I should talk to him competing with
the feeling that I should pretend it never happened. Cleopatra was the
queen of denial and she always won. Afterwards, I felt cold and empty.
I started listening to my namesake for the first time. I bought a Billie
Holiday album and played it alone in my room. It was just my speed.

"My man don't love me. Treat me oh so mean." I would sing to
myself in my closed room. "But when he starts in to love me, he is so
fine and mellow." I would never admit out loud that I understood the
music. I understood the lows and highs of a man. Billie had the sound
of ecstasy and pain in her voice and I knew exactly what that felt like. I
wanted so badly that wanting. When Vaughn wanted me, really wanted
me, there was no resisting it.

When I was caught listening to Billie Holiday I'd just say 'I love
her style.'

"Oh my God. That's slit your wrist music." Zondra would
complain.
But the girls had no idea who I was inside. They had no clue about
Vaughn. Because he was my secret I never had to explain myself to
anyone. I didn't have to justify seeing him now. I didn't have to justify
waiting by the phone. April was winding down and he was missing
again. It'd been two weeks since he'd called and soon he'd be leaving.
Was he leaving me now? Was it already over? I couldn't call him with
no voice. I had to wait, and time felt like a dull knife dragging across my
breasts.

162

DChristy Eves

My notebook, with the pages torn and the receipts and napkins
spilling out, was too tired for what I was feeling. Even though my outlet
for poetry was gone, I'd gone out and bought a blank book. It was an
antique distressed and dirty looking pink with grey faded roses on the
cover and soft, gold paint on the edge of the pages. I sat with my music
and wrote.

I pass through trees

Of thick and leafy green

Swallowing the sky

And urging me down the

Throaty rood

That road which leads to the

Bed I know

The sheets I've smelled

That scent of familiar space

Of distinct smell

Of no further growth

On stunted blooms

Stagnant roses

Hung to dry frozen

In their stiff brittle stems

And in blood colored blooms

With petals paused in time

When handled their

Beauty into dust

And your bed smells

DChristy Eves

Of old rose dust

From other blooms dissected

And yet I go

You call me I go

And I come

Through the trees

That swallow the sky

That covers the road

That lead to your

House

The grey tomb

Of indecision

23

IT WAS JUST ANOTHER ORDINARY WEDNESDAY, and I was getting ready to go to bed. It was about 11:30 p.m. and I was pretty tired. I had been thinking about him for the past few days and how badly we needed to talk. I had just talked to Dr. Pinter and I told her that I wouldn't see him anymore without asking him about that night.

I would never understand how a man so popular among the young ladies at FAMU, not to mention his girlfriend, would have to take sex. It wasn't violent. I honestly felt like he didn't know what he was doing; but he did do it nonetheless. And I was worse than him because I continued to go back to him, knowing he had little concern for me. My compassion and empathy for him was ten times greater than it was for myself. I thought, *Funny how you lose control. Funny how you can just wake up one morning and it's just gone... the control. Without even realizing you've surrendered, your control is gone and some man with a pretty smile is stealing your soul. I guess life is funny that way.* I tucked myself under the covers and had just put my head to the pillow when the phone rang.

"Hello."

"Simone."

"Hey!"

"I miss you." It had been almost three weeks.

"Really?"

"Yeah. Come by and see me."

"I'll be there in ten minutes." Speak of the devil… And he shall appear.

I jumped out of the bed and screamed. I was so excited. I was going to see him. I was going to look at his beautiful, caramel face and pretty smile. I loved the way he smelled. Clean. He always smelled like clothes fresh out of the dryer and a body straight out of the shower. Like soap. Fresh. I was going to look at him. I was going to touch him. Smooth like silk. I shook my head, *Snap out of it Simone. Snap out of it. You WILL talk to him. You will ask him the question. You will ask him why……….why?*

I got myself as cute as I could in five minutes. I washed up, threw on some lipstick and eyeliner, my cutest jeans and a shirt that would stop at my midsection, just high enough to see my belly ring. I slid into my black boots with the perfect heel and I was off. I tripped on the vacuum cleaner in the hallway in the dark. I ran down the stairs. I started my car and headed towards his house.

As I began to drive I had excitement lodged in my throat. But, the excitement slowly subsided as I began to realize what would happen as soon as I saw him. *I can see the sex in his eyes from here, a mile down the road and in the dark. And I can smell the words on his breath.*

166

"You miss me Simone?" *"C'mere."* I remembered him calling me a "serious encounter." That's what I was to him, "a serious encounter." And yet I could still taste him on my lips… a mile down the road and in the dark…… already on my lips.

When I turned onto his street my stomach started to knot up. *I can't believe I'm doing this……. Yes, I can, 'cause I always do.* I pulled into his driveway and stared at the light on in his bedroom and I made a last minute attempt to remind myself that he and I had to talk about what happened. *You better do it Simone.* I walked up to his door and knocked. *Any second now…..his face……any second…his face. How will I react to it….seeing his face again.* When I heard he'd left the city last year, I didn't know how to react. I thought, 'what am I supposed to do now that he's gone and all of the words are still burning on my lips?' I hadn't been able to bring myself to say anything to him, since he'd returned and I knew that this was my last chance. He was leaving next week. Any minute….

Click. Click

The door opened and his face appeared from behind it. And he smiled.

"Come on in."

"Hi."

"How've you been…What's going on…How's classes?"

"Fine. Everything's good."

"Give me a hug."

He smiled big and reached his arms around my waist and pulled me really close. He slid his hands down the back of my pants and inside my panties and squeezed my butt. I kissed his neck and cheek, and he mentioned that he'd busted his lip the other day. I didn't know why he said it. I was wondering if he said it because he thought I was going to kiss him and he didn't want me to. But then he kissed me back on my neck. When he turned me loose he grabbed my hand and led me to the kitchen. He leaned against the counter and grabbed me tightly again. He told me to take off my sweater. I did and I dropped it on the floor. I knew this would happen. I knew he'd want me immediately. I was nervous, but in my own way, I wanted him too. I wanted him to touch me. I wanted him to kiss me. I wanted him to be near me. I wanted him close enough for me to smell him. And most of all I wanted him to want me the way I wanted him.

Soon we were upstairs in his room. In minutes he was inside me. Pumping away his frustrations of a less than perfect life, of whatever problems he had that he couldn't share with me. I was no more to him than one of those little stress balls that you pick up at the grocery store and squeeze when you're under stress. He squeezed me with the process of relief, not affection. I could feel it in his touch.

As I was lying on my stomach trying to piece together his words and his actions, "you're the best" "you feel so good" "did you miss me" "c'mere," out of nowhere he jumped up. *What in the world?* Then I heard the doorbell ring. He picked up a towel and went out on the balcony.

"Who is it?"

I guess he heard a car pull up before the bell rang. I couldn't hear a response, but he continued to talk back and forth to the person. Then I heard a woman's voice.

"You gon' let me in?!" She sounded angry.

He answered, "Hold up" and came back in the room and told me to "Get dressed."

"What's wrong?"

"That's my girlfriend….. You're gonna have to sit in the room with Marcus."

"Oh God." I laughed.

For some reason I wasn't scared or nervous. It was funny immediately. Right away I knew that when she came in she'd know what was going on.

"Wait for me?" He asked. In that second I saw his face… his eyes.

For a split second, he was real.

It took him forever to answer the door. He took his time, gathered his clothes, went to the bathroom, washed up a minute. Meanwhile, she's ringing the hell out of the doorbell. She knows. She would have to. I went in the room with Marcus and he started complaining. Vaughn walked me in there and told Marcus,

"You're gonna have some company tonight."

"Man, I can't believe you got me involved in this shit."

"I'm sorry." I told Marcus, it was our first time meeting. He sucked his teeth and growled. I sat on the floor at the end of his bed right near the door. I could hear everything. He made his way downstairs as if he had no rush in the world. I was beginning to wonder if he had feelings. It's amazing how a man who only cares about himself can be

so sweet and turn around and show you his indifference. It made me
wonder why he was sweet to people in the first place.

He opened the door. I could hear the clicks. I really couldn't
hear her words but her voice was compelling. It was knowledgeably
angry and hurt.

"What are you doing here at twelve thirty at night? And without
calling."

Then I could hear, "You got a girl in here?!!!"

"What are you talking about? And how did you get over here
anyway."

"I don't believe this shit...." Marcus broke in.

I just looked back at him. Even though he was here, I was alone on this
one. It was completely unreal. Not only was I caught having sex with
another woman's boyfriend, but I was hiding and listening to the
argument. *She's coming upstairs. I know it. I wonder what she looks
like.* I'd heard how pretty she was. I knew a guy in one of my
journalism classes that was rumored to have slept with Vaughn's girl
after one of their notorious fights. I was just curious. She was a cheat
just like him. So she shouldn't have anything to complain about. I
didn't feel bad at all. I was just upset that she ruined my evening. I
wanted to talk to him, and she blew it. I wanted to finish, and she blew
that too. Now, I would never see him again and I would never talk to
him. Dr. Pinter said I should write him a letter, but he's not the type of
man you write a letter to claiming that he raped you. He would kill me.
I had to talk to him in a subtle way.

I could hear the voices upstairs now. First, in the bathroom down the hall and then in his bedroom next door.

"I do not have a girl in here."

"Vaughn, are you lying to me?"

He paused. "You're crazy."

Then there was a knock at Marcus's door. Even though I knew it was coming it surprised me. She cracked the door open and from her position in the doorway she could only see Marcus in bed by himself.

"I got company." He tried to tell her, that's when she stuck her head in a little further and noticed me on the floor, at the end of the bed, fully dressed. She knew I was there for Vaughn.

"Are you here for Vaughn or Marcus?" She addressed me directly. I couldn't see her face because the light was behind her head. I could only tell she had long hair. *Big deal. I had a head full of long hair my whole life and cut the shit off.* I didn't answer her because I didn't feel like lying to the sister. I felt like saying, 'I'm here for Vaughn.' But instead, since I knew he had a girlfriend when I got involved, I felt obligated or better yet, it was part of the deal to keep quiet. Marcus answered her quickly,

"Naw, naw, she's here for me."

Now, come on sweetheart, I know you don't believe this shit.

"I'm not talking to you Marcus! I'm talking to your friend. Are you here for Vaughn or Marcus?"

I paused briefly and answered, "I'm here for Marcus."

My voice was sarcastic. She knew I was lying. But I did appreciate the tone she held with me, very 'woman to woman.' I wanted to say, 'Yes sweetheart, I'm fucking your man; and have been for the past year. And I've been hurt by him and if you want him, take him. I don't want him anymore. Matter of fact you and I could do much better. Vaughn is nothing but a face and a body. He's not real.'

She left the room. Some time passed. But after a while it was quiet and I heard the television. She would forgive him. She probably already has. In the moment of silence as my own anger faded, I wondered had I forgiven him too? Was I still sitting there hoping she would leave and I could go back and sit on his bed? Was he really not coming back to get me? I got up without a word to Marcus and left.

24

MAY CAME—despite my pleading with it to stay away. May came and Vaughn never called again. He was gone and I could feel it. I threw the lavender dress away with the trash. He'd left me....without one word. The marks he left on my skin were all faded. I cut the rest of my hair off with a pair of scissors in the bathroom mirror. I looked like a boy. My hair was short and curly. I could see the real texture without my perm. I stared at myself in the mirror. I looked completely different. I wasn't even sure I recognized myself. But like it or not.... there I was.

Eli packed up her things and left for good. We all watched her pull off with her sister taking her back to Pensacola. Her boyfriend was leaving too and they thought they'd have a life together. They told us all they'd be back next year. She was secretly pregnant, but I knew. Cat told me and I kept it to myself. It was like watching a funereal procession when she left. *Where the hell does she think love's taking her,* I thought. I thought she was naïve and throwing away her life for that guy. I couldn't figure out why it made me so mad. And I couldn't figure out where she'd gotten a nasty bruise on her arm that was turning all green and yellowish in the middle. She was already long gone to us, but it just occurred to me that I missed her. I missed her smile.

Cat moved in with us and the atmosphere changed in our house with Laurie gone. With Cat as our roommate, when we invited people over, they came. No more empty living room with just us girls; guys couldn't wait for the opportunity to sit close to her. The spill off of men was fine with me. Smoke, men and liquor were my biggest sources of distraction. Now we had all three anytime we snapped our fingers. Cat would say,

"You feel like smoking?"

I'd say, "Sure."

She or I could call any boy we knew and they'd rush right over with weed, drinks and food. We never paid for anything. It was summer and both Cat and I had one summer class to worry about and that's all. I took photography and Cat took calculus. We had way too much free time. Z was working all the time and would come home to find Cat and me in the living room filled with guys and smoke. She would flash that granny-glare and head off to her room.

Cat and I being left alone in the apartment was like leaving the kids in charge of the classroom. I was having the time of my life and every second I tried to fill with something. I couldn't sit still and let my mind talk to me. Maybe he would be hiding in the corners of my mind waiting for me when silence opened the door. I wasn't sure if in some way Cat needed the noise of our friendship too. I wondered if she was blocking someone from her mind. We seemed to be on the same mission.

Everything had its price though. Pleasure and pain were two sides of the same coin. Even Cat's friendship came with a cost. Derrick had a crush on her. He came by sometimes with his crew of friends to see us. He would openly flirt with Cat. She never accepted his advances but there was an unspoken competition waged and she was the clear winner. He was sitting next to me on the couch one Thursday night and Cat was sitting on my other side. We were pretty squished and Cat kept wiggling on the couch, uncomfortable. Derrick had just passed the blunt to me and Cat called out,

"Billie, my God, you're so skinny your hip bone is cutting into me!" She laughed out loud. Her laughter had a harsh tone. The room went silent when she said it. Men are not that perceptive to women's feelings, but they can sense the beginning of a cat fight in a flash. They waited for my reaction. My faced turned red. I said nothing. 'Skinny' was like a curse word to our group. Black men like meat on a woman's bones. We were all just over a hundred pounds and we would weigh ourselves to see who weighed the most. Cat and I were both the same height and taller than Laurie and Z, and we weighed the most. I was 108 lbs. and Cat was almost 110 lbs. *It has to be her breasts*, I thought. She had the breasts, I had the hips. We were the same size otherwise. I couldn't tell her that her outburst cut me a little, but she knew it and it was in her eyes. The winner's smile. I was the runner up. My prize— Derrick after his attempts had failed with her and he'd given up. He was the only guy around during the slow summer I'd met that I felt like sleeping with, so he still made his way to my bed. It couldn't be empty. He filled it nicely and reminded me of his trademark hold that lasted all night.

On campus I was enjoying my photography class. I had a cheap little camera and took pictures of things around campus. There was a garden near campus that was set up for growing something that hadn't appeared. There were rows of wooden crosses with sticky, brown vines with no leaves climbing them. I took pictures of the empty crosses ready to bear in black and white. Cat hadn't made such a wise choice of summer class and she was failing calculus. But she did mention an interesting guy she'd met. He was helping her study, which was about as effective as Derrick helping me forget Vaughn. But, we stayed our courses without thought or waiver. Eventually May was kind enough to leave us for June.

One Tuesday, on my way up the hill to class, I noticed a familiar afro. Rasheed.

"Hey!" I called out.

"What's up girl??" He still sounded like he was rapping. He smiled.

"What are you doing up here? Taking classes?"

"Yeah, I gotta graduate at some point. You still writing?"

"Yeah. I don't read anywhere though."

"You disappeared from poetry group after your thing with Grant huh?"

"I thought that would be best.... How is he?"

176

"He graduated. He's back home now. He got a job up there."

"Well, that's good."

"Hey, I'm working with Jaheim Bonds on this poetry magazine. It's called *Think Tank*. You should submit some stuff."

"Really? Well, I'll look some stuff over and see if I have anything publishable."

"Yeah, you should. Call me. I wanna read you some of my new stuff."

"I will." I gave him a hug and headed off to class.

Later that night, I was back home and curled up in my bed by the night light. I flipped through my pages and considered a new poem.

> Some things you don't tell your girls
>
> You don't tell them about last night
>
> You tell them everything went fine
>
> Some things you don't tell your girls
>
> You don't say that he was rude
>
> You tell 'em he was sweet as candy
>
> Some things you don't tell your girls
>
> You don't say that he grabbed you a little too hard
>
> You tell 'em he held you tight
>
> Some things you can't tell your girls
>
> You don't say that you told him no and he grabbed you
>
> and said
>
> Yes
>
> And that he hurt you
>
> And that you cried

And that you went along because you were afraid

And that you wanted to be back in safety's arms

You tell 'em it was a long night

And when they ask have you seen him since 'that night'

You smile and say sure

I dreamed that everything was fine

I dreamed that he was sweet

And he held me tight

And in the morning he made me breakfast

Not that he threw my clothes at me

And took me home

I thought about the poem a minute and put it away. No point in publishing that one.

25

"I LOVE THAT ONE about roads. The way you describe the black of the road and the direction that's unknown. That was really good." I said.

"Thanks. It's between that one and the one about chasing that beautiful girl." Rasheed said and went back through his book. He had a big, wide, black journal with one gold line down the margin on the front. It looked like an encyclopedia. I had given him a call and he wanted to stop by and go over some poems. It was a week later on Tuesday afternoon and I was home alone, bored and welcomed the company.

"So, what girl is that about? Is that a real story or imagination?"

"Nah, that's true. I was hanging out with this girl who had a boyfriend. Now, her man was a real dog, classic cheating and being mean. She was fine, super fine. She was tired of his shit one day and I was lucky enough to be right there, being her friend as usual. But, she didn't want to cry on my shoulder. She wanted to give Rasheed the booty." He laughed.

"Rasheed! What happened after the booty?"

"She went back to him."

"Were you hurt?"

"Nah… She was fine though. I was trying to see her again. That's where the chasing came in. But you know beautiful girls are a trip."

"Beautiful people in general."

"Yeah, they own the world… do what they want. Speaking of which, where's your girl?"

"Cat's gone to class. Man, does everybody have a crush on her? What am I chopped liver?"

"No wait," He laughed and back peddled. "You're fine too..."

"Stop now. I'm just kidding."

"I know. But listen, you're not the mean, beautiful type. You're beautiful. You are. You're beautiful inside too, that makes it different."

"What do you mean?"

"I mean that you've got a good heart. But, there's something about that mean streak in a girl that makes her extra beautiful on the outside. I think when they're young they get over too much on everybody and it makes 'em extra attractive, like they had to hone the skill of beauty or something."

"You may have a point there. It's a sense of entitlement. I never had that growing up."

"I'm surprised you weren't spoiled being the only girl in a house full of men."

"Nope. Overprotected and ignored. The men in my house were like a brick wall. Nothing came passed them. The Hazard men are all tall, strong, and known to fight…well. The guys in the neighborhood couldn't even think about checking me out. They would pile up at our house and I'd be stuck upstairs listening through the floor. Sometimes I'd go down to pretend to get a drink or something, and I'd see them laughing and having fun and talking about girls and who was fine. They would find me lingering a little too long and send me away." I said remembering.

I got up to get myself a drink. In the kitchen I could see my dad's face in my mind, that Cheshire cat grin. I remembered him opening the front door one day to find a beautiful, full grown Latino woman at our door.

"Can I help you?" My dad asked her, stunned at her presence.

"Yes," She answered and had an accent. "I'm here to see Dexter."

"You here to see Dexter? My son?" My dad pulled his head back to take in her full breasts, tight waist and wide hips stuffed in tight jeans. She had to be in her twenties.

"You must be here to see me." He was incredulous. Dexter came to the door.

"Dad. This is my friend." Dex cut in.

"Goddamn." Dad stared.

"Can I go Dad?"

Dad thought a minute, patted Dex on the back and off they went.

"Goddamn." Dad touted once more watching the woman walk away.

DChristy Eves

Later that same day it rained and my friend called from a payphone nearby. He was my classmate; a sweet boy with a kind face who always carried transformers in his backpack. He had ridden his bike over to my neighborhood. He asked if he could drop by and come out of the rain and see me. I was too young to have boy company but I asked anyway.

"Dad, can my friend Wesley Chapleton Jr. come by and hang out just for a little while?"

"No. No boy company."

"But Dad, it's raining outside. Only for a little while. Please." I begged holding the phone with Wesley listening on the other end.

"I don't care if it's shitting outside. I said NO!!" His voice boomed. All I heard was a sigh and then a click. Wesley hung up.

I stared down at my glass in the kitchen. I laughed a little at the memory and went back to the living room.

"Rasheed, being the only girl, I spent all my time making my Barbie's kiss their Ken's alone in my room while my brothers ran the streets." I said still laughing at the thought.

"What about your dad? Were you Daddy's little princess?"

"No princess here. I was and still am his Little Girl. I had a whole set of rules that was different from the boys. When I asked about sex he told me he'd sit me down and tell me everything when I turned eighteen. I think I'm still waiting on that talk.

"My dad was a big flirt with the women. He would take me with him places and women would smile at him and give him discounts on things, and he'd stick out his chest and grin. He used to take me to bars

182

when I was really little and sit me up on the counter and the women would go, 'Oooh Otis Jay Hazard. You sho' make some pretty babies.' He could get free drinks and show off his skills at baby-making.

"Listen, I was not even close to being spoiled. I was totally invisible, except to my mom. We cleaned together and talked. I'd help her in the kitchen. I was her baby. The one she'd waded through three boy babies to get to. But when I asked her about sex, she hid her eyes and changed the subject."

"Damn. Well, I'll tell you what. That's explains it." Rasheed got up to stretch and refill his cup of juice.

"Explains what?"

"You." He called from the kitchen.

"What do you mean?"

"You're getting a rep girl." He came back and plopped on the sofa next to me and patted my leg.

"A rep?"

"Yeah. It's all over that you cheated on Grant and were trying to get with Sam and you were messing with some other guy too."

"What?!"

"Yeah. Don't worry. I don't listen to gossip. I think you're cool. The thing is you can't raise wolves and rabbits together."

"What the hell are you talking about, wolves and rabbits?"

"Wolves and rabbits. Your dad was doing what men do, raising his boys up to be wolves. That's how my dad raised me. But you can't raise a sweet little rabbit up in the same house. That part's you. You're just asking for the rabbit to get eaten alive. Either that or they have to learn to become wolves too."

"Rasheed. Are you high?"

"You're a rabbit, who *thinks* she's a wolf." He laughed. "Anyway, if you been waiting your whole life to get some of that male attention shot your way, no wonder. Anyway, fuck them. It's just that crew we hung with. No big deal. I don't even hang with them anymore. Me and Bonds got the magazine and we're getting a new poetry group set up next year when the school year starts. You should hang with us."

"Rasheed. You think I'm a slut?"

"Slut? Nah. I think you're cool. Don't worry about that stuff. I shouldn't have said it. Just like that girl I told you about. She stepped out on her man and she's not a slut, it happens. No big deal. Her man is supposed to be all that. Vaughn Cruz. Even his name is pompous."

"Vaughn Cruz?" I sat up straight from the couch.

"Yeah. You know him." I couldn't believe it. We were all in bed together. *Classic.*

"Not really. He was in journalism too, that's all."

"He graduated. She's still here, in the same class with me. And she can't resist me forever." He patted the 'fro.

"It's a small world."

"Small campus. Anyway, like I was saying, don't worry about that stuff. Old news."

"Rasheed. Wanna smoke?"

"Blaze it up man."

26

BY THE END OF JUNE, the summer was rolling in, slow and hot. I'd never felt heat like the Florida summer. It was hard to breathe. And despite our best efforts to keep things live, a new kind of reality set in. Most students had gone home and it was pretty quiet. My money was dwindling and I needed a job. With only one class to attend, summer had a whole new face—boredom.

Cat and I had seen every made-for-TV cable movie, talk show and soap opera ever aired. When we weren't watching television, we would hit the thrift shops and find great clothes and costumes to wear. We'd dress like mandarin ladies one minute, and the next we'd find '60's mod outfits. We took pictures with lit cigarettes in our mouths. Cat liked all the same crazy stuff I did. We kept some guys on tap for weed when we needed it and a good laugh at their expense. But Derrick and his crew were the roosters of the hen house and when they came, everybody else was a non-thought.

Derrick and I were having an interesting relationship. Rod had come by several times without Derrick to hang out with me. He'd manage to luck up on times when the girls were out and he and I would smoke and talk. I knew he had a crush on me and I didn't do much to discourage it, but I never encouraged it either. But he was easy to talk to. Rod had kind eyes and I liked the way he looked at me. Before he'd leave, he'd always give me a big hug that I enjoyed. But that was the end of it.

Derrick apparently knew his brother was visiting me and I think it raised his eyebrow slightly. My phone rang late one night at 1:20 a.m.

"Hello?"

"What's up B.?"

"Derrick, what's up? It's late."

"It's early."

"You win."

"I wanna come over."

"Then come over."

"You alone?"

"Don't be silly, come on."

He was there pretty quickly. I had unlocked the door when he called so he could just come on back. He opened my door, kicked off his shoes and got in bed with me and started asking me questions.

"What's up with you and my brother?"

"Derrick. Nothing. Just because Rod's interested in me doesn't make me interested in him. What's up with you and my roommate?"

"Look, she's cute, that's all. It's not that deep. You've been spending time with Rod. You read Rod your poetry?"

"What? Maybe once when he was over here hanging out. He asked to see some. We're friends, that's all."

"Read me one."

"It's almost 2 a.m. and you want poetry?" I stared back at him. He had slid up behind me and with my back to him he was lifting my white spaghetti strap Calvin Klein night gown and rubbing my stomach. I was glad I'd worn it; I knew he'd think it was sexy. He smiled. I got my book from my bedside table and flipped.

"Here's one for you.

I like to fuck.

Or maybe it's the fucking attention.

I don't know,

But I like to fuck.

Fucking is fundamental.

It's fun—damn—it's mental.

Get with your fucking mind

And do it all the fucking time.

But is it the fucking

Or is it the fucking attention?"

"Funny. You're supposed to read me a real one." Derrick let me go and rolled on his back.

"It was real. As real as I get this late." I was laughing, but Derrick did not think it was funny. I put my book back down. There was no way I could read my book to Derrick. Too many of my poems now were about him now. There was something about the combination of honesty and sex between us that was beginning to feel like it was trying to find a root inside me. It felt like the photo I took of the garden that was waiting for something to grow. All the posts were in place to support the crop. It was just waiting for rain. I wondered if he was starting to feel it too. *Maybe that's why he's over here looking for poetry in the middle of the night.* His brother was no more than the first trickle of rain.

I knew that trick. I'll reveal myself to him, feel close, make love and think I'm in love. Hell no. Jealousy was love's best trick. Just when you thought you could hide safely in the casualness of an affair, jealousy would come along and whisper in your ear that possession is nine tenth of the law. Derrick just didn't want his brother getting something from me he didn't have access to.

I put my head on his chest and wrapped my arms around him. It was quiet for minute. He asked me what I was thinking and I said nothing. I had a lot of thoughts floating by but I couldn't tag one. Not a safe one. Right then he gave up trying to talk to me and started kissing my neck. I had no defense for his kisses. It was like a rush of alcohol to my head. I felt light-headed. He pulled me up to him and held my face in his hands as he kissed me more deeply than he'd ever done before. The next thing I knew he'd taken off my thin nightgown and I was on the floor kneeling between his legs. He asked me to take off my panties. I did. A whirl of passionate and faceless sex took place. I did things to him that should only be saved for a lover, not a luster; but if he asked me I had to comply. And when everything was done I rubbed him down with a full body massage. I even rubbed his ugly ass feet. I touched him with everything I had in me. I touched him like I would touch the love

188

of my life. The need I had to love was just pouring out of me and I couldn't damn the flood.

As we fell asleep together tightly snuggled in my bed, I felt sick. How could I allow myself to be so stupid? I got up to go to the bathroom and he grabbed my arm,

"Don't go." He looked so sincere, I felt so special. I remembered the last time I was at his place and he held on to my shirt when I got up to leave his bed in the middle of the night after making love. He told me,

"Don't go. Don't leave."

I said, "You want me to stay?"

He held on to me, "Spend the night with me."

I couldn't leave him that night, or any night. He had me. And I hated it. I turned back and looked at him. Why did he want to trick me and make me feel loved when he only wanted to fuck me? Why did he need to swallow me whole? Was I supposed to turn into his girlfriend, a girl who'd be sitting in his lap while his other lovers blacked-out from jealousy? I touched his face.

"I'll be right back."

I went to the bathroom and avoided the mirror. When I came back he was lying there waiting. I sunk back into his arms and he locked me inside his chest. I hoped that he didn't think I was like this with all the guys. It was just him now. I took a deep breath and filled my lungs with his cologne—his potion—and fell asleep.

27

Z HAD A NEW BOYFRIEND, Ben. He was from Miami and
was a real guys' guy. He was very protective and had that daddy vibe
about him. Cat had started to bend her attention to the guy who'd been
pursuing her in her calculus class. He was very intelligent and handsome
in an off beat way. But there was something really sleazy about him. It
was in his eyes. When he'd come by, he'd stare at Cat like she was the
last supper. As soon as Cat would leave the room he'd look over at me
and give me a long piercing glare. I knew that look. It did make me feel
better about Derrick's crush on her.

Faults and all, by the closing of the summer everybody had their
man. Derrick was mine. He stopped staring at Cat. He'd spend the
night, stay for breakfast sometimes. He didn't have a girlfriend anymore,
or she was gone home for the summer. Who cared why; I was getting
the brunt of his attention. We would go to the movies together, get high
in the parking lot then go in and crack up at whatever was on. We saw
Dumb and Dumber at the dollar theatre high and it was so funny we were
crying and falling all over each other. When he'd spend the night he'd

make me feel so special. He knew just what to do with me and he always held me afterwards. I didn't want him to, but he was getting to me…getting inside my mind. He knew how to stay away just long enough and then come back and be just good enough. I was hanging in the balance of his absence and affections.

July was the worst month for heat and we did everything we could to stay in the air conditioning. Derrick and his crew of guys were over on a Friday night doing the usual puff, pass, movie and drinks-go-round routine. Derrick, Rod, and two of their friends were over. We had been hanging out in the living room laughing loud and smoking and irritating Z. The short guy with the weak chin was obviously infatuated with Z and offered to sit with her in her room away from the smoke. While they escaped our shenanigans, Cat and I laughed at the top of our lungs at who knows what and played cards with the rest of the guys. There was a knock at the door and Cat got up to answer it. She looked through the peep hole and said,

"Oh shit!!" She turned around. "It's Ben."

Ben, Ben, Ben… I turned the name over in my head trying to make a picture.

"Who?" I couldn't remember.

"Ben. Z's boyfriend! She's got a guy in there with her."

"Turn out the lights!" I screamed. Cat turned out the lamp right in front of the window and stood there like the cops were on the other side of the door.

"Shhhhhh!!!!!" She yelled to the guys. "Nobody say anything."

191

Meanwhile, Ben hearing all this was starting to get very mad. He began bamming on the door.

"Open the door! What's going on in there??" He yelled.

"Go wait in my room." I waved the guys away. Derrick got up, took the joint and moved like he didn't have a care in the world. The guys followed him. Cat and I tapped on Z's door.

"Z, Ben is out there knocking on the door." I told her.

"What the hell are you guys doing out here? What's going on?" Z came out of her room.

"Ben is out there, but we got rid of him for you." Cat continued, she was laughing. Z took one look at us, our red eyes, our crazy high selves and she realized very quickly that we pretty much ruined any chance she had of politely playing the situation off.

"We aren't even doing anything in here. Why didn't you just tell me he was here?" Z was pissed.

"OPEN THE GODDAMN DOOR!!" Ben was livid and beating on the door now. He switched and started bamming on her bedroom window which was in the front.

"WHAT DO YOU THINK I'M STUPID OUT HERE??!!! I KNOW YOU'RE HOME!! YOU GOT A MAN IN THERE?!" Ben started to sound like a real thug outside. His voice was deep and gruff. The guy was cowering down in Z's room and looked scared. Ben was strong and looked as intimidating as he sounded.

"Go out there and tell him to leave." I told him.

"Fuck you." He said back scared to death. He picked up the phone in Z's room and called 911.

"What a loser." I said staring at him. Cat shrugged her shoulders and went back to my room with the guys. Having been high also, this seemed perfectly logical and I followed her.

"Relationship drama." I said as I waltzed back there.

Z was left to clean up the mess. She went to the door and tried to get Ben to calm down. He was out there calling her every name in the book and threatening to come inside and kill the guy in her room. During the fiasco, Cat and I sat with the guys hiding in my room. We were sitting on my bed with all the lights off. We were all whispering for some reason. I was lying with my head in Derrick's lap and he was combing through my hair. It was growing back fast and it felt so good. After a while we all forgot why we were sitting there in the dark.

"I wish we had doughnuts." I said.

"Oooh. That's sounds good. Is Krispy Kreme open?" Cat sat up.

"Yeah, they're open all night." Derrick said. There was a hungry beat; we all eyed each other.

"Let's roll." Derrick grabbed his keys.

We all got up went to the living room like marching zombies. Z and Ben were still in a heated argument.

"If that nigga back der, he need to come out, be a man and face me!"

"Ben, this is between me and you. Please just go on home and we…." Z saw us coming. We simply walked passed Z standing in the door with Ben. They stopped for a second incredulous and watched us file out. As soon as Derrick's car started they started yelling again.

"Tell that mothafucka to get out here!!!"

When we came back, with a dozen or so assorted doughnuts, they were still arguing and we passed them again breaking the beat of their fight. We headed back to my room. Soon the police came and made Ben leave. We did nothing to help, nor did we check on Z. We ate all the doughnuts and starting falling asleep. Eventually the guys left.

The next morning in the clarity of sobriety, I realized I had made a terrible mistake. Z was not speaking to me. I went to her door.

"Z?"

Nothing.

"Z?"

Nothing.

"Come on Z. I'm sorry…….. I was high……… I wasn't thinking."

"I know you weren't thinking."

"Z. I'm so sorry."

"Ben could've beat my ass last night and you went to get doughnuts??"

A little laugh slipped out.

"I heard that!"

"I'm sorry. Please let me come in." I tucked my head in. Z was giving me the stare. "I'm really sorry."

"Fine. Whatever." She let me come in and talk, but I could tell she was getting tired of my foolishness.

"You okay?" I asked.

"…..I'm fine….. We broke up. He called this morning and told me to never speak to him again."

"Z, I'm sorry. I'm so sorry."

"Whatever. It's fine. I knew we weren't gonna be forever. He really liked me and he treated me nice, that's all."

"What was up with that guy? What were you guys in here doing?"

"Nothing."

"Nothing, all that time before Ben got here?"

"……Well, he kissed me."

"Really, so you *were* getting a little busy in here." I laughed.

"No. He just kissed me once and told me how much he liked me."

"Well, who can resist the sunshine of adoration from a man? No one."

"You and Cat…. You guys need to stop smoking so much."

"It's summer. What else should we do?"

"I don't know but it's not cute."

"I'm tired of being cute anyway, so whatever."

"Billie…."

"Yeah."

"Nevermind." She sighed and knew it was pointless to talk to me about any of my vices. Even in our drifting apart she knew me very well. You can't erase where you've been with someone. And Z and I had eleven years of friendship under our belt now.

28

BY THE END OF SUMMER, August told us that the months of distraction were coming to a close, and I finally found my way to the beach. Rasheed told me about St. George Island. It was a tiny, little strip of beach on the gulf coast. It was tricky to find but I knew we were getting close when the houses lining the road all sat up on silts. Rasheed showed me the way one lost Saturday when the girls were both occupied with their men and Derrick was busy playing Now You See Me, Now You Don't. He gave me directions while smoking in the passenger seat.

"Right here, turn left."
 I looked and saw a tiny, little, two-lane bridge that looked like it went straight out into the water.

"That little bridge?" Suddenly I wished I hadn't smoked. The bridge lurched upward like the track of a roller coaster, and when we got to the top of it you could see the whisper of an island. It was all covered with what looked like snow and periodic blades of tall grass.

We drove onto the island and turned down the island's one road. It was like a black belt through a white pillow. The sand dunes piled high and rolled on one side and on the other there were little cottages on silts. When I looked through I could see blue water. The sky above was bright and a few clouds puffed out. There was a silence on the island that ushered away the world. I rolled my window all the way down and drove so slowly, we could have been walking.

When I got out I could feel the sun all over my skin. It felt good. We got out and headed toward the water. The sand was so soft it was hard to walk. I took off my sandals immediately and it felt like powdered sugar. The breeze came off the gulf slow and soft on my face and hands.

The beach was nearly empty. This was what I was looking for. I dropped my towel, my shoes and took off my dress and headed straight for the water in my bikini. I left Rasheed standing there.

It was as warm as a bath. I headed straight in and let the water climb up my body as I submerged. I let myself go and floated up with my belly to the sun. I lay there floating, thinking nothing; just feeling the warm water, the salt, the sun and the sand when I let my feet touch the bottom.

When I got out I turned to see the beach behind me. The little houses were shy on the coast. Rasheed was sitting on the towel and looking out at the gulf. I came and sat next to him.

"Rasheed. Thank you."

"You're welcome."

"I love it here."

"I know. Is this the most beautiful thing you've ever seen or what?"

197

"It is."

"I come out here by myself a lot and just sit here thinking."

"You don't get in?"

"Sometimes. I like to write here."

"I can imagine. You can feel the earth here. Not our little lives and our little dramas, but the earth."

"Yeah. And you really can't get high here." Rasheed nodded his head.

"What do you mean?"

"I mean you can smoke here, and somehow, you can't get that high. It's like the wind won't let you go too far or something."

"Actually that's true. I was high as hell crossing that bridge, but now I'm fine."

"See."

"I can't believe school starts back in two weeks."

"Yup."

"What happens after you graduate? You think people just fall off the end of the earth?"

"Yup." Rasheed laughed. "I'm joining the Peace Corp."

"Right." I laughed. "I'm ready for school to start back. I need some boundaries."

We sat there taking in the sun and the silence. We stayed for hours until the sun set. The sky was orange like fire and then the purple and blue pushed it down until it faded into the water. If my body hadn't betrayed me with hunger, I don't think I would've come home at all. I would've slept on the sand. On the drive home we listened to Sade's

"Cherish the Day" and Rasheed made me promise not to tell 'the fellas' he liked her.

29

ANOTHER BIRTHDAY was rounding the corner. We were juniors; we had our clique and our freedom two years under our belts. Surely by now we were women, and not little girls. I was turning twenty. This year my friends were throwing me another party. Of course with Cat no longer my roommate, attendance once again waned. Actually waned is generous; no one showed. I was hoping Derrick would come by and right the wrong of my birthday last year, but he was a no show. I guess it was becoming a tradition that no man would push himself inside of me while chanting happy birthday in my ear. I couldn't help but notice that Derrick's attention faded with the summer. All that remained of the season was the heat.

Back on The Hill, Voice and Diction Theatre was my newest class. Broadcast journalism students were required to take it. The professor for the class was the most regal looking beautiful woman I'd ever seen. She made me feel like I was twelve years old and had my shoes on the wrong feet. She wore a natural and had it cut low on the side and high on the top, which should have looked terrible, but on her… it was Nerfititi's crown. She had brown skin, high cheek bones, sharp almond shaped eyes that looked like they'd been drawn on her face and she had an hour glass figure with a bust line that sat up high and proud. She did not walk; she floated into the room and talked like Clair Huxtable. Every syllable was pronounced and not one single dropped 't' or 'g' after 'ing.' And she looked at you like if you were up to something she already knew about it.

We were just wrapping up a class about breath and speech and packing to go when Ms. Champion fixed her eye on me.

"Billie Simone." She motioned for me to come over to her. I went quickly.

"Yes."

"Did you see the flyer outside about the audition?"

"Audition? For the play?" I asked.

"Yes." She was matter of fact and looked at me like I'd missed an instruction to check the board.

"Uh… no."

"Please read it. There's an audition coming up and you need to audition."

"Me? I've never done anything like that."

"Read it then come talk to me." She said and smiled a little, packed up her leather satchel and left.

"Okay, Ms. Champion."

I went outside to check the Theatre Board. It was pricked with posters, announcements and notes. There was a flyer for *Fear Itself*, a new play, on the board. Auditions were to be held in two weeks on the stage. I'd done my fair share of pageants but this was totally different and I wasn't sure I wanted to do it. But, when Ms. Champion asked you to do something... you just did it. And that was that. I signed my name on the list for auditions and swallowed the knot that was already forming in my throat.

30

"HEY MOM. I'M AUDITIONING FOR A PLAY."

"Really? A play? That's sounds wonderful. I think you'd make a great actress."

"You think so?"

"Oh yes. You've got stage presence. This is perfect. When's *our* audition?"

"Next week. I'm nervous. I picked out a few poems to use for the audition. You wanna hear some and help me decide?"

"Absolutely. I have to learn my lines so *we* can do a good job." Mom laughed and I read her the poems over the phone. She listened closely and *we* decided which would be perfect for *our* audition.

I was excited about having something new to occupy my mind. There was a weird feeling in the house since the year started back. Z and I were just passing each other and not landing our words.

After I hung up from mom, I got up and went out onto the deck in the back and sat staring at the trees. It was early September and the air was still thick and moist. But there was something hanging in the air, I couldn't place it. I wondered for just a second what Vaughn was doing and where he might be now. I wondered if he ever thought of me. Then I shook my head and stood up and went inside. I checked my caller ID again. No Derrick. I sat and wrote in my journal. My caller ID had been naked of his name for a month.

Love is like a trap

I was lured in by your warm scent

And before I realized it

I felt the cool breeze

Rush in as the gate slammed

Shut.

And every time I feel like

Running I remember that I love you

And I can't let go

And every time I scream

It's because I need you so bad

That I wanna run

I wanna run out into the world and forget you.

Your prickly hands caress me

And peel back pieces of

My flesh

And I wanna run

And I slam my face against

The gate and taste its iron

And I look back for the

Warm spot that led me

inside

And damn it's cold

And damn I'm trapped.

You make me wanna run

You make me wanna scream

You make me wanna make love

You…

I prepared all weekend. Mom and I had finally settled on a piece—an angry woman rant poem. All day I went over and over it. I went to Ms. Champion's office and she told me to visualize a man in the audience who I was mad at, she even said,

"give him a line internally to make it more real for yourself." I was mad at a few men. But maybe it was more madness than mad. Anger didn't flow easily to me in real life. But then again, this was fantasy—my specialty.

Cat stopped by to hype me up before I left. I did my piece for her and she critiqued. She picked out something simple for me to wear—a black sleeveless pant suite with my funky silver arm bracelet. She even gave me her gorgeous, silver, antique thumb ring to wear for luck. I'd been admiring it for months (and I know she noticed). I was touched she was so invested in my success.

I arrived early, filled out the audition sheet and signed the list. I waited nervously until we were all called as a group into the theatre. I sat behind Mr. Proctor, the director. He explained that the sheet we signed was the order in which we'd do our monologues.

"That means I'm third." I said out loud and hadn't meant to.

"Yes dear." Mr. Proctor nodded.

We all filed back outside the theatre and we were called in one by one. It wasn't long and third was present. They called my name and I got my audition sheet and went into the theatre. As I walked down the aisle, I listened to my heels click all the way. I stood almost apologizing for myself and the clicks at the end of the aisle.

"Do I hand this to you?" I asked Mr. Proctor.

"Yes."

I handed him the audition sheet and made my way to the stage. I looked at each black stair as I stepped up. *The stage—I made it this far. Things should flow smoothly from here*, I thought. Ms. Champion called out to me to find the light. I did. It was warm on my face. I introduced myself. I put Derrick in the audience, since I was still freshly mad at him for missing my birthday and pulling another disappearing act. I took a deep breath and let go. I performed the piece well and with fiery anger.

They all smiled.

"Good! Now, do it over.... seductively." Mr. Procter's voice lifted.

What!!! Seductively? It occurred to me that I had no idea how to be sexy. I had never *tried* to be sexy in my life. So I tried. He stopped me. I tried again. Again he stopped me.

"You started something... and then you pulled back." Mr. Proctor instructed from the seats and he was behind the light and sounded like the Great Wizard of Oz. I was silent.

"Do you want a stool?" Dr. Champion asked, trying to save me.

206

By this time tears had spitefully begun to build behind my eyes and underneath my lower lid. I had no control over sexy. I couldn't produce it on my own. I could pull girly, innocent and even attitude out of the hat, but not sexy. There was no man there to kiss me on the other end of it or hold me all night afterwards. I had no way to find it on my own. I thought of my mother and how she hoped "we" would do well. She said she'd fly down if I got the part in the play. I was disappointing her. And much more, I was disappointing myself.

It was too late to fight it. I was in third grade stuck in the principal's office watching my whole class board the yellow school bus to go on a field trip, that I'd missed because I left my permission slip at home. I cried as I watched all the other kids walk by the office with their lunch bags and permission slips in hand. I was crying before I could stop myself.

Ms. Champion came up to the stage, and I bent to talk to her. Her voice was sweet and powerful like a queen's—not soft, but sweet.

"What's wrong? What happened?" She said.
I tried to explain but I was overwhelmed.

"You want to go backstage and collect yourself? Go backstage and I'll be right back there. I'll just tell Mr. Proctor to give you a minute." The heavy burgundy curtain was pulled closed on the stage. I turned without facing them and walked backstage. By now I was crying hard at the fact that I was twenty years old and crying in public. I felt weak and defeated.

Ms. Champion came back quickly and she gave me a hug—a long hug as I pushed the last of the tears out and she chanted,

"Relax, relax…" When she let go I kind of sighed and laughed. We sat down.

"I blew it huh?"

"No. You gave a good audition. What was the problem with sexy?"

"I don't know how to be sexy."

"The issue here is intimacy. You're thinking about someone who you want to be with, and if you don't know how—pretend. We women have to do it so much anyway. Get someone else in the audience, a man that you want."

I nodded. Funny how the men in your life you were mad at were usually the same ones you wanted. It was the wanting that made you mad.

"If you don't feel comfortable doing this, don't do it. You don't have to." She put a hand on my shoulder. But that was just it, I *did* have to. She left me alone to regroup and compose myself and she said she'd be back in ten minutes. I was alone behind the curtain. Intimacy……I imagined what it would feel like to say out loud the things that surfaced inside my head when I was with a man I really wanted. It was my heart, my softness that I thought would repel. I was always sure the sound of my voice mixed with the thoughts in my head would scare any man away. But I wondered and then indulged the feeling I might have if I decided to not give a fuck, for just a moment and tag those thoughts with my open mouth……… I was ready.

Sitting on the stage behind that thick velvet curtain, I felt a sense of comfort and belonging I'd never experienced anywhere. Ms. Champion came back. I was smiling. She knew everything was fine.

She told me I was next. On my new turn, they called me out, placed a chair and I walked dead center.

Sexy wasn't what I thought it would be. In front of that man in my mind I did something I had never done before—I opened up, with my heart and my voice, not my body. When I was done, they all smiled. Mr. Proctor said,

"You liked that huh?" They all quickly agreed.

"Yeah." I beamed.

"Ok Billie, I wanna see you back tomorrow. Come by my office some time in the morning." It was an immediate call-back. *YEESSS!!!* I hopped and bounced off the stage. I was light as a feather. I gave them all a goofy wave and I ran outside.

I quickly found a pay phone and called my mom.

"We did it! We got a call back!!" I felt like Blanche Devereaux, and gave a southern accent. "That's the most fun I've ever had standing up."

"Billie!" Mom said.

"Sorry Mom." I giggled.

31

LATER THAT NIGHT I headed out to poetry group. The
meetings were held at Rasheed's place and fell on a lot less ceremony.
We piled in at around 7 p.m. and sat around the room on his old sofa or
comfy chair or on the floor. Some people were so pumped with vigor
they stood the whole time. Bonds rarely sat. It was like improvisational
jazz; we just built on each other's energy and never apologized for the
way the music went.

Rasheed pulled out his trademark encyclopedia book and read
first. His rapper's style and cool composure made him seem like he was
buzzing and humming at the same time.

"Don't lie to me

Cause I can see

All that damn animosity

Lock a Black man in a cage

With six white rats

Too many cameras, lights and all that

If a nigga ain't funny

DChristy Eves

He got to be hard

Angry and violent and

Breaking the law

I watch enough TV

I know what you see

But that don't look like

Real Black men to me

If a sista ain't a fat non-sexual Thea

TV images make her be a

Loud mouth bitch

Or light skinned witch

Or maybe out on the streets

Turning tricks

This is the shit they call

The real world

Whose world is this?

It ain't ours, kid

After all the lives we've lost

We're trapped in a moment of silence

Watching too much TV violence

All that shit on the news don't just be us

And get that camera on us as we bout to cuss.

It's like all we got left is our style of music

But every time I turn around they be trying to use it

It's been passed down and evolving from generation to

generation

But you'll steel our style like you invade

A nation.

Taking shit that was always ours

Your kids grow up and they become stars

My brothas stay strapped or locked behind bars

Deep within the dark, dank dungeons

The smell of defeat becomes

dramatically pungent." Rasheed put his book down and sipped his water.

"Rasheed, that was cool." A guy standing in the corner got up and dapped Rasheed with a hard double smack. We all weighed in on our thoughts about the image of Black people on television and how it was so different than whom we really were.

"Okay, who got next?" Rasheed facilitated. The next girl read a poem about women taking responsibility for their own heartaches. She repeated the line,

"I got my own heart to blame for the rain. He may cloud me, but I got my own heart to blame for the rain." She said.

"I think that rain is growth. It's pain, but it's growth too." I told her. Then I shuffled through my book and found one to share.

"If I fly

If I lift off the ground

Soft beneath me the ground

Begging me to come back

Land softly

If I fly

DChristy Eves

If I lift off the ground

I'll leave that earth, that dirt beneath me

And I'll let go

It's hard and cold below

The grass is a liar

Soft and green

But I know the black earth would burry me

If I fly

If I lift off the ground

Don't tell me goodbye

Don't let that empty grave call me down

Just let me go

Just let me let go."

I finished and put my book away. Rasheed was sitting next to me on the couch and he bumped my arm after I finished and smiled at me. He pointed at my leg and, although it was covered with jeans, he touched my tattoo. I nodded.

The meeting went on and we shared our secrets with each other and no one judged. We just left it all on the floor exposed and real. Bonds made the announcement before the meeting was over that the first publication of *Think Tank* would be coming out next month.

"I want all y'all to reach inside and find yo tightest work. Don't front. Get real wit' me." Bonds was tall and skinny with dreads and a serious expression that rarely cracked. He tapped my shoulder on the way out.

"Don't front. Get at me wit' somethin' good… a'ight. Y'all women need to preach to these young girls wit' dat real shit."

"I'll find something, let you read it and see what you think."

"A'ight Ma." He patted my back and let me go.

Dat real shit?…... I thought about it as I left.

32

"I WAS SO NERVOUS."

"I bet. But you got it! I feel like I won something."

"Me too. I couldn't believe it when I checked the call board and saw my name. I thought the call back went well, but I wasn't sure. I heard this morning the list was going up at noon. And sure enough, there was my name. Billie Simone Hazard!"

"I'm so proud of you. I can't wait to come down and see my star."

"Mommy. Hey, is dad there?"

"Yeah, sure."

"Did you tell him yet?"

"Oh yes. He's excited. He's all ready to tell the guys at work and brag about his daughter, the famous actress. He's really proud of you."

"Can I talk to him?"

"Yeah, sure. Hold on." There was some shuffling and then my dad's gruff voice broke the short silence.

DChristy Eves

"Hey baby girl."

"Hi Daddy!"

"How you doin'?"

"I'm good Daddy. Did mom tell you about the play?"

"Yeah, she did. That's great. That's real excitin'."

"I'm really nervous, but I think it'll be a great challenge for me. I feel so different in the theatre than I have in my journalism classes. I don't know, maybe this is it for me. Maybe I'll change my major and become an actress."

"Well, now the play is good. It sounds like alotta fun, but don't go changin' your life. You cain't get no job in theatre. What chu g'on do with a theatre degree? You better just enjoy yourself and get on back to business."

"I was just thinking that's all. I just like the theatre so much more that's all. It feels like... I don't know, like me. Journalism is just... not me."

"Well, a good job is everybody. You'll be you with a job and some money in your pocket. You can have fun doing alotta things, but you always gotta watch out for the three bears at the end of the road waitin' for you—bare ass, bare stomach and bare pockets. You learn how to deal with them, then talk to me about what feel like you."

"I'm just trying to be happy. That's all."

"Happy is for folks that already took care of they business first. Shit, You happy. You in college down there having a good time being in the theatre. I had to drop outta college to take care of you kids and feed and cloth you. And I did that. And I'd do it again if I had to. You got the whole world on your little string. You plenty happy. When you get outta school you betta had put more than happy in your backpack." There was a beat and we both said nothing. "Now, it was good talkin', here go your mother. Be good."

"Okay Daddy…. Bye."

He handed mom back the phone. I thought about what he said. I tried not to feel stung. I tried not to let it rain on my little parade. I shook my head and cleared my thoughts. Whatever he had to say had to be on hold. I had work to do.

Busy. If someone asked me to describe my life now I would say—Busy. It was a great feeling, the swell of work in front of me. I didn't have time for thinking, I didn't have time for partying, and I didn't have time for missing anyone. It had been three weeks since I was cast in *Fear Itself* and six weeks since I'd had sex. It was hard not to let what Derrick had done to me sink in, but I was crafty and used it to my advantage.

My character, Ivory, was an erratic, emotional and invasive woman who was in relentless pursuit of her man. Pursuit was a quality I'd never experimented with, but I understood the motivation behind it. I wanted to hunt Derrick down for disappearing again. He spent the whole summer in my bed and prying himself into my heart, and now on a whim he was gone. I closed my eyes and saw him when I was Ivory and my castmate would become him. It was more natural than I thought it would be. After weeks together, soon I wasn't even looking for Derrick

217

anymore. Ivory was looking for Truman. And I was looking forward to opening night.

I spent my days in classes and doing homework between them. I spent my evenings in rehearsals. I went round and round on the merry-go-round of rehearsals and classes for weeks. It was my redeemer. The theatre filled out my empty spaces and I found a place to just be. But, I wasn't dead and the thoughts did creep into my mind with the lights low and the quiet finding me alone in bed. There wasn't much to be done about it; at least not much that I had the energy to do. So, I snuggled in bed holding one of my pillows close to me and breathing the scent of my own fresh cotton sheets. I had a new cream textured comforter with little wooden buttons on the front. I had six pillows on my queen sized bed. And I had no problem lighting candles for myself and writing in my journal in the golden glow.

33

"WHAT'S UP B?"

"Derrick?" I stared at the receiver and looked over at the clock. 6:15 p.m.

"What's up with you tonight?"

"I have a rehearsal tonight."

"Until how late?"

"Ten."

"You coming home afterwards?"

"That's the plan."

"Let me come through and see you." He said. I sank down on the couch and put my bag down. I was on my way out the door. It's a call I could have easily missed.

"Where've you been?" I heard myself say it and sound like one of 'those girls.'

"Around." He was dry.

There was a brief silence.

"You know where to find me. You just haven't been looking." He continued.

"Right. Yeah, that's been the problem."

"Billie, we haven't talked in a while and I thought I'd call my girl and see what was up with you. If you don't want to see me, that's cool."

I paused. "I do."

"I'll be by after ten then."

"Alright."

I hung up and headed out to rehearsal. It was early October and rehearsals were getting serious. We were getting close to opening and tonight was a costume tech rehearsal. I was anxious to see my costumes, but the thought of being snatched back to my old world with Derrick was putting a damper on the evening. I didn't know if I was relieved to finally hear from him or angry. *Two fucking months.* He pulled the classic guy move of turning the situation around on me. He knew I couldn't call him. He knew it was his job to call me. He'd had no problem calling all summer, now suddenly I was the one who'd dropped the ball. But the empty spaces inside me couldn't let it go. I wanted to see him….badly.

I went to the theatre and the routine was totally different. We were all asked to go down into the green room in the basement of the theatre and look over our costumes. The crew was there and helped us find our racks. Ivory's first look was a thin, silky, white nightie. I immediately looked at the crew member and said,

"I'll be half naked in this."

"Oh, no you won't be able to see through it. At least I don't think you will. We'll see tonight under the lights how naked you are." She went on about tucking clothes on racks and sewing the hem on another dress.

The order of business was to go through the blocking of the play in full dress for each scene. The stage lights were up for the first time and it was already starting to feel real. My first monologue opened the show and was down center in the naked nightgown. I walked barefoot onto the stage and waited while the voices in the dark theatre decided if I was too naked or just naked enough.

"Can she have something on underneath that?" It was Proctor's voice.

"Uh, huh. I can put a little black slip underneath and that should do it." The costume designer's voice—his voice lilted and I could hear him making a note in his book. I wondered if it said, 'too naked.'

"Okay, Ivory. Next." Proctor yelled. I left the stage and changed into my next outfit which, thank God, included clothes.

By the time the night was over, we'd run a little long and it was ten-thirty when we were done. I didn't want to rush, but I couldn't help but drive a little fast on the way home. When I got there Z was in the living room watching television and Laurie was in the kitchen heating up a bowl of soup. I checked the ID on the phone and it had my mom on it and that was it.

"How was rehearsal?" Laurie asked hearing me come in.

"Good. Turns out I'll be naked in the first scene."

"What? Really?" Z looked up from the television.

"No, not really. But, it felt pretty damn close."

"Girl, I wouldn't put it pass the theatre." Laurie was sipping her soup from a large mug.

"As long as you're not a stripper, a little nudity won't kill you." Z laughed. "I'm kidding. Don't hit me." I was pulling a toss pillow off the sofa. I sat down next to her.

"What's wrong with you?" Z noticed my mood.

"I'm fine. Nothing…. Derrick's on his way."

"Hmmp. Can't get rid of that man, can we?"

"I guess not."

"I thought we was free! Then here come Mista." Z was still joking.

"Stop." I was fighting a smile.

"I'm over y'all don't worry. Have your fun." Z pushed her glasses up on her face.

"I haven't had anything close to fun in two months." I said.

"That's nothing." Z waved the air.

"Two months? How long for you?" I was curious since she's broken up with Ben.

"It's been three months."

"Damn." Laurie was tucked into our arm chair with her robe and slippers on.

"I'm assuming that means you're not having a drought Laurie." I said.

"Nope. Pride is guilty a few things, but letting me go without, isn't one of them."

I got up and high-fived her. "You get it girl."

She laughed. "And get it good."

"I don't miss it yet. But, I'm thinking about letting Frank get some." Z said.

"Frank. Derrick's friend from the summer?" I had an image of him hiding from Ben in her room and calling 911.

"Yeah. He's really nice. He calls me all the time and he really likes me."

"He doesn't seem like your type." I was surprised.

"What's my type?"

"The daddy type." I was quick to call it.

"That's true." Laurie interjected. "You like the big daddies. Actually, I'm not sure what my type is. I never really dated before I came to FAM. I went to a Catholic high school and it was almost all White. The White guys weren't trying to date me and I wasn't really trying to date them either. It wasn't until here that I met the only two guys I've ever dated. I guess my type is somebody who's really into me. Now, Billie, you like dogs."

"Oh God. I like dogs?" I was stunned.

"Yeah. You love those barking, womanizing dog types. If he's smooth and has women hanging all over him, picking and choosing who he wants to be with, you're all 'oh, there's something about him.'" Laurie was laughing hard now.

"Now, that's true!" Z high-fived Laurie.

"Wait a minute…. Really?"

"Stop playing. You know good and hell well you like dogs. Derrick, Rasheed, Horatio…" Z continued.

"Rasheed and I are just friends. Wait, what about Grant?"

"You dogged him." Laurie jumped in.

"You love it. You wanna beat out all the other girls and take him home and change him." Z was laughing.

"Now, that part's not true. I don't give a rip about other women, and I don't want to change any man. I just want who I want, when I want them."

"When they want you, you mean." Z continued.

"Why are we all of a sudden ganging up on me?"

"Tough love Billie." Z patted my leg.

"Well, no thank you on the love, okay……… Really? Dogs."

"I can't believe you're acting like you never knew this." Z was unfazed.

"Don't get mad Billie. It's fine. You don't like relationships, so dogs are usually really fun. You seem fine to me." Laurie said settling back down.

Then the doorbell rang.

"There's the king of the dogs now." Z got up and got the door while I sat on the couch still wrapping my mind around the new label I'd earned. Dog Lover.

"Why look who's here. It's our old friend Derrick. How we missed you so." Z said opening the door with a flourish. She laughed at herself.

"Hey girl." Derrick gave her a big hug. "Ladies."

"Hey Derrick." Laurie waved.

"You're not getting up to give me a hug?" Derrick motioned for me. I got up and gave him a hug. He still smelled like powder and fresh cotton. He sat down on the couch. "What are you ladies watching?"

"Law and Order." Z sat back down.

Derrick was in no rush and leaned back on the sofa and got comfortable. His particular brand of patience after absence was causing a progressive tingling between my legs. We watched the rest of the show with the girls and then everybody started filing out to their rooms. We went back to mine.

"What's been up with you?" He spoke as he closed my door behind him.

"Working and rehearsing."

"That's cool. I can really see you in the theatre. I think that's a nice move for you." He relaxed on my bed and I cut on my stereo and played him "All Blues."

"Really?" I said.

"Yeah, you're the artsy type. You're hair's growing back fast."

I put my hands up into my hair. "Yeah it is. So, who told you about the play?"

"It's a small campus and I'm up on you." He smiled.

"Up on me huh?" I couldn't help a smile that leaked out of one corner of my mouth. "What's new with you?"

"Well, it looks like I'll be leaving soon." He said.

"Leaving? Leaving where? Leaving school?"

"Yeah. I've got some family things up back home and I'm gonna have to go home after this semester. I may be back later, but I'm going home in December." He dropped the bomb on me like he was telling me he'd be choosing the black socks over the brown ones.

It was quiet for a moment. "Wow……..leaving." I was dumbstruck.

"Leaving Love." He said, and I decided to ignore his calling me 'Love.'

"You don't know if you're coming back? Is everything okay?"

"Yeah. Well, not really. My mom is sick and we have to tighten up on money. They need Rod and me to come on home and help."

"I'm sorry. Is your mom gonna be okay?"

"Yeah. She's strong. My mom is amazing. It's mostly a financial decision."

"I wish I knew what to say. I hate to see you go." *Campus without Derrick?* I kept trying to imagine it. I couldn't.

"Are you going to miss me?" I was so happy to see that smile. That slight gentleman's southern accent draped on his words like the hanging grey moss. He managed to pronounce every syllable and still have a southern accent, like a news anchor.

"Like crazy."

He kissed me. *He's the devil*, I thought. *My evil.* He picked at every weak point I had and still charmingly enough that I couldn't resist. He always gave me enough, just enough. Just enough sex that I wanted more and was not tired. Just enough of his face that I wasn't sick of seeing it. Just enough to make me jealous, but not too much that he couldn't explain it away. He was just the right amount of pain, so that it still felt good. I broke the fast with him. The night was slow and it was starting to rain. Maybe God watches us and knows when it should rain. It rained all night and it thundered and tapped on the window. Derrick's sand colored skin on his sleek frame moved in and out of the covers, in and out of my mind and in and out of me. While on top of him, I looked down at him holding my waist and watching me move. He pulled me down onto his chest with his right hand and kissed me soft. What on earth was this feeling I had for him? *You can't love someone you don't have. Can you?* It was the not having. It was the wanting. It was the absence that made his presence glow.

"God you make me crazy Derrick Vaughn."

"My last name is Welsey, crazy girl."

"I know your name. I'm renaming you." I bit his ear and kissed it. He flipped me on my back and dug deep into me.

He whispered, "Call my name."

"Derrick…..Derrick."

He was smooth and perfect and I buried my face in his neck and my nails into his back until I shook my self loose. He slowed, smiled, and then finished.

"So, you gonna spend more time with me before you leave me?" I was curled in his arms.

"Yes."

"Really?"

"Yes, I'll try."

"Try? I know all about your girlfriend and who ever the hell else you see. I couldn't care less. I only care about the time you spend with me." I got close to his ear and thought of Ivory. "Ain't I good to you baby?"

"Very good." He tightened his grip around me.

"I got what you need?"

"You got it girl." He smiled sleepy and kissed me. He held me. I'd missed it very much. I wasn't sure when I felt the wetness on his chest what it was, then I realized I was crying. I wiped my eyes and hid my face. He closed his eyes and fell asleep.

I realized something lying there in Derrick's arms. He was worse than Vaughn. He was worse because he was after my heart. It wasn't the poems, it was my heart. Vaughn could only be so dangerous because he only wanted all of my body. He wanted no crevice off limits to him. He wanted my eyes, my lips, my hair, my mind, my inhibitions on the balcony, he wanted my sweat. When I had the audacity to refuse him any part of myself, he simply took it. It was his after all. It would have to hurt. It was his and he wanted it.

But Derrick wanted the last piece in the set. He'd waited very patiently. He waited for Vaughn to release my bruised and broken pieces and he was right there to collect them. They were more than hunters— they were collectors. Derrick had bided his time sneaking the discarded pieces. Picking them up as I stared elsewhere to the moon. While I watched the stars shine. He'd collected my self. He had all now but one—the most dangerous piece of all. Most men would stop at her self. Actually most men would stop at her vagina; leave that sharp-edged,

228

sparkling, red glass in its case behind the ribs. But he was not most men. He wanted to break in past the guards, under the red beams of light shining from my eyes and slip inside my rib cage and retrieve my heart from its pillar. He wanted to put it in his trophy case next to whose ever else's carefully guarded heart he'd stolen. He didn't want his brother to even glimpse it until he'd taken it.

Just then I knew there was no way I could be a man. Love was woman's burden. Adam's sons spent generation after generation trying to retrieve that rib given without his consent. The price for having his rib—he'd take it back and have my heart too.

I knew my quest to be like a man—to make love like a man— was futile. There was nothing for me to take from him except my own pleasure. When men made love they took things from a woman and left her with empty spaces inside. Spaces he'd fill up with his presence. In his absence those hollow spaces he'd carved would come alive. He needed to come inside her and leave her to face the emptiness so she would know he'd been there, that he'd taken back his rib. You could see the difference between girls and women marked by the caverns. When you looked in a girl's eyes after the first time she'd made love you could see the small space left by the first plunder. The space inside would knock her balance and caused her hips to sway. It was the emptiness that ached. Vaughn took more of my self than anyone before him. And Derrick was finishing me off. My emptiness ached for them both.

He was still holding me when I figured this out too late. The holding…the holding…the holding me all night. The steady heat and scent of his body had slowly, ever so slowly, melted the ice protecting me. My heart was in his hands, in his arms. I was trapped. So trapped I didn't even own the piece of myself that had the will to resist. All gone. He'd be inside me long after his absence had grown vast like an ocean. I kissed his fingers laced over my chest and released my eye lids to close.

That night I dreamed of the ocean.

Black, high tide, full moon....

Vast.

34

BY MID-OCTOBER, OPENING NIGHT was upon us. There were tears the day of audition, tears at the first blocking and now tears at Opening Night.

"Wash away the scared child and push through," Mr. Proctor would tell me. We mixed and blended day by day from a room full of strangers to friends. I could not see doing anything else. We were taking everything we worked for over a month on and sliding it into a two hour show.

The set rose right out of the black floor and stood with wooden walls, furniture, lights… life. All the rainbow colored lights were hanging now in position waiting for the music to cue up. I was backstage in my nearly naked nightie with the tiny, black slip that really couldn't have been helping that much, waiting on the blackness to arrive so I could make my way to position. The stage manager put his hand on my shoulder.

"You ready?" He asked. I was nauseated but nodded yes anyway. I was freezing and shaking and I could feel my mother and brother Jay, who came down with her, in the audience. Derrick was not there. I could feel that too.

"Cue black out..... Black out go." The stage manager pointed to me.

I hit the lip of the stage in the blackness and found my mark and I waited for the lights. When the light came up, it turned me on. Click. All of the words just arrived in my mouth.

It was the most amazing two hours of my life. I'd done it. I'd committed myself to something and I saw it through to the end. When I came out afterwards to the dressing room my mother had sent roses backstage, a full dozen. It was the best feeling in the world.

Mom and Jay stayed at the house with me and the girls. I got to show them the campus and let them meet my friends. They both told me they loved the play. Mom said,

"Ooh, you were so good. And I was so nervous standing up there by myself. You'll see one day when you have a daughter. It's like your self is up there. But worse than your self, because it's your baby up there. You were beautiful."

"Thanks Mom. What did you think Jay?"

"It was good Billie. Just one thing I didn't like." Jay said.

"What's that?"

"Why did they have you coming out there naked in that first scene? That night gown was too small. I started to say something to that director guy. He coulda covered you up more than that. And what was that scene where you had to grab that guy's crotch, that Truman guy?

What kind of play was that? But you were good." Jay said it and was done with it.

"Et tu Bruté?"

"What?"

"Nothing. Well, that's just the nature of The Theatre."

I figured something out about the theatre during the run of the show. Even the theatre was a man. The ultimate man. You could bring his nasty undercover work right out into the light. You could curse out loud, grab for a man's crotch and stand out there half naked, all in front of your parents, family, friends and faculty. You need only say 'It's in the script,' and they had to accept it. It wasn't your fault. The Theatre had demanded it. You could talk openly about sex and it was called visceral. Lust was revered, anger was easy and drama was oh so right. Life was pulp. We squeezed its juices and laid them out on stage. The heat generated was considered a part of the process. 'A Show Thing,' as cast members snuck off to consummate the building tension. There were always romances that bloomed under the lights.

Then in six weeks, just long enough to be hot, and not so long as to cool, the rush of excitement would peak. Everyone came and the applause was heaped onto you out in the open, under the bevy of lights. Then everything that he was to you, his show would end. And strike. The set would tear down and the black stage would act as if nothing ever happened. But if you were still and very quiet, you could feel the passion smoldering on the boards waiting for the next show to trickle in.

In typical fashion of a girl with a new man that was exciting and mysterious, I'd lost interest in other things. My grades were slipping.

233

DChristy Eves

Journalism was a cold, old boyfriend in an argyle sweater introduced to me by my mother. I couldn't see him any more. I missed classes and did work in the theatre. I would work on anything my new man had to offer, it didn't matter the work. I'd pass out flyers, post notes, clean the shop, help in the office and run errands for Ms. Champion or Mr. Proctor. Once bitten, never the same.

35

"WELL, WHAT HAPPENED?"

"She lost it."

"Lost it?"

"Yeah. He kicked her in the stomach and she lost it." Cat's voice was matter of fact.

"My God. Does her family know?" I asked.

"Her sister knows. She had to go and stay with her."

"I can't believe she would let him do that."

"I know. It's crazy. And….they're back together now. That was three months ago."

"Why would she go back to him?" I asked Cat.

"I don't know. When she was here in August she was getting away from him and she and I talked. She just said that he loved her so much it made him crazy. He always thought she was cheating on him. He never trusted her. I knew he couldn't handle being with her. She's too beautiful for him. She was his drug."

"But why does she love him? That's the part I don't get."

DChristy Eves

"It never makes since why we love the men we love. We just do. But why we stay and what we put up with is another story." Cat went through her drawer and found a tee-shirt.

"I could never let a man beat me." I couldn't imagine Eli being in such a situation.

"Shit, I would beat a man's ass if he tried to hit me. Sometimes I feel like I have this rage inside me that if someone crossed me, I mean really deserved it, I could do some vicious things...really get my revenge." I looked in Cat's eyes and I could hear in her voice a sound that I'd noticed before. It was a sharp tone that was just beneath her regular tone of nonchalance. It gave her voice a duel quality of both indifference and venom. She had never expressed any anger in all the time I knew her, but you could feel it just beneath the surface. You could hear it when she laughed. I knew she meant what she said. I also knew she'd be one person I would never cross.

"I wish she would have just stayed here." I exhaled.

"She's not even the same person anymore." Cat said and shook her head.

Driving back home from Cat's I could picture Eli's face. I remembered the weird bruise on her arm the day she left. How long had this been going on? I shook it off and turned the volume up on my radio.

When I got home I was surprised by what lay on the other side of the front door. It was Derrick and Rod. Derrick had not been MIA since his return, although he did manage to skip my play, but I always knew when he was coming.

"Hey." I greeted them.

"What's up B?" Derrick smiled from the couch. Laurie was in the kitchen stirring something and Z was watching something on television with Rod and Derrick.

"Hey girl." Rod got up to hug me. Rod asked to use the phone in my room so he could have privacy. I nodded hugging him back.

"What are you guys doing here?" I asked Derrick.

"Just in the neighborhood....wanted to pay you ladies a visit." Derrick was relaxed on the couch. I dropped my bag and sat down next to him. His eyes left the television and focused on me for awhile. A smile formed.

"Come relax with me." Derrick said getting up, taking my hand and heading back to my room. Rod was just hanging up the phone when we came in.

"Hey kids." Rod said sitting on my bed. "Listen, man, I'll be right back. You wanna stay here while I make a quick run?" He got up.

"That's cool." Derrick said and plopped on my bed. He grabbed my book off the night stand and began to flip through. Rod gave me a wink and headed out. I grabbed my book back from Derrick.

"Get out of my stuff."

"Alright fine. Have your secrets."

"You have yours."

"Show me that roller of yours." He was lying back on my bed.

"Oh the one I got from back home?" I dug through my bottom drawer where I kept all my drug paraphernalia, which was basically the roller and a carved weed pipe in the shape of dread man's beard I'd gotten from a crummy little store near campus.

237

"Yeah, show me how it works. Let's roll one." He pulled out some weed and I showed him how it made joints look like cigs. I heard a car pull off in front of the house and saw that Rod had already left and Laurie was heading off too. We smoked a while and then Derrick started telling me about getting ready to go home.

"You know what girl?" He said as he took the first puff.

"What's that?"

"I'm gonna miss you."

"Stop lying." I took the joint from him and puffed.

"I'm serious. You're a cool chick. We have fun. I can talk to you. You and your girls are just cool to hang out with. I feel like the Big Poppa over here. You ladies have no idea how rough it is out here. Y'all just sit in here with your books, good grades and good looks and just chill. You've got a good life."

"What about your life? You've got friends and respect and your life is good."

"Sometimes it is, sometimes it's not. Depends when you catch me."

"Caught you," I grabbed his arm. "What about now?"

"I'm hanging in here. Gotta make moves now and worry about the rest later." He took my hand off his arm and put it on his chest. "I wish I could stay longer. Finish."

"I wish you could too. You just have to make sure to come back."

"I will. Maybe I'll come back for your lips." He smiled. "I'll come back, get these lips and put 'em in my pocket and take 'em home

238

with me." He pulled me to him and gave me a shot gun kiss. I was immediately high. It didn't take long before we were laughing and kissing and touching. He turned my stereo on and played the FAMU radio station up loud. "Purple Rain" was playing.

"Come on baby, gimme those lips." He whispered in my ear and gave me a look.

"You were too good sweetheart. I'll have to take care of you later." He said smiling. I crawled back up to his chest, kissed him and cuddled in his arm. I wasn't sure how much time had gone by but I heard laughing in the living room. I noticed Rod and Derrick's car back out front. We went into the living room and Rod was there with another friend of theirs, some guy I recognized but couldn't remember. They were laughing and slapping hands. Z was out there and looked irritated. When she looked at me she rolled her eyes and went in her room.

"What's going on out here?" I was concerned they had done something to offend Z.

"Nothing girl, we were just admiring yours skills." The other boy laughed.

"Man, shut the fuck up." Rod pushed him and sounded serious. They other guy couldn't help himself from laughing.

"What are you guys talking about?" I asked Rod directly.

"Nothing. Forget it, he's crazy." Rod shot his friend a look. Derrick grinned and sat down. Something was up. I went in Z's room to find out what.

"Z what's going on? Did they do something to you?"

"You know what, I'm sick of all this crap with you and those guys. I don't want to be involved with them anymore."

"What are you talking about?"

"You and those guys."

"Me and those guys? I was back there with Derrick. You were out here with them."

"They were back there with you. I just let them in and they went back to your room."

"Back to my room? They weren't back there."

"Yes they were. They were back there standing at your door watching you give Derrick head."

"What?!"

"Yeah. I heard them giggling at your door and I went to see what was funny and I look in there and see you and Derrick… I was disgusted. I left."

"Z? You just left?"

"Yeah. I do not want to know you like that."

"You didn't make them leave? Or even make a noise to let me know they were out there??"

"I thought you knew."

"You thought I knew?! What, you thought I was putting on a show?"

"I don't know what you and your friends do."

"Z!! But you *know* me. I cannot believe you let them stand there…" The thought of me down on my knees with Derrick and the guys out there laughing…my throat started to close. The thought of Z

240

just letting them watch and not defend me clamped down on my neck. And worst of all the thought that Z seemed indifferent was the final straw.

"I don't wanna talk about this anymore." Z said dryly. She sat on her bed and put her glasses on and picked up her Econ book and opened it.

I turned out into the living room and the guys looked like three little boys caught skipping class by the teacher.

"Go home." I said and went to my room. Derrick and his friends left. He did not follow me back to my room to apologize. I watched him walk out to his car. His shoulders were straight and didn't hold even the slightest hint of a bend. He had an unapologetic swagger. I saw his face as he got in, his eyes. Nothing. And for once I didn't even care.

What struck me most was Z. She'd betrayed me and was mad at me about it. Is that what she thought of me? I was that low to her? She thought I was the kind of girl that would let a guy's friends watch? We'd been friends for twelve years. She always came home and stayed at my house, not hers with her own family. She was my sister. What was she now? I knew we'd been pissing her off with our friends and our smoking, was this revenge? Was it payback for the Ben incident? She knew me too well to think I *wanted* Rod and his friend to watch me with Derrick. It was revenge.

Sitting in my room in the silence that followed their exit and Z's coldness, I could see Z's face. I could see the face of the girl in glasses that came up to me the first day of school in the 8th grade. She'd run up to me as soon as I came through the door and said,

"Remember me?"

She'd been gone for two years in California with her mom. We were friends in fifth grade and danced in a recital together to "Mr. Telephone Man." It took a second to recall, she was too close and in my personal space—something I've always guarded carefully.

"Uh… yeah. Zondra, right?" I told her after the image of our leotards sunk in.

"I'm back!!" And she was. We were inseparable from that moment on.

I never liked making friends and felt awkward in front of everyone at school. I was the kind of little girl that stayed seated next to her mother at the playground. When my father would come to the playground with us he'd eject me,

"Go'n over there and play with the other kids so me and your mother can talk." I'd stare at my mother for rescue and he'd jumped back in. "Go on." I'd go and stand near the other kids and wait for enough time to pass that I could just come back and sit with my mother again or go home and play by myself in my room.

Z was my first real friend. She chose me for some reason. I wasn't funny, cool or outgoing in any way. But for some reason she wanted to be my friend. Her selection of me as a friend felt both strange and good. I didn't understand her choice then, but the longer we knew each other the more I saw us as halves growing up together. Where I was weak and painfully shy, she was social and butterflied among people. Where she was scared and non-confrontational, I was aggressive and quick to defend her. We weren't Billie and then separately Z in school, we were Billie and Z. There she was with little, round glasses with cheap wire frames and fastidiously braided hair, back when her mother still did her hair for her, and a bright, shameless smile and inch from my face saying,

"Remember me?"

I sat until the sun set. I sat until I knew what to do. I got up, grabbed my keys, my journal, a pack of cigarettes and a bottle of tequila that Derrick had left and headed for the beach. As I drove, I drove out the image of the little girl in the glasses, I drove out the image of myself kneeling before Derrick with Rod and some guy watching, I drove out the image of Vaughn grabbing my waist and pulling me towards him. I drove out until the blue black night forced the day to retreat. It took over the sky and defended me. By the time I reached the little bridge that lurched up into the night sky, I could already see the moon. I drove along the tiny road and the dunes caught the moonlight.

I parked in front of what looked like an abandoned vacation home that was attempting to ward off invaders with timed lights. The flood lights flashed on, but no one was home. I parked in their driveway and walked through the shy houses to the beach. I found a place in the sand near the water and sat down. It was late November and the air was cold. I pulled my leather jacket close to me and wrapped my scarf around my neck and tucked it inside my jacket to warm my chest. And I listened to the waves.

Rush…

Pull…

Rush…

Pull….

The sound swept over me, calmed me. The stars were so close to the water it looked like they might jump in. The crests reflected the moonlight and perforated the black ocean with their rhythm. Rush…Pull…Rush…Pull….

I opened my tequila and took a sip. I lay down on the sand. And I realized with or without me, the world would move forward and the tide would continue to roll onto shore and the night's sky would remain black and the stars would always be the only thing that could break through the sky. I blocked the wind and lit a cigarette.

The more I drank and listened the more another image was rushing into my mind. A dream I kept having. The night of the shot gun kiss and the circle of guys at Derrick's. That night we went to bed and he swallowed me in kisses. I'd had no idea how many pineapple juice and rum drinks I'd had because Derrick kept refilling my glass before it was empty. I slept hard. In the middle of the night, my mind clicked on like a television and I could see darkness in front of me that began to come into focus—it was dark green carpet. There was a glint of silver that caught the light. Gum wrapper. I could hear a smacking noise in the distant. It was rhythmic. I turned my head behind me to see where the noise was coming from and saw a pelvis behind me and realized, seeing my own hips that, I was on the floor. I caught a chill on my skin and realized I was naked. The smacking continued. I couldn't lift my eyes high enough to see the head of the pelvis but then I could hear the deep radio voice.

"Go 'head man. Do it."

I turned my head forward to see where the radio voice was broadcasting. Another pelvis in front of me revealed an exposed penis hanging so close to my face it looked like a monster. I jerked. The monster noticed my spasm. The new pelvis spoke,

"Naw, man. I'm not doing this. This the kinda shit you end up catching a case for." The pelvis put the monster away inside his jeans. The familiar voice disappeared. Smack, smack, smack. I could still hear the smacking as everything disappeared back into blackness.

Was that real? Did I dream that? I couldn't decide. I didn't *know*. I didn't even *know* if I'd been book-ended by the brothers Wesley. I couldn't recall. I took another sip of the tequila and fell back into the sand. I took a drag of my cig. The immense black sky moved above me. The sand beneath me felt soft. I was in a soft bed of white pillows under a velvet black cover. I wanted to feel something, but I realized something else. Rasheed was right about the beach. You couldn't get too high here, and you couldn't get too low. You were hovering somewhere in the middle. The waves were floating you somewhere between yesterday and tomorrow. I felt one tear stream out of my left eye. Z was right all along too; he was different than I thought.

36

THANKSGIVING CAME AND WENT. Finals arrived and retreated. The era of the devil dogs was over. Derrick had gone home. Not a word. Not a trace. All gone. I was left with a new feeling— indifference. I no longer cared to hide anything and said the word "rape" alone in my room. I followed the word with action by taking the "Some Things You Don't Tell Your Girls" poem to Bonds. I let him review it or throw it away, I didn't care which. I had only one copy and no longer wanted it.

I forgave Z because what else could I do. The energy to remain angry was too great. When Z came home from work she behaved as if nothing had happened. I eventually let it go or stored it someplace. I didn't know which.

When the new semester started, Rasheed told me Bonds loved the poem I submitted and he was publishing it. I had the notion to wonder about its reception, but it fell off my mind like a pen rolling off a desk. The indifference had grown in my chest and filled out some of my empty places. But I needed more filling.

DChristy Eves

There was Rich from New York with a sexy, east coast accent and everybody called him Rise. He had the biggest hands I'd ever seen. When Rich put his hands on me they seemed to cover me like a blanket. He was tall and built largely and muscular. Like a wall—brick and hard. He lowered his head when he walked to counter his size and intimidating stature. He wore a red Eddie Bauer headband, a flannel plaid shirt, jeans and boots. Tims. Headphones. He was never out of his home without his headphones and his Tims. I wasn't sure what was going to happen until he bit into my ribcage and strolled his hands across my breasts. This giant could swallow me whole. His hands overlapped as he held my tiny back in his arms. And the more he undressed me, the more I wanted him. He felt so very good. Plunging deep inside and stroking those very special places. He was intense and passionate. It was wonderful. I hadn't felt that sexy in a while. I hadn't come that hard in a long while. In a deep whisper he said,

"I love your body." A deep growling voice.

I would go to his house and watch him fold laundry and wait for him. I would put my head in his lap when he sat down. He would stare at my hair and touch it. He placed these light kisses on my ear and slid them to my neck. And neck became chest became stomach became pelvis became breasts became body. Other times he'd take a moment to view my body. He'd bite his lip and breathe like a soldier just home from the war savoring the moment before he tastes his momma's welcome home meal. The taste it seemed he'd waited so long for. His taste—me. I was his welcome home soldier meal. I thought of him and his body, his massive hands, his words most of all. With other men I'd imagine different beautiful women I wanted to become. Models. With him... I was the beautiful woman. I was not afraid. To him I could compare to those women, even beat out a few. He'd undress me and couldn't wait to kiss my body in any spot his lips could land. He couldn't wait to feel me. My skin. Me. When I looked in the mirror I saw it, I felt it. He brought out the beauty in me.

But it could not last. He was a conscious brother and he was looking for a woman to really be with him, to open herself up to him and exchange hearts. He even wondered if we'd slept together too soon. Too soon was foreign to me and I had no heart left to give. I simply took my pleasure and moved on.

Then there was Lawrence, I called him Law. He had the blackest skin I'd ever seen. It shined and glowed in candlelight. He was from Florida and had a thing for light skinned girls, the more mixed they looked, the better. I was just mixed enough looking for him to forego my not having an actual non-Black parent. He loved to call me and harass me. My caller ID lit up in the weeks we shared. His attention was like a sleeper's mask covering my eyes from the daylight. I would crack my eyes open in the morning, totally rested. With that still sleepy feeling lingering I'd look around my bedroom and see morning light creaking in clear and new. I'd see my lover, Black and luminous. His skin as Black as last night in the bright morning. He would lie sleeping against my cream sheets and head pressed into three of my fluffy cream pillows and next to my cream colored skin and sandy brown hair.

"Wake up sweetheart." I'd whisper to my knight in shining armor—Black skin had to be armor. We would make love in the morning with the sun penetrating my blinds—glowing. I would watch his body move and silhouette against the cream room. He was like the black center button on the face of a numberless clock. Beautiful.

But it could not last. He was falling in love with me. He had a daughter and a real life and he was trying to figure out how I could fit into his life, maybe even if I should fit in his life. Maybe he could find an actual mixed girl to bring home to his tiny nameless town in Florida and meet his Papa. In his indecision, I took my pleasure and moved on.

Then there was Xavier. He was new in the theatre department as was I. I'd finally woke up one morning and decided I didn't care what my dad thought and I switched my major to Theatre. Mr. Procter warned me against it as well, saying that I'd have to stay an extra year to finish all the theatre requirements. But I was decided and I didn't want to leave anyway and fall off the edge of the earth. That's when I met Xavier who played the role of a king in a children's play we'd put on for the locals. The cast was mostly kids and a few college students to anchor them. Dr. Champion directed the play. She had gone from Miss to Doctor and the switch made me proud. I loved to say Doctor and joke, "what's up Doc?" She would smile and I knew that accomplishment belonged to us all. Not just her, but the university. She brought me in to work on the play as assistant stage manager. I did mostly busy work and ran errands for the show, but I was there for every rehearsal and saw them place the crown on Xavier's head. He looked like a thin version of Tyson Beckford to me. He had a girlfriend in the theatre that was beautiful and sang like a recording jazz artist. She was flawless. And yet, he had the wandering eye and though they shared a loft off campus, he frequently

shared my bed. He'd bring me red wine and Cassandra Wilson CD's.
We drank wine from wine glasses only. I didn't have any so he bought
me a pair. We sipped, talked about life and its processes. How the
changing and growing twisted and molded you and wrapped around you
like vines. Vines that burrowed through your skin and found your weak
places and investigated there with their curling leaves. We traded
philosophy and made love to female jazz vocalists. He was Jamaican
and it showed in the movement of his hips.

Of course it could not last. He was a wandering prophet with
other women to visit upon. I didn't blink for the opening or closing of
the door. I enjoyed my pleasure and moved on. I thought briefly of his
very sweet girlfriend and tried to care but couldn't manage it.

Then there was Anna. Anna worked in the theatre and wore boy
cut jeans and white tee-shirts almost everyday. She had the kindest eyes
I'd ever seen. She looked into your eyes without aversion and smiled
from within. She had a crush on me and I could feel her fantasizing
about me. It didn't even feel strange, just warm. I let her join me and
my friends for movies at the house. They all eyed her through the
corners of their eyes noticing her lack of lipstick, bra and other feminine
accoutrements.

One night I'd taken Anna with me to pick up the Girls' Night
movie from Blockbuster. The stage manager from *Fear Itself,* was there
working and spotted us picking up "True Lies" and gave me a surprised
look. Next a rumor would spread that I went both ways. I could sense
that she was ready to make her move and I could no longer enjoy the
sunshine of her adoration in innocence. So one day we took a short

DChristy Eves

deviation on the way to her apartment. I was giving her a ride home from the theatre and she wanted to stop in a dark parking lot to smoke. We did. I could feel her nerves and she mustered up the courage to speak. After a brief silence slightly broken by puffing and passing, she spoke,

"You don't know how bad I want to kiss you right now." I wasn't as ready for it as I thought and realized I had no plan of what to say back. But the smoke took the lead and sent out a small giggle. I followed it by the greater evil and said,

"That's something I should hear from a guy." I puffed again. She sat in her seat and the bottom fell out. I could feel her heart receive a slice from my tongue. She said nothing. The emptiness filled the car. I wondered if I was capable of stealing parts from her and leaving her with caverns. Had I just carved a little space somewhere inside her? I wondered with scientific fascination, no emotion stirred. I wanted an emotion to rise up. I wanted to say something better. I wanted to have compassion, but I felt none. I didn't have it to give.

I drove her home in silence. She got out and closed the door. The gentle click of my car retrieving its door was the last time I heard anything from her or even saw her. She never returned to the theatre and I never saw her again. I wondered where she'd gone and hoped it didn't have anything to do with me. But with not much feeling in my chest I moved on.

Stealing things for my own pleasure conjured up a new hobby. Stealing. I'd learned how easy it was to take the lavender dress for Vaughn. Now I stole just for me. I stole Calving Klein nightgowns and underwear from Burdines. I stole baby tees and new socks from JC Penny. I took jeans and khakis from Sears. I taught all the girls how to steal too. Z, Cat, sometimes Laurie, and I would all head to Governor's Square Mall and plunder the racks. Z got so good she once stole a heavy, black, leather coat that tied at the waist. When she'd wear it out to the club over her dress she'd pull the belt tight to create a waistline and hips on her tiny frame. Cat would whisper in my ear,

"Look how tight she pulled that belt." She laughed her laugh of duality. We would simply put the stolen clothes under our clothes and in some cases, a riskier move was to go into the dressing room and put an additional piece in our half full shopping bags. The "half full" part slipped Z's mind one day and she brought an empty bag into the dressing room. When she came out it was half full. We were on our way out of the door of Sears and into the mall at large with Burdines on our mind when a short stocky man with a printed golf shirt came up behind us just as we crossed the threshold of the department store.

"Mall security, come with me."

He took us through the store, down the elevator and into a part of the basement where regular shoppers were not allowed. We got into a small grey room with metal file cabinets and other storage items. It had an old wooden desk shoved into an opening with a rotary dial black phone on it. He asked to look in our bags. Cat looked over at me and I just stared back. I heard myself protesting the entire way down to the basement and defending the girls and myself. I think Cat even tried to signal me to shut up, but I was on autopilot.

252

DChristy Eves

By the time we were faced with opening our bags it was obvious we were guilty.   He found numerous items in Z's bag. She had belts, skirts, tops, dresses, pants. Cat had a slick blue dress with a halter neck and a couple of baby tees. I had only one stolen item in my bag, although I was wearing a pair of flat front black Audrey Hepburn slacks under my khakis. He reached into my bag and pulled out a boat neck dress that was identical to a dress Cat already owned. When he held it up I was silenced. Cat's eyes darted quickly to me with first a flash of surprise then a smile that preceded a laugh that did not arrive as she'd recognized the flattery of my copy.

The short, stocky guy was joined by a taller, dark skinned guy with a beard that clearly felt sorry for us. We began chatting with them and I asked how they knew we'd stolen anything. The short one pointed to Z's bag and said,

"She went into the dressing room with an empty bag and it came out full." I tried not to be pissed that she'd made such a rookie mistake. She'd gotten too comfortable and too greedy. But it was me who'd even planted the seed. So any anger I thought to have quickly relented.

They told us we'd be alright, the items we'd stolen weren't enough to land us in any real trouble but they had to report it.   We heard him calling the police and reporting a petty thief. When the police arrived and put the cuffs on the girls we all realized we were not hanging out in the basement with kind teachers who were going to let us off with a slap on the wrist and send us home. We were being handcuffed and taken to jail.

They cuffed Cat first, Z second and then me. When I heard the cuffs click behind me I started crying. Cat looked at me and said,

"Billie. Don't." But it was too late. There I was. There were my missing emotions.

"See, it's always the tough ones doing all the talking that be the first ones to cry." The taller guys said and they laughed.

We got to exit the mall through a private back door, but we had to ride right down the middle of Appalachee Parkway handcuffed in the back of a squad car. I could feel people turning to stare. I kept my eyes down and composed myself. At the station we were photographed and printed and put into a tiny cell alone. We called home and got the machine and left Laurie a message. We knew she was at work and wouldn't be home until late that night. We sat in the cell for hours waiting. While we waited groups of cops came by to stare at us and laugh.

We sat there in our peddle pusher with neat, black flats and tucked in shirts. We looked like girl scouts without cookies. After long hours feeling like a display of idiots, Laurie finally arrived and took us home. We were given a court date that butted up against the end of the semester and all of our flight plans for the summer.

When I told my mom what happened I could hear my dad yelling in the background.

"Good! They need to put her ass in jail. Gimme the Goddamn phone! You ain't doing shit but babying her. It's half yo fault." He told my mother and then I heard his voice close to my ear. "I ain't paying shit for no fine. Sit yo ass in jail!!"

DChristy Eves

The semester ended and the court date arrived. We all showed up together to meet the judge in the big wooden box. He dropped our charges pending a $175 fine and ten hours of community service to be served picking up trash from the side of the road in July. In Tallahassee, in July the heat and stench would be unbearable.

Two days after the court date, we moved all of our stuff out of the little house in the woods on Van Buren Road. Rasheed came and helped us put our things in storage. While packing my things to go home, I'd come across the picture I took for photography last summer. The rows and rows of crosses. It occurred to me; they were not waiting for something to grow. Those brown vines were dead. Something had grown there and died. There was nothing left but the dried up vines and the rows and rows of crosses.

Senior Year

37

TWENTY-ONE WAS A JOKE. I turned the legal drinking age and I'd already had blackouts, hangovers and regrets under my belt. But the new year did bring some wisdom other birthdays hadn't afforded me. I was not waiting for any man this year. I was resigned to spend the day with my girls and was actually looking forward to the absence of pretense. We all headed to BW3's—Z, Cat and I. BW3's had a twenty-one and over section that was guarded by a really strict string of bouncers that did not buckle or look the other way for cute underage college girls. Laurie wouldn't be twenty-one until October but she was not absent because of age. She had not come back from the summer.

Another subtraction of our circle. We had gone from five girls freshman year to just the three of us in the home stretch. There was a lot to survive in college, but even though it didn't feel like it anymore, the goal was to get a degree. Wasn't that why we came? Like my father said, I'd better put more than happy in my backpack. And I did. There was way more in there. Mine was full to choking.

The summer was a long slow one home again. I worked all summer trying to save up for my $175 fine and to have money saved up for a security deposit on a new apartment. My dad was close to done with me and wasn't willing to help me dig myself out of the mess I'd made. I had to pay for my own flight down to Florida in July to pick up trash. I landed in Tallahassee and Cat picked me up from the airport. Z drove in from Atlanta where she'd had a summer job. Cat had decided to stay for the summer so we crashed with her.

It was over ninety degrees with a choking humidity that clung to us. We had to ride in a truck with a bunch of guys boosting an assortment of gold teeth, spiky hair, bad breath and unhealthy dull skin that already looked cooked from the sun. We wore orange vests and used long pick-up sticks to stab bits of old McDonald's cups and God knows what else along the highway. Luckily, we were so far out on I-10 we weren't in danger of being seen. The only saving grace was a brief rain that came in the middle of the day and sprinkled us to relieve the scorching heat. I'd never seen it sprinkle in Florida. When it rained, it poured. But that day we got a light misting that cleaned the sweat from my face and wet my tee-shirt under the vest and felt so good. We all lifted our faces and there we were, three Black women in the rain with eyes to heaven and not a care about our straightened hair.

Back home I worked for the Detroit Police Department supervising Police Cadets as they volunteered in the community, which translated to babysitting high school kids at old folk's homes. I hated the

stench of pee in the air and candy on the breaths of the cadets. There
were only so many hours to work and the pay was only so much, so I
learned something else. There was more you could take from a man than
just your own pleasure. You could take money.

Detroit was just the place to learn this lesson. The men in
Detroit seemed to *expect* to give a girl his money. There was an
understood exchange between men and women. And it wasn't money
for sex. It was money for the possibility of it.

At Emmanuel Steward's, a nice club downtown, I met a new
man. He was in town visiting from California. He called me, courted
me and took care of me. I was attracted to him but bided my time
carefully. By the end of the summer I had enough money to do what I
needed to do. Pay my fine, put down a deposit on my apartment and
have something to start up my senior year with. When we finally made
love it was slow and sweet he was kind to me. It was just the kind of
relationship I needed—one with a clear end point.

I managed again to further disappoint my father before I left for
school. He'd been inside my car washing it for me the Sunday before I
left. It started as a lesson in how to properly clean and care for the dash
board and ended in him taking over and cleaning it for me while I
feigned interest from the sideline. When he opened my ashtray he found
a joint roach. His eyes shot up to me standing there and I tried to
remember why on earth I would forget such an obvious detail. Since it
was a misstep made under the influence there would be no recalling it
and the offense remained like a sign post. Bad Girl. My dad's eyes
creased and the deep folds in his forehead squeezed together. There was

no explaining it away and the image of his "little girl" faded right before my eyes. She was forever lost. The woman standing before him was detestable. His mouth seemed to feel the acrid taste of my character. He spit. He didn't even try to reach me. In his eyes, I was gone. He said nothing and walked away. I said nothing, and this time I didn't even cry. I left for school shortly there after with the knowledge that somehow my womanhood was an offense against my father. It was our second soundless goodbye.

And like magic, there I was, back in Tallahassee at the start of my senior year, at BW3's with Cat and Z. We were showing the bouncer our ID's and entering the zone that had always been off limits to us. When we got inside the roped area it was… well just like the rest of the place except with drinks. So I ordered,

"Rum and coke." The girls got their drinks and we recalled our summers.

"I can't believe Laurie's gonna have a baby." I started

"Yep. Pregnant." Z said.

"Pride?" Cat asked.

"Of course." Z nodded.

"What's she gonna do?" I asked.

"Keep it. She loves him, so she's staying in Macon and she's gonna have the baby there." Z reported the details.

"Wow. I can't believe it. I told y'all, Get On The Pill! What is so hard about taking a tiny little pill every morning? It's a lot less trouble than getting pregnant." I said looking at Z.

"I take mine now." Z shot back

"Eli had her baby. She had a son and his name is Shawn Jr." Cat said with a raised eyebrow.

"Is she still with him?" Z asked sipping her fuzzy navel.

"They're back and forth." Cat explained.

"Well, we're seniors now. Is this anybody's last year?" I laughed.

"Not mine. It took me too long to decide my major, so I know I'll need the fifth year." Z said.

"Well, it depends on how this year goes. I'm going out for this internship I heard about. It's eight months long, so that would put me into a fifth year." Cat surveyed the room for any sight of men we knew.

"Well, I could have graduated this year, but I did not want to take one more journalism class. I'd rather stay *two* more years. This year I have all theatre classes." I smiled.

"Well, here's to seniors and super seniors. And Happy Birthday Billie." Cat raised her glass. We all clinked and I wondered what this year had up its sleeve.

Already the drama of moving into our first two bedroom apartment had kicked off the year. Z and I could not locate one single man to help us move. My heavy oak bedroom set sat there like a two ton 'I Told You So' from my dad. My mom and I could hear his voice,

"I told you not to buy that Goddamn expensive ass big ass bedroom set for that girl!"
We had to make trip after trip loading all the heavy furniture and boxes to the apartment.

DChristy Eves

"I cannot believe we just did that." Mom's voice lifted as she finally sat down. She suddenly sounded like one of the girls. "WE did that. No man. No Daddy. Just us. When I saw all that furniture I wanted to cry. But I thought, well, that won't do any good. We can't crack up. The men...they would have us thinking we couldn't do it. And I would've thought, 'well, they're right. Thank God the men were here.' And look at this, we did it. Daddy would have had me going to the store to buy stuff to make sandwiches for everybody. But we put our little women's arms together and got it done!!"

My mom had a look on her face I'd never seen before. All the berating and belittling my father heaped upon her, all the questioning of her ability to calculate the simplest measures, all the hurt mixed with the confusion of love served to orchestrate a carefully constructed internal monologue of self doubt that my mother took with her everywhere she went. But somehow the effort to lift furniture in the Florida heat proved too much for the monologue and it took a break. Underneath it, like scraping back the rust off a piece of old metal, shone the shiny silver of her self confidence. And for a brief moment it was brilliant in the sun.

Z had a new job at a furniture store and a new daddy. His name was Ray. He had a big barrel chest, a big car, never let her drive when they went out and always walked on her outside for protection. He knew the rules of where a man should sit in relationship to a door in a restaurant. They were inseparable.

It didn't matter much because I had a schedule full of theatre requirements. The theatre required enormous amounts of time and

261

commitment. We had a big show coming up and we all kicked in hard to audition for The Essential Theatre's afro-centric take on *Macbeth*. It was the show of our dreams. I practiced and hoped to play Lady Macbeth. Instead I was cast in three small roles that when combined did not equal the amount of stage time and lines in a cat food commercial.

Crossing The Set on the way to class one day, a thing I did less and less now, a strange girl stopped me.

"Hey!" She said and ran up to me. "Are you Billie Simone?"

"Yeah. Do I know you?"

"No, no. I read your poem in *Think Tank*."

"My poem?"

"Yeah. *Somethings*." Her eyes were bright, but she lowered her voice when she said 'somethings.' I blinked and tried to remember.

"That poem woke me up." She touched my arm. Then I remembered. I didn't know what to say, so I just stared at her.

"I think what you said is so important. I'd been so afraid to tell someone what happened to me. I hadn't said anything to anybody and all of a sudden when I read that I realized I wasn't the only one. I was dating this guy and... well, let's just say I can relate. I talked to my mom about it immediately. I just wanted to tell you that... tell you it helped me." She sort of tilted her head and smiled and left me standing there stunned. I didn't know how to feel. I felt at once exposed and in front of a stranger. That my poem helped her, I thought, should make me feel good, so I stood there for a moment longer waiting for the good feeling to follow. It didn't. I needed to see the magazine.

I detoured my paces and found the magazine racks outside the Student Center. Nothing. I checked the stands in the sitting room of McGuinn, the old ladies were still sitting there examining the new crop of young girls and going, "ummm hmmmmp." Nothing there. I checked the lobby of Tucker Hall. Nothing. Finally, I found this short guy from poetry group last year coming out of a class on the first floor.

"Hey, have you seen the latest issue of *Think Tank?*" I stopped him.

"Yeah. Bonds just put out a new one. It's the first one this year. Wait, I have a few in my bag." He rustled through his things and pulled out a copy. "Here. You gotta give Bonds your new number so he came keep you up on the progress."

I took the neon green, homemade press paper in my hands. It had graphic art on the cover that looked like a comic book drawing of a muscular Black man on the cover holding the world on his back. *Think Tank* was smacked across the globe.

"Thanks."

"Hey, that poem of yours was deep." He gave me a look. "Damn girl, I didn't know all that happened to you. You okay?" He touched my arm like the strange girl. He was looking at me as if I had a gaping wound that needed attention.

"I'm fine." I took the magazine and headed off to the library for privacy.

I sat on the steps of the library and sat a minute listening to the spray of the fountain. I opened the magazine and flipped slowly through to see if I could spot my name and my phrasing. And there it was on the seventeenth page. In print. My words. The only tangible evidence that Vaughn ever existed. I had no letters from him, no stuffed bear won at a carnival, no cheap necklace with half a heart, no man's tee-shirt stuffed in a drawer. Just this poem that told the world that he threw my clothes at me. Empty had a bottom. I'd just reached it. I could feel the falling stop.

I could almost feel Grant over my shoulder trying to read the poem and when I turned my head no one was back there. I knew then that no one had my back and that I was my own protection. I closed the magazine and tucked it inside my backpack and headed off to the theatre for Intro to Costume Design.

38

IT WAS SEPTEMBER and the girls began to disappear more. Cat started dating a new guy. If there were a president to the Five-Year-Plan guys, he would've been it. But now suddenly they were inseparable. I had no clue what she saw in him, although he was nice. Z and I both stared at each other when she brought him by the apartment while we hung out. He would just sit there barely saying anything. He was like her purse. She even began to change her style to match him. Gone were the sexy backless tops, the perfect cut jeans or the stylish silver jewelry. Now she wore knit twin set tops and khaki pants. I think I even caught sight of her on campus one day in a headband.

With everybody paired off, campus was lonely. I was soaked in work from the theatre so that kept me busy, but I couldn't help but miss the girls... I even missed the guys. I could never hate men. I gave it a try alone in my room one night. I fantasized about sauntering up the line up of bastard men we knew. I was going to tell them all off and smack their faces. But, somewhere in there the daydream slipped and I found myself dreaming about Vaughn's soft skin on his hard legs. I could hear him saying, 'Simone. C'mere.' The bottom line was that I loved men. I loved the way they smelled, the way they walked, the way they touched your lower back when you entered a room before them. I loved them when they were mean to me; I loved them when they were kind. I loved them when they made love to me and I even loved them when they left me.

So, I learned to sew costumes, I learned all about lighting, and I became aware of the artistry in set design. I met a whole new crop of friends. I had a theatre family that was colorful and different. I flooded the images in my mind of caramel skin, dark eyes, being held all night, the illusion of friendship, beautiful forearms—I drowned them all in work.

Theatre people are different than regular people. Gossip is more than just a notion to them, it's blood in their veins. Oddly enough this blood-work of gossip didn't turn them into enemies, it turned them into family. They had each other's back when it came right down to it. The same girls that would gossip about one girl sleeping with somebody's man, would be the ones that would be there to let her cry on their shoulders when her heart was broken. They were there to support... and of course to get the juicy details.

Everybody gave one hundred and ten percent of themselves. And I realized something else—Theatre was not at all like a man. If anything Theatre was like a woman. Those black boards of the stage never forgot a thing. Every show was her child. The theatre gave birth to those shows. She labored and involved her whole family in the process. She required nothing less than our best and we were all in the highest love with her. We gave the theatre all we had. In return she gave us the spotlight and her love. She took nothing from us, leaving us empty. She filled us up.

39

IT WAS A COOL EVENING in early October. That night we were learning the waltz for the royal banquet scene in *Macbeth*. They paired me with a tall, large and light skinned guy named Luke. Luke was a sweet kid. He was just beginning with the theatre and was a football player also. All the girls in the show eyed him and blushed if he even looked at them. He was not at all my type. Young, sweet, kind eyes, religious, morally coded, no bark, no bite. No thank you. No vapors here. But he was really funny and made me laugh during the long rehearsal scenes.

Apparently theatre was a well suited transition for many southern Christians. The theatre was overrun with bible thumpers. It irritated the handful of non-religious folks and made for a nice balance of condescension and comparisons. The chief complainer for the unholy team was Rasheed. The theatre had the power to convert too and Rasheed took a cue from me and crossed over to the dramatic side. I couldn't have been happier to see that fluffy 'fro enter a room. He was a running commentary on the comedy of religion and theatre.

After the waltz scene was finished he slid beside me.

"That young boy don't have a clue who he messing with?" He said to me in my ear laughing. No one else noticed Luke's subtle flashes of teeth and twinkling eyes, but Rasheed missed nothing.

"What are you trying to say about me buddy?" I shot back.

"Don't worry; I'm on your team. Take 'em all down." He laughed hard under his breath. I smacked his shoulder. "Hit me if want to, you're still on my team." He grinned.

The next day, although I had planned to be gracious, not getting the part of Lady Macbeth bothered me. Curious about how I went wrong in my audition, I went to the queen to find out the truth. Dr. Champion was in the office and I peaked my head in to find her packing up her things into her leather satchel.

"What's up Doc?" I started.

"Billie Simone."

"Are you busy, heading out?"

"Not too busy. You can walk with me if you like. I'm heading to my car."

"Okay." We walked and I got my thoughts together.

"What's on your mind?"

"Um. I'm trying to really focus on my acting and become stronger. I guess I'd like to know what I did wrong in my audition for *Macbeth*."

"What do you mean 'did wrong?' You were cast weren't you?"

"Yes. But I didn't get Lady Macbeth."

"Oh. I see. Well, sometimes we are just not right for a part."

"How was I not right?"

She stopped. "Why we do or do not cast someone in a role is based on a lot of factors Billie Simone. Not getting a part is as much a part of the theatre as getting the part. In fact, more so. Is this really what's bothering you?"

"Yeah. Yes, why?" She was looking through me and saw something.

"I don't think so. I believe there's something else."

"Like what?"

"You tell me." Her eyes had frozen me and I stood there silent and still. Unlike my mother she would not let it go and she took my arm and escorted me to the theatre. The auditorium was nearly empty and only the shop manager and one of the tech students, Gregory, were on stage starting the building of the set for *Macbeth.*

"What's really wrong?" We sat down in the back of the theatre. I could hear the power saw turning off and on and the hum of work between the two men. They were building the illusion.

"I thought he was my friend." I started to cry. I didn't even know if I meant Vaughn or if I meant Derrick. I told her what happened with Vaughn. I still wasn't sure if what happened with Derrick really happened. I couldn't bring myself to believe it. So I just focused on the beginning. Vaughn. I told her how he hurt me and how I let him and how I still went back to him.

"Why did this happen to me? What's wrong with me?" I cried.

"Don't' do that. Don't do that to yourself. Listen, there are men out there, people out there, that will absolutely take your power if you let them. Now, he was wrong, don't misunderstand me. And I'm so very sorry this happened to you. But you have got to take control of your own power. You can't just give it away and hope the person you give it to will handle it correctly. You have your own power in relationships, in your career, in your life. This is *your* life. You have to stand up for yourself and if someone wants to take something from you," she leaned in and took my hand, "give them the fight of their life."

"Fight?" I thought about it. I'd never been in a fight in my entire life. Once a boy in school belted me in the stomach for not liking him. I cried and told my dad what happened when he picked me up from school that day. He quickly dispatched my brother Jay, who was always tall for his age. He marched right up to the boy in the hallway and in a very calm voice asked,

"Did you hit my sister?"

"Well...uh...I..." The stuttered non-answer was confirmation of guilt. With the guilty party correctly identified, Jay threw him high up against the locker so that his feet dangled.

"Never touch my sister again for the rest of your life!!"

After that he and everyone else in the school knew I was not to be messed with. But down here at FAMU, I was alone. All I knew was to lean on a man. But the men here were too slippery to lean on.

"Don't you see yourself? Look at yourself. You are so much stronger than you think you are. Billie Simone, look at yourself." The way Dr. Champion said my name, even I believed it. Billie Simone. It sounded like a woman I wanted to become. I knew I could never be pulled together like Dr. Champion, but maybe I could be Billie Simone.

"You don't have to just accept the way someone treats you. So many times we just give in because we're afraid of losing a man. But you have to think, 'shouldn't he be afraid of losing me?' If he were afraid of losing you, then he wouldn't have hurt you. And if he's not afraid of losing you, he's nothing to hold on to. Let him go. Hold on to you and let him go."

I put my head down and cried.

"It hurts. Learning to let a man go is a part of becoming a woman. You can do it. Open up your heart and politely tell him to get out." She smiled. "Are you ready?"

"Not yet…"

She let me cry. I sat there in the back of the theatre with the hum of work and the sense of order in the rows and I cried until there was nothing left. Then I breathed. *A woman?* It was sad. I was so anxious to get away from those overprotective men that circled my life back home. But now in the great Out-There that I so adamantly wanted, I realized I had to do their job…throw my own boys against the locker. I wasn't sure I could.

When I collected myself, Dr. Champion rose from her seat and took me with her to lunch. She said what we needed was,

"…not the food but the fellowship."

40

I ONLY KNEW TWO SOLUTIONS to mounting self doubt—one was work, the other was sex. As the campus cooled, so did I. I was cool... a gentle new feeling that had energy. At that, I decided work would be the suitable distraction. I focused on *Macbeth*. When *Macbeth* ended, I quickly found another show. I busied myself with production after production. I never let the quiet accumulate.

By December, Cat was on the verge of leaving us for California and a new eight-month long internship. I knew campus would be lonely without her. She was my hanging partner. She and I were the ones to start all the fun. She would now be taking all the fun with her to California. I would be forced to entertain myself.

There will always be a man whose eyes manage to cut through daily life and see me, see some secret thing about me that other people missed. He did that. The new semester brought about a change. I didn't notice Luke much at first, but he continued to smile at me and twinkle his eyes. We shared several classes together and he would always greet me warmly. But we were friends.

The gossip mill spun his vitals out to me; he was from Memphis, Tennessee and was a Christian. Southern Christians had a dogged determination to be "Christians," whatever that meant to them. Mostly it seemed to drive underground sexual urges and relegate them to the devious category of 'worldly' or sin. Certainly not my type, but there he was smiling that smile at me.

The semester made its way to spring and in late March the rehearsals for the season's musical were underway. On the first night of rehearsals for *Godspell*, he saw me walk in theatre and he gave me a strong hug. A small, warm, feeling snuck inside.

"I was wondering where my baby was. Here you are. I'm so glad to see you." He said. Twinkle. He tried to thinly veil his attraction to me behind the pretense of friendship. But if there was one thing in this life I could spot, it was when a man wanted me. *Careful Billie.* I thought.

But he convinced me further of his intention for friendship. He chatted with me, but not too much at rehearsals. I was the assistant stage manager and he was cast in the show. He smiled, but not too brightly. He didn't hug me any more at subsequent rehearsals. He worked diligently on his role. I think I spotted him one day in colored denim… *not sexy.* I thought, *this will be fine.* One night after rehearsal he asked,

"Billie, can I get a ride home from rehearsal?"

"Sure. Where do you live Luke?"

"Really close. Not far at all."

DChristy Eves

"Alright."

We rode the short distance to his apartment. We talked along the way. He told me that he was not doing well in Spanish. I'd been taking it since the fourth grade and was close to fluent.

"I can help you. It's easy." I told him.

We began meeting every night after rehearsal. We talked about life, theatre, men, women, sex. Sex. He said he didn't have it. He was a virgin. He was trying to walk the walk. He had a girlfriend back home. *Shit, who doesn't have a girlfriend back home? Damn, maybe I have one.* We sat in my car for hours outside his apartment talking. It wasn't like Derrick fishing for usable information to snare me. He seemed genuinely interested in me as a person. I didn't feel the lock of holding myself back. I actually talked to him. My words were free and fluid and we bounced the ball of conversation back and forth between us comfortably. Every night after studying I'd try not to spark a discourse, but every night one would spring up on its own. He'd put down his book and throw his pen.

"People always think there's something I can do for them. They always want something from me. I just want somebody to want me for me."

"What about your girl? Doesn't she want you for you?"

"Yeah, she does. But then there's this pressure to do things right...to be, I don't know, a role model. I feel like that with my family too. I've got little brothers that are looking up to me to be the best and do the right thing... all the time. My church, they expect me to be a success at everything I do—football, singing, now the theatre... life. It's

275

a lot of pressure. Sometimes I just want to be. You know what I mean—just be."

"You can't please everybody. You have to live your own life. That's what I'm learning. I'm this constant disappointment to my father. And I feel like my mom wants me to be this girl that I'm just not. And I want to be one of those simple girls that sit around waiting all innocent for love and the right career with money and prestige, but I just don't care about those things. I *want* to be happy."

"I love talking to you…the way you put things. There's never any judgment. You just listen and offer your thoughts." He put his hand on mine; the static electricity charged his touch. "I need a friend like you."

"I like talking to you, too." I blushed.

Luke and I would go on like that for hours. He would never make a move. Then it occurred to me he was a big guy not because of fat or an accident of genetics. He was full of muscles. *My God. He is sexy.* He wasn't shy or quiet as I thought before; he was sitting disinterested like a lion. I began to look into his eyes. They were beautiful.

I began to dream of him. The tension of pretending we didn't want to touch was overwhelming. I craved touch like most people craved food. But I thought, *Careful Billie.* I resisted. I drove him home nightly and we'd sit there pretending it wasn't getting later and later. We saw 2:30 a.m. on many occasions. I was his Spanish tutor, but if he was relying on me, a failing grade was in his future. Was I a wolf in rabbit's clothes? I did not want to be Derrick. I didn't want to bite Luke. I wanted to be better than that.

It was a Friday night in early April and the show had just opened. The cast was having a party at Bennigan's afterwards to celebrate. Z came to see the show and I gave Luke a ride over to the restaurant with us. On the way to our table a girl at another table grabbed Z's attention.

"Hey Zondra, right?"

"Yeah, hey. I remember you from Paddyfote."

"Yeah, I lived on your floor." The girl smiled. "Can I talk to you?"

"You guys go ahead. I'll be right back." Z said and stayed to talk.

We made our way to the table and the whole cast was there. We had a huge table and Luke broke from me immediately and sat with some of the guys from the crew. I held a seat for Z.

When Z finally returned from talking with her old floor-mate, she had the business Z look on her face.

"What's wrong?" I said.

"Ray is fucking that girl over there."

"What?"

"She just told me that her best friend lives next door to Ray and she had slept with him a couple times and then he stopped calling her. She saw me show up at his place one day and she thought she'd pump me for information about him. She didn't know I was his girlfriend."

"Ray, Ray, Ray." I shook my head. "Don't the men you date have sense enough *not* to get caught?"

"I'm going over there as soon as we leave to confront his ass." I knew after that the evening would get cut short. We hung out awhile longer with the cast then I told everyone we needed to head out.

"Alright y'all, I gotta head out. That's my ride." Luke got up to leave with us. I dropped Z off first at home so she could get her car and head over to ambush poor Ray.

"So, what do you think about what happened with your friend?" Luke asked once the car was empty.

"What do you mean? The cheating?"

"Yeah."

"No big deal. It happens. Ray is a really good guy. I like him a lot. I'm hoping he can talk his way out of this one. Z loves a good drama where men are concerned."

"So, you don't think you would be mad?" Luke pressed the issue surprised at my nonchalance.

"What, if I found out my man cheated on me? No, not really. I just would rather know nothing about it. Keep the details away from me. Z's going over there to gather up all the dirty details. That's a patch of dirt I'd leave covered. Cheating isn't even enough to really anger anybody. It's just a doorway. The real anger comes in the details. A person needs the details to conjure the fury. Was she prettier than me, uglier than me, do I know her, did you do it at our place, in my car, at the bathroom at the Wendy's where we first met, is her hair longer than mine, how light is she, how dark is she, was that my sister, my best

278

friend, that time you were late, was I in the bed passed out at the time? All of the details swirl around the calm center of cheating—the eye of the hurricane. It all makes me laugh." I explained.

"You're a different kind of girl, do you know that?"

"I've been told. Would you be mad?"

"Yeah, I think I would be. But then maybe I wouldn't. I guess in some ways I can understand."

"What do you understand?" I asked him.

"What it feels like to be caught up. We try to be good, as good as we can. We live and take our responsibilities seriously. But at the end of the day, we're human. And that's inherently flawed." Luke explained.

"Beautifully flawed."

"Yeah, I guess there is beauty in the flaws." He stared at me.

We kept talking under the moonlight. The morning hours slid their way into the car. His eyes softened and he spoke in a relaxed voice. Then, in the chill of the night air he broke his own rule and kissed me. He kissed me slow and then harder. We kissed for so long time melted behind us. It was the kind of kiss you have when you're sixteen and all the sex is in the kiss. When he broke from my lips he looked at me and he'd simultaneously drained his urge and filled mine up to the brim. At that, he backed out of the car and retreated home. But not before asking me to keep it a secret. I agreed. I knew the rules. Christian or devil dog—same thing. I had to wonder what made my kisses the kind that needed to be kept secret? And why did men get girlfriends anyway?

DChristy Eves

The torture mounted. And busy with work I wasn't meeting any
other men. He began to grow in my empty heart and block out the rain.
He covered my thoughts. He covered my dreams. When he smiled at
me in waking hours I would almost shake with anticipation of his touch.
If he hugged me, I closed my lips tight to prevent slipping out my tongue
and licking him. By the close of the school year I was in a full fever.
Yet, he seemed relaxed. With the show over, we no longer rode home
together and he went on about his life. Again I had to wonder if it really
happened or did I dream his kiss. I searched his eyes. There was no
secret longing there, just kind, friendly and light eyes. It was a puzzle.

41

LUKE LEFT CAMPUS for the summer and left his kiss on my lips. The longing was hard to ignore. But when I got my report card for the semester in the mail I opened it to find straight A's. 4.0. I had sixteen hours and aced every single one of them. They were like five golden apples. Their juice kept me sated and lessened the longing. It was my second set of apples. I aced the fall semester as well and this gave my father some hope that maybe one day his little girl would return.

May was here and there was no theatre to keep me occupied.

"Hold on to myself?" I thought about what Dr. Champion told me. "How the hell do I hold on to myself?" Fortunately Ray and Rasheed had the answer.

Z had forgiven Ray. He had the right amount of sorrow on his breath when she confronted him. He didn't play the 'what's the big deal I'ma man' card. And it helped that he really loved her. Z and I were holding down the two bedroom apartment for the summer in Tallahassee. I was without my chief partner in crime so that seemed to make me less annoying to Z. Plus Ray had her fine and mellow.

Ray, for some reason unbeknownst to Z, had a black video tape with him on one visit. A little boxed treasure he wanted to stash in my room so Z wouldn't see it.

"Put this in here right quick. You know Z go through my stuff sometimes." His New York accent jumped and danced.

"What is it?" I asked.

"A video."

"I can see that. Of what Ray?"

"It's just a little porn my man brought by the shop for me to hold." He tried to say it fast so it would sound less seedy.

"Ooh. Just a little porn, eh?" I snatched it from him.

"Damn, can you stop playing and just keep it in here a minute 'til I can take it home?" He looked over his shoulder to see if Z was out of the shower. "I don't want her to give me that look, you know. She looks at me like my grandmother...all disappointed."
I knew that look and couldn't help but laugh.

"Oh, I'll keep it alright. You can have it back later."

"What, you g'on watch it or something?"

"Oh yeah."

He stared at me puzzled. "You a trip girl."

"What's the big deal? You were gonna watch it."

"Whatever, that's cool." He shook his head a little. "Your ass is crazy, you know that right?" He gave me a big relieved smile.

"That's what they keep telling me."

I took the video and closed my door. That night was an interesting night. I watched the video. It was poor quality and clearly comprised of uninspired male fantasies. *Making noise is good, it keeps a man on track, but this is over the top,* I thought. But when you got right down to it… it did the trick. If I were to be alone, I was going to need some tricks up my own sleeve.

The next day Rasheed came by to hang out. It was Tuesday and I was counting how many pairs of jeans I had. The boredom and lack was turning me into a neurotic woman with a penchant for clean floors, drawers and pores. I bought several of those new nose strips to clean my face.

"What's up girl?" Rasheed said at the door when I opened it.

"What's up with you?" I let him in and he sat on the couch.

"Nothing. I'm heading out of town to Miami tomorrow. Take some videos of hot chicks on the beach."

"Don't get any more original or we'll have to patent the idea."

"Excuse me then. What's your big plan this weekend, got any more Christians to dismantle?"

"I'm not dismantling anybody."

"Yeah, okay. Tell me anything girl. You know you'll break that boy off something."

"Why are you so concerned with what I do to 'that boy'?"

"I'm not concerned about that boy. I'm more concerned about your girl. Where's Cat?"

"Cali."

"Damn. When y'all g'on invite a brother to watch?"

"You are sick and crazy. And I love you dearly." I hit him in the head with a pillow.

"Alright, girl. I'm out. I just wanted to holla at you before I bounced. I got you something." He went in his pocket and pulled out a small brown bag.

"What's that?"

"Open it." He handed it to me. I took the bag and pulled out a long sliver wand.

"What is this?"

He laughed out loud and hard. "Are you serious?! You don't know what that is? Oh my God. I came into your life just in time. It's a vibrator."

"A vibrator?"

"Yes. A woman should never be alone without one. You can thank me later." He pulled up the corners of his mouth and a few of his teeth peaked out. I studied the sliver wand and didn't know whether to be afraid or intrigued.

"I'll call you when I get back to town... that is if your hands are free."

"Get out." I aimed for his head. He dodged me like he knew it was coming. He gave me a quick hug and headed out the door.

Maybe this summer won't be so bad after all....

42

"HAA-HA!! I GOT YOU NIGGA!!" Ray threw his cards down on the table and it shook.

"Careful Ray. Don't knock down my drink." Z braced her glass.

"Sorry baby. I'm just the man, that's all! The Man. That's twice in a row. Don't want to make anybody at the table feel bad... but...uh... I'm killin' it!" Ray was doing a winner's dance in his seat. It was Friday night and spades was the distraction of choice. Ray was there with his friend Kurtis.

"You ain't shit. I won the last one son." Kurtis's voice never raised its inflection. He remained perpetually at one note. "I'm ready to blaze one anyway."

Kurtis was a close friend of Ray's that had a reputation of systematically going through the women in our class. He was incredibly handsome with cocoa brown skin, a well trimmed beard and shining white teeth. But he had a mean streak that was too close to the surface for me. He never got women through charm. He got them through sheer look and swagger. He played his good looks like a card. His Brooklyn born attitude did the rest.

"Go right ahead. And just to correct you... **I** won the last one son. Z, want a drink?" Z nodded and Ray got up from the table and headed to the kitchen.

"Why you didn't ask if I wanted one Ray?" I shouted.

"Cause I already know yo ass want one."

"You don't know me...fool. You just owe me...cool." Z and I sung in unison.

"Double Mint twins." Kurtis's one note marked a slight trace of amusement.

Ray came back in the room with three drinks held into position with his hands and chest. Z and I took ours and left him to his Bacardi and cranberry juice. It was getting close to eleven. The evening had the hang of too much effort and too little product. Kurtis was not the most entertaining person I'd ever met. But at least he brought weed.

"You smoking B?" Kurtis began to empty a blunt.

"Yeah."

"I'm assuming you straight nigga." Kurtis looked at Ray who was sitting on our loveseat with Z in his lap. Ray never smoked.

"Yeah, I'm cool. No smoke for me and my girl." Ray's lips parted into a wide grin. "No smoke, but I'm hoping for some fire."

"Quit Ray!" Z giggled.

"We'll be back. Y'all be good." Ray got up and took Z back to her room.

DChristy Eves

Kurtis and I listened to the stereo and passed back and forth the finished blunt. I wasn't really in the mood to smoke, but it seemed the natural conclusion to the evening so I went along with it. We sat next to each other on the sofa with Mobb Deep's "Survival of the Fittest" playing in the background. I didn't guess Kurtis wanted to listen to Sade or Miles Davis. We chatted mindlessly and covered all the general bases. I'd had enough and stopped accepting the passes and he continued to smoke on his own for a few puffs.

The sensation of being high with Kurtis seemed off. I was used to smoking with close friends and although I'd still become paranoid about a sound or possibly the choice of hairstyle I had at the time, I always felt a sense that everything would be ok. Now, I felt odd and awkward. I couldn't laugh. Nothing was funny. Cat and I always found something to laugh at, or someone. *Maybe I should call her; it's still early in California.*

After a few dry seconds, he put his hand on my leg and it laid there like an inanimate object, foreign from his body. I was just beginning to wonder what it was doing there and why it was so dry and rough on my exposed leg—I was wearing khaki short shorts and a white tank. He pulled my leg toward him like he was opening a door. I was still in scientific fascination with the oddity of his rhythm when he was suddenly on top of me on the sofa coming for me with his equally foreign lips. Before I could say 'wait a minute!' his tongue was in my mouth. It happened so fast and my mind was moving so slow. I pushed his chest back and he hovered over me with a determined look on his face.

"C'mon. Quit playing with me. I know all about you." He advanced towards me.

"Get off!" I pushed again and this time with more force and he slipped back off the couch. Then he grabbed me and pulled me down on the floor. There was a tussle of arms and legs and I was pinned with my head underneath the glass coffee table. Something in me began to cook, simmer and then boil.

"Get the FUCK off me!!" I screamed.

"Fucking bitch! Think you gon' smoke all my weed and be done." His voice left its one note parade and hit the 'd' in the word 'done.'

"Bitch?!"

"I said Bitch!"

Then I saw my tiny, peachy, beige arms with clenched hands like a cat clawing his face. *Give them the fight of their lives* was ringing in my head. He grabbed my wrist and tried to hold them down. But not before I drew blood from his face. At that, Ray and Z came out of the room and Ray jumped in and grabbed Kurtis.

"What the fuck happened out here?!" Ray said holding Kurtis. Kurtis touched his face and felt the blood. He wrenched loose from Ray's grip and lunged for my neck. We fell back on the floor. This time my claws found his balls.

"GODDAMNIT!!!" He screamed and by then Ray was pulling him off him.

"Fuck this bitch! I'm out." He gathered his keys and headed for the door.

"Yeah, nigga. Get the fuck out! What is wrong with you?! I brought you over here to be cool and chill out. What the fuck are you doing?" Ray's chest was raising and he stepped towards Kurtis. Kurtis looked at Ray. It was clear his size and stature trumped Kurtis's smallish frame. Kurtis suck his teeth, shook his head and left.

"Wait here, I'll be back." Ray followed him out.

I got up and sat on the couch. My head was spinning.

"Billie what happened?" Z sat down next to me.

"Do I have a fucking sign on my head? Good Times. Take One."

"Did he try you?"

"Yes! We were just sitting here. He just started trying to have sex with me. Out of nowhere, he was on top of me and he was trying to kiss me and take off my clothes." As I tried to replay it in my mind I couldn't believe it.

"I actually had to fight him. I had to push him off me. He wouldn't let me go. For a minute, I thought, 'he's too strong.' Then I thought again, 'hell no.' I'm not letting Kurtis overpower me. I've had enough of this bullshit."

"I knew there was something I didn't like about that guy. He was just g'on force you to do it out here in the living room, with us in the other room? Idiot."

Ray came back in the apartment.

"You alright?" He looked at me.

"Yeah. I'm ok."

"Look, I'm sorry about that nigga. He just ain't used to a whole lot of rejection."

I exhaled. "I'm going to bed."

"You sure you're alright?" Ray's face was sweet.

"I'm sure. Thanks Ray."

I got in bed with my clothes on and curled under the covers. I wasn't as unnerved as I thought I would be. I didn't just go along with him and give in. I was proud of myself for standing my ground. But one thing bothered me. He said, *'I know all about you.'* What did that mean? What did he think he knew about me that made it okay to just attack me? Still high, the room lit around me in the glow of my low lamp. I couldn't close my eyes. I reached into my nightstand and pulled out my shiny, silver, magic wand. I thought about Rasheed. But I wasn't in the mood for that kind of magic. I waved it in the air and thought of Derrick. I drew his face in the white ceiling. Tonight would be a good night for holding. I could use my magic wand and erase the hideous night. *Poof. All gone. He could appear and put his arms around me and lift the hair from my neck and kiss the nape. When I get up to go to the bathroom, he could grab for my arm and ask me not to go.*

"God, nobody could hold me like that man." I said out loud to no one.

I sat up and remembered Gregory lived in our complex. Gregory was a tech student and was so quiet and shy. He always wore thick, silver bracelets and heavy leather belts. He kept his head low and never wavered from his course. He had style but never asserted himself. He

290

reminded me of that song "Nature Boy." I knew he had a crush on me. I could feel his eyes when I entered a room, but he never attempted to make a move.

It was a rainy night and I grabbed my umbrella on the way out of the door. When I got to his door, although it was midnight, I saw a soft light on in the front. I knocked. When he opened the door he just stared for a moment in shock. I could feel him eyeing my wet, white tank and tanned legs.

"Uh.. Hey... uh Billie?"

"Hi Greg. Can I come in?"

"Of course. Sure, yes, yes. Come in." He hurried, opened the door and watched me come in. His apartment was cool. It was a studio with all things concerning living in one space. The bed anchored the middle of the living room and a small couch sat in the front near the window. A poster of Miles Davis playing his trumpet hung near his kitchen. And a jimbay held court beneath a pillar in the center near his bed. I knew then I was in the right place. The lights were dim and Coltrane was playing, "Naima."

"Hey. I'm sorry for bothering you so late. I just really needed someone to talk to." I started wandering around his apartment assessing his style as he stood frozen. I opened his cabinets and checked out his glasses. Plain, blunt, four-set round glasses. Clean, plain, white plates. A few mugs for tea. His shy eyes filled me with a sense of entitlement.

"That's perfectly alright. I'm glad you chose to come here to talk.... What made you come here?" He was still standing.

I sat down on his bed. "You're walking distance."

"Okay." His breath suspended.

I laughed. "And I consider you a friend."

"Well, I'm pleased to be a walking distance friend." The exhale led him to sit across from me on his sofa.

"I just had a fight with this guy and I don't want to be alone. Can I hang out here for a while?"

He blinked. "Yes. Yes. As long as you need. Just relax. Can I get you something to drink or some chips or a sweater or a blanket or anything you need?" I watched him try to relax and fail. Power crept into my consciousness.

"No. Just come sit with me."

"Okay." He got up and sat next to me with his hands in his lap.

"I'm just so tired of being hurt. I so tired of being hurt by men. What is it about me that says I'm some kind of target? I just don't understand."

"A target for what? What happened?" He was genuinely concerned and listened closely.

"Pain." I wasn't sure that was what I meant. I didn't know what men thought of me. Maybe I was just a fool.

"Let me play you something. Is that okay?" He waited for permission.

"Yes." He got up and went to his stereo. He clicked off his Coltrane and silence slipped in for a moment. Then I heard the first piano strokes of the melody of "Blue in Green." I knew it would only be a few more seconds until Miles's trumpet would be touching my ears. *Perfect.*

"Can you hold me?" And Miles was in my ear now.

"I can do that. I can definitely do that." He gently put his arm around me and I laid myself down on his bed. He wrapped his arms around me and held me tightly. He slowly moved one hand free and carefully began stroking my arms. He gently rubbed my back, my hair and my face. He stayed away from my holy trinity and gently pet everything else. I felt like a cat. He covered me with blankets and I drifted off to sleep. Every time I woke up in the night he was there petting me. He couldn't have slept all night. I could smell in my faint memory something clean and wooden.

And I slept beautifully.

43

I FOUND A NEW BAR to hang out in. I'd go there solo and listen to the music and order red wine. It was an odd Wednesday and I went there to collect my thoughts and journal. The MC strutted to the stage and announced the night's entertainment—spoken word artists. I closed my book and raised an eye to the stage. One by one poets came to the mic stand and behind them a drummer made beats to accompany their poems. At the end of the night I signed up to read at the next session.

When I got home it wasn't too late and Ray and Z were up watching the tail end of a movie. I waved and went to my room. There was still something nagging me when I was alone and I couldn't shake it. But I tried for peace and went to sleep. In the morning I heard the front door close and I assumed Z was on her way to work. I got up to have breakfast and found Ray in the living room finishing a bowl of cereal.

"Morning."

"Whassup girl?"

I got a bowl and accompanied him on the sofa.

"Ray, can I ask you a question?"

"Shoot kid."

"What did Kurtis mean when he told me 'I know all about you?' He said that when he jumped on me."

"He said that huh?"

"Yes, he said that. What does that mean? Are there rumors about me?"

"Well, look, I'll tell you. You got a rep. It's not a bad one 'though." He kept eating and smiled a little.

"Well, what is it then?"

"You got a good rep. Very good."

"Will you quit being evasive and tell me what the hell you're talking about."

"I'm saying the word is you know all about it. You take it there. It's not at all that you're easy to get or anything, or that anybody can have you with a word and wink, but that if a brother is lucky enough to get next to you…. you know how to handle it. You're like a grown ass woman in bed. That's why brothers be giving you the extra 'Hello,' 'How are you?' 'How you doing?' They trying hard to get next to you." I was completely stunned. I had no idea men talked like that. They were worse than women with gossip.

"Who is saying all that?"

"I'm not putting nobody out there, but men get in the barber shop and they talk. And yeah, you've come up. But don't worry… it's a good rep. Very good." He patted my leg and took his bowl to the kitchen.

295

DChristy Eves

"Alright Billie B. I'm out. Gotta head to the shop now. I'll see what else I can find out today. You're a heartbreaker." He laughed.

"Whatever. Get out. And take your tape off my dresser on your way out."

"Oh yeah, that's right. You enjoy it? Haaa Haa." He was still tickled at my surprise. "You a trip girl." He grabbed the video and headed out the door.

I sat with the image in my mind. This is all Vaughn's fault. I never knew anything about passion before him. But after him I craved it. He was my first hit of a drug I couldn't get over. The total separation of love from sex. His sex was a spirit he'd slipped me. Like being bitten by a vampire and turned into one. He was still inside me. That tattoo was inside me with his name on it. How long would it be there? Forever? Could I love? Could I be loved? Our last encounter was so unfinished...unfinished in everyway. Is that how I fell into Derrick?

The thoughts wore me and never let me go. I dragged them with me the following week to the poetry set. The poets each read with the drummer. It made me think of Gregory—his jimbay like a promise under the pillar. He may not have known it, but he would be getting a visit later that night.

One by one the host called us to the stage. When he introduced me he called me "The Beauty from Detroit." And his voice lowered for Detroit, as if it were some secret place that produced a special kind of honey only born of our grey streets and sky. I read and the drummer sent the rhythm out to the crowd. I was suddenly aware of the candied eyes that met me on stage. How many of them had heard that I was some

296

kind of wild child? Were they thinking it now? I felt again that mix of something private making its way to the public without my escorting it there. But there it was. Vaughn's bite for all the world to see.

After the set I drove straight to Greg's apartment. Maybe I could love him. That's something I could do. I could break the chain and love. I went there to his door. I saw the low light. I knocked soft. He opened the door and his eyes widened to see me standing there. The sensation of power hit me again.

Maybe I was doomed.

44

"HEY BILLIE, WHAT DO YOU WANT to do this year for you birthday?" Z asked.

"Birthdays are for children." I said flatly.

I was focused. The school year started and I knew this would be my last year. I knew that if there was a tomorrow beyond this place of trees and heat, I was getting ready to stubble upon it. My first order of business was the fall semester auditions. Dr. Champion was directing *Pretty Fire*, a one woman show broken into five vignettes. It was a huge part. And I wanted it badly. It was my last chance to take on a lead role and really grow as an actress.

On the day of rehearsal, I dressed myself without Cat's coaching. When my heels clicked up the aisle on the calling of my name I didn't buckle. I found the stage and hit center without looking. When I finished I felt the smile and nod of the queen. She could see I worked hard. And it was hard work that meant the most. It was work that had the yield. Life, love, magic—it was all chance. Work was the only thing you could control.

A week later I made my way to Tucker Hall to check the board. And there it was. I got the role and I would be performing the title vignette, "Pretty Fire." I had spent the rest of the summer resisting the urge to dominate Gregory. I knew I could love if I tried. We spent nights together. We touched. We never went all the way. But love was nowhere to be found. But work, reliable work, here was the yield—the title role. *What a waste of time love is*, I thought.

Rasheed was in class with me and so was Luke. Everybody made their way back from summer and we were all here in the soup of September. Luke held his hello hug a second or two longer than necessary. But I wasn't biting. Rasheed of course noticed.

"What's up with ya boy?" He asked at the end of class.

"Why are you always in my business?"

"Because I'm your conscious."

"If you're my conscious I'm in trouble."

"You aren't in trouble, you are trouble. I see you." He laughed.

"I'm not messing with him. Okay. I've moved on."

"Got another target in mind?"

"What target? Can't I just date, do my work and graduate like normal people? Why do I have to have a target? That's predatory." I argued.

"You're a predator now. Don't fight nature."

DChristy Eves

"Who's on *your* target list? All in my damn business."

"These girls ain't ready for me. Theatre girls. I've got girls that give me what I need."

"What's wrong with 'Theatre girls'?"

"Don't worry I don't mean you, you're something else."

"Can we get off the subject of me please?"

"Fine, I don't want to upset you. You might bite me or something; I know how you wild animals are." He laughed again. "I just mean these girls already think I'm up to something. You're the only one who really talks to me here. I don't know what I did to these folks."

"Nothing. I think you're just too honest for most people. Too open. People love a good show. Plus, you really see people. I think that's the worst part. People don't like to be seen." I said.

"Why don't I bother you?"

"I like seeing up front what I'm getting. I've had enough of dark hidden corners."

Rasheed put his arm around my neck and hooked it. He gave the top of my head a kiss and pushed me back. "That's my girl."

"Please, don't say that." I laughed.

That night, tucked back in my bed, I dreamed of a large cat slinking from the trees in my backyard back home. Instead of one lone tree that my mom kept circled with flowers, there was a forest. Out of it came the large, yellow, lion with no mane. She made her way towards me and I knew she could outrun me, but I made my way to the back door anyway. I ran. She flew. I got the door open, but couldn't close it

300

behind me. She'd stuck in her claw and ripped at my skin. I saw my mother behind me in the kitchen making dinner and I asked her why she never told me there was a lion in the yard. She shook her head and hid her eyes and continued cooking.

When I woke up I was alone in my bed and somehow unnerved. I tossed for awhile trying to get comfortable then I remembered my magic wand. There was silence in the room and when I turned it on, the buzzing bothered me and I smothered it under the covers and smooshed pillows over it. When the buzzing was so faint I couldn't hear it, I relaxed. I took a deep breath and let the magic take me away.

45

TECH WEEK IS ALWAYS AN EMOTIONAL and unemotional week. It's emotional giving away the show that had felt private and sacred to a new crew of people that hadn't been there since the beginning; unemotional to find your mark on the stage only uttering the endings of each bit to mark your blocking for the designers. But as the week went on emotion won the tug of war and I was feeling the pressure of a huge role on my hands and the absence of family to witness the feat. My mother would not be making it down to see me. She said they simply didn't have the money for her to fly down. I didn't push. I didn't want to add to their burdens, but I was hurt. She couldn't find a way to see my final show and my biggest role.

Opening night arrived the next week, my stomach filled with butterflies. On my way out of the door my phone rang and I saw that it was my mother. I stood for a moment listening to the rings. I wanted to answer but I didn't want her to hear the disappointment that lodged in my throat.. He didn't want her to come, I was sure of if. He probably convinced her that they couldn't afford it. They both worked full time and had well-paying jobs, but they couldn't scrape $200 or so for a plane ticket to see me? He didn't want her to leave. He wanted her at arms length. Choking distance. I didn't want to be mad, but I was frozen in place until the ringing stopped. When it was over I left for the theatre and a cool, October breeze was at my back.

The house was packed. Every seat was filled with a humming presence that shifted in its seat and flipped open its program. My butterflies turned to monkeys and they were jumping in my stomach. My hands were turning a weird, greenish color. Thank God my vignette was third. And thank God all my girls were there. Cat was back from California. She and Z had front row seats.

You could feel the show's momentum. In the wings my feet had air underneath them; I was floating. On my cue I went out in blackness and the black boards were underneath me. On stage I could feel the ground. When the lights went up, the presence in the seats went with me. We were all transformed. It was magic. But the best kind—the kind I'd worked to make appear.

46

PRETTY FIRE ENDED and we struck the set. The black boards were back. The holiday season was different. I was different. The family was different. They weren't asking 'how's college?' anymore. They were asking, "So what's next Billie?" I'd never thought of it. What was next for me? I didn't know. The question was like that lion in the yard. It slunk down from the trees unseen, but it was somehow always there. It had claws and was now very real. And although I had to have known she was coming, I had no clue how to fight her. So with no real answer I feigned cool disinterest and said,

"Whatever's next is next."

"Well, you just come on back home when you're done. We can figure it out later. 'Lotta college kids come down to the factory and make pretty good money managing. Even some women." Dad was resigned to my womanhood and soothed by my outstanding performance as a student. I spent the break sojourning with my family and not smoking weed, drinking or finding random guys to stay out all night with. I felt good. I felt like his girl again. We stayed up late talking about life. He offered his views on the world and we watched nature shows that my mother hated

"I can't believe you like that kinda show Billie. You are just like your father." Mom said wrinkling her nose and heading to the kitchen.

"Yeah, nature is interesting. It's life." I touted back.

"That's what I'm always telling mommy. You got to look at life as it is. Real life, not Disneyland."

"I like my fantasy movies with nothing serious." Mom yelled from the kitchen.

"I agree with you Dad. Real life is endlessly interesting. People, animals, life. I'm not sure about the Chrysler thing 'though dad. I don't know. I can't see myself up there. But I'll figure something out. Oh, look at the babies, they're so small." I was pointing at the screen watching a mother bear hide her young.

"Well, I'm not supporting any wild fantasies of yours when you graduate. You better figure that out, how you g'on support yourself. I'm trying to help you." Dad said.

"Well, I'm trying to help myself. I want to find my own way."

"Listen Billie, I didn't get this old and this ugly not to know anything. You think you know everything. Been to college, read some books, now you know every damn thing. What you don't know will fill a library. There are things out there in this world that will eat you alive if you ain't ready. You ready? You think you know how to survive? Talk about life. *This* is life. And life will tear your ass apart if you ain't ready. You don't think I had plans? I had plans. I had a lot of plans to be happy and all that bullshit. Then life woke my ass up and told me 'Go to work Otis.' You got this opportunity in front of you, to make something solid underneath you.

"I was in college. It was my second year and your mother was about eight months pregnant and Dexter was two. Out of nowhere, she started bleeding. They put her in the hospital; kept her up there six weeks. Then one day I get a call they rushing her for an emergency c-section. Our baby girl. She only lived nine hours and then she was gone. She died right there in my hands." He held out his creased and wrinkled hands. They were large, leathery and hard like baseball mitts. I could almost see a baby fitting inside them the way he held his fingers to cup.

"I had to take care of your mother and Dexter. I didn't even have time to cry. Mommy was devastated; she had to quit working for awhile. I did what I knew how to do. I went to work. I told my professor, I say, 'Man, I gotta take care of my family. I can't do this now.' He told me to go on and leave, but make sure to come back. But that was it. I never made it back. Chris and Jay came next and then you. You look just like her when you were born. Just like her.

"I want you to be happy, don't think I don't. I wanna see you smile and be happy and one day make a family and get me some grandkids. But you gotta think. It's time to grow up. You ready?"

I couldn't carry the dreams my father laid down to raise us. I couldn't carry the dreams my sister could've had if she'd lived. I couldn't resign myself to give up on chance, happiness…my dreams. Just take any well-paying job to lay my hands on security. The creases in my dad's forehead reported a safe ending to his dreams deferred, but they were like a scroll that told the story of all he'd given up. They never left him, his dreams; they just hung above his brow and carved into his every expression.

47

BACK ON THE HILL in Tallahassee for the spring semester, Luke re-entered my radar. He'd come by the apartment to welcome me back from the holiday.

"How was your break?" He said coming inside. Z was in the living room with Ray, so I took Luke back to my room.

"It was good. Got to see the family, eat some good food. How about you?" I said.

"Good. It was really good. I love getting together with the family seeing how big my little brothers got. My mom made a huge meal. I know I ate too much. I indulged myself." He lay across my bed with the ease and comfort of a man who'd been it in before, although he hadn't.

"So, what made you drop by and see me?" I was curious and lay on my stomach next to him.

"Nothing. I was over here and I remembered you lived down here, so I thought I'd swing by and see you. It's been a while since we hung out."

"Yes, it has been. I've been pretty busy."

"I know. I wanted to leave you alone during *Pretty Fire*. Let you work. You did really good by the way. It was a great show." He smiled and I tried not to notice his soft scent.

"Thank you." I was suddenly nervous. "You want something to drink?"

"No I can't stay long. I've got a late class, I just wanted to stop by and say hey."

He stayed awhile longer and we talked. He had a way of listening to me that made me light up. *Listening…hmmm, feels like holding all night but better.* He gave me another hug. Too long. When he left I was suddenly pissed off. I couldn't figure out why it irked me. His tight hug and soft scent. His casualness. I lay back on my bed after he was gone and his cologne remained. By that night it still hung on to my pillow.

This dance went on. He'd come by, hang out in my room, leave his scent on my pillow—seeds in soil. He watered them each visit with his touch; he'd find a way to touch my arms or legs, gently. He smiled at me and his eyes still twinkled. He opened himself to me and told me things I knew other people didn't know about him. I relished in the privilege of knowing a man other women longed to know. The petals of my heart colored rich and deep and opened under the sunshine of his attention. But in public, his sun was behind the clouds. Nice short hellos with his voice lighter than his private tone. He was creeping back into my dreams with his scent periodically in my bed.

309

I tried to remain focused and make my escape plan. Since I knew that asking my folks what I should do was out, I thought of my own plan.

"I should move to New York. Get an apartment. Audition. Act. Live." I announced to myself in the mirror. Dr. Champion had pulled my coattail to an audition in New York for The University Resident Theatre Association, URTA. It was a huge audition for graduate schools with MFA programs in Acting. I wasn't sure about grad school, but it was on option and a ticket to New York—a soft landing. I signed up immediately.

Late one evening in early February, my phone rang with Luke on the other end. He wanted to know how I was doing and if he could stop by. I told him I was hungry and to bring food. He laughed and came over.

"I was serious, I'm hungry. You didn't bring me any food?" I said searching his empty hands at the door.

"No, I'm sorry, I thought you were joking. Come here, don't be mad." He pulled me to him and hugged me. He let me go and smiled. "I'm heading to a dinner party at one of my friend's house after this. You can go with me and there'll be food there."

I was a little surprised because all of his friends knew about his girlfriend. I thought they'd wonder who I was and why I was with him. I thought better of going, but I was hungry.

We got in his car and he drove us the short distance to the area where the party was. He didn't exactly know where the house was so we pulled up to the dark street and he looked around the car for his directions.

"I think I left them back at your house. We might have to go back. I don't know the address." As he spoke the moonlight crossed my mind.

"How come you never show off your chest? Let me see it." I smiled laughing a bit.

"No." He smiled back shyly.

"Come on, let me see."

"No…" He tried again.

I reached my hand across him and touched his chest.

"If I can't see it, I at least want to feel it." I reached my hand under his shirt and playfully felt his stomach. My hands were cold and he jumped and laughed. He reached across to me and put his hands on my chest, on my breasts. He looked surprised that I didn't move or smack his hand away.

"You're not going to stop me?" He asked.

"The question is… you're not going to stop me?" I said and lowered my hand into his pants.

The heat flooded the car and the little game of chicken that he'd played with other girls at church picnics had just met its match. He put his hands into my pants. I went into his underwear and undid his pants. He unzipped my pants and put his hands into my panties.

"Yes." I responded. I could feel the dissatisfaction in his kiss this time. Desire always wanted the next level. His foot slipped off the breaks and we started rolling down the street.

DChristy Eves

"We're moving." I warned. He remembered to break but would occasionally roll and stop. But he didn't take his hands off me to put the car in park. I was getting a little nervous we'd hit a parked car so I said,

"Let's go back to my house."

We drove down Appalachee Parkway locked in touch. When we got to my apartment and I led him up the stairs; I could sense the nerves surfacing. I knew he wasn't ready. I could feel the pause building up as we ascended the stairs. I could feel it mounting as we crossed to my room. I could feel it stack as I shut the door behind him. But.... you can only play with me for so long. I wanted him.

And then.... After making love to the man I'd dreamed about for over a year, I turned to face him he was standing on the other side of the bed pulling up his boxers and dressing to leave. Leaving. Leaving. I wanted him to spend the night. I wanted a moment that sex could not encompass. I wanted an absolution that I couldn't reach lying with him on an accidental night.

I realized that sex wasn't what I wanted at all. I wanted him, and now I was a regret. I could see it in his eyes from the back. He didn't face me. I thought of one of Ivory's lines from *Fear Itself*, "He came and went." I didn't rise as he left. I listened for the clicks as the door shut. I lay there twisting my hair in my finger tips and thinking. The scented emptiness from the other side of the bed was glaring back at me.

Mine were the kisses of a clandestine lover. I was the lover of other women's men. Other women were the safety belt I used to ensure that love would never crawl down that tree and slice into me. But there was no way to hide from it. It wasn't the animal that lurked in silent

312

prey-er. I couldn't conjure love when I tried and I couldn't avoid it when I hid. It was the grass underfoot of desire. Desire—the ceaseless, unrelenting juggernaut of hunger. I sat up and dropped my hands.

"Stop." I said to no one in particular.

He called later that night to ask it I was okay. I said I was fine. I had taken his virginity, but still somehow he managed to take something from me. The separation between love and sex snapped. He muddied the water and he left me with the mess.

48

PASSION IS IN THE STOMACH. It burrows a whole in the pit. But apparently love is in the mouth. I couldn't keep his name out of my mouth. Luke. Luke. Luke. Every time anyone asked me a question I found a way to say his name.

"What time is it Billie?"

"I'm not sure. I think Luke is wearing a watch."

"Billie, I'm trying to decide what to have for lunch. What do you think?"

"I don't know; I saw Luke with a ham sandwich. That looked good."

I couldn't stop myself. I was like a cup spilling over. Jocelyn and Angie, two of the theatre's angels, noticed my melancholy and set about uncovering the cause.

"You don't look right. What's wrong with you?" Angie sat next to me in the green room during a break from classes.

"I'm just...I don't know. I don't feel well." I tried to imagine myself as sick. Luke wasn't even calling to check on me anymore. Even the casual visits were through. I like dogs better, at least they always wanted a second, third, even twentieth time. *I am sick*, I thought.

"Well, you should go home and get some rest." Angie put her hand on my leg.

"Yeah, go home." Jocelyn was about as good at comfort as I was at relationships.

"Thank you for your great concern Jocelyn." I held my head in my hands.

"Hey Luke!" Angie smiled and shouted out. I lifted my eyes in time enough to see him pass by and wave. His eyes caught mine and there was a look in them I couldn't place. I stared to figure it out. I stared to soak up his presence. When he passed, I noticed Jocelyn staring at me.

"What was that?" Jocelyn asked.

"What was what?" I resettled myself in my seat.

"That look." Jocelyn persisted.

"What look?" Turns out actor training does not help in awkward life situations. I was transparent.

"Your look at Luke. What's up with you and Luke, I notice y'all was all buddy buddy before. Y'all not friends all of a sudden?" Jocelyn leaned in.

"We're friends. We just…" I got up to leave.

"Wait, wait, wait." Angie pulled my arm. "What's going on?"

"Nothing. We're just not friends now I guess. I guess I did something wrong." I was starting to cry. I hadn't meant to. The third grade had crept into the green room and accosted the woman I thought I was.

"C'mere." Angie and Jocelyn pulled me by my arms to the bathroom and gave me tissues. Angie continued. "Now, come on tell us what's wrong. I can see you're hurting. Talk to me. It's okay. We've all been there. You're brokenhearted, I can see that. What happened, you got a crush, told him or something and he's not interested."

"Not interested. Please. He was interested alright. He was interested until he finished." It flew out of my mouth faster than the thought that birthed it.

"Finished?" Jocelyn piped up. "Finished what?"

"Look, forget what I said. I gotta go." I tried to get out of the bathroom, they blocked me.

"Finished what…. You had sex with him??" Angie voice got low.

"I…I… a little."

"Oooh my God! Not Luke!" Angie threw her hands in the air and called the lord. "Lord Jesus."
I hadn't meant to get Jesus involved.

"No you didn't." Jocelyn was still staring. "Goddamn light-skinned girls."

"Listen, this is private. Please forget I told you all this. Please, let's just let this all go. Forget about it." And I found myself saying something that I'd heard many times but never uttered myself. "Please don't tell anyone."

They both nodded in unison, "We won't tell."

It was a nod I knew would result in the immediate broadcast of my affair with Luke. But in the meantime, Angie gave me a hug and patted my back.

It didn't take long before the news reached Luke. It wasn't hard to figure out the look he shot me after that. It was a look that read both disappointed and done. At least it was over. I managed to keep Vaughn a secret for four years. I couldn't keep Luke a secret for four days.

49

MY TWO WEEKS IN NEW YORK for the URTA auditions sang by like the sound of Coltrane's "Afro Blue." Movement and energy. I realized that you could nail an audition for something you didn't want. I didn't really want my future. I couldn't see it. I felt like I was resisting a fall but riding in a barrel headed straight for Niagara.

When I made it back to Florida the sun was out and it was a beautiful March morning. Z was fixing breakfast in the kitchen and lumping butter and sugar into her oatmeal.

"Hey." She looked up and said.

"Hey."

"How was it?"

"I killed it. There's already several schools interested in me. I got so many call backs I had to take a separate cab back to the flat than the other girls. They were done hours before me." I gave her a bump and laughed. But my heaviness wouldn't let the brag ring true. It was true although, I had never been so successful at anything I'd attempted before. It was confusing.

"That's great! I'm so proud of you." Z's voice lifted.

"Really. Proud? Why?" I said making a cup of tea.

"Well, you need something. You're always searching for something. You're never quite satisfied. I've been thinking you need to figure out why you're so unsettled, but maybe this is the thing you need. You found your place in the world and you should pursue it."

"My place… I don't know what that is anymore. I feel like I don't know what I've been doing here other than escaping Detroit and my family and trying to grow up. I was thinking I never want to be in school again. I'm tired. I'm tired of all this drama. I just want to breathe."

"Are you tired of school or drama? There's a difference." Z explained.

"I don't know. School some place else won't be like it is here. Grad school will be all White. What kind of theatre do White people do? Everybody's been warning me to be careful in front of all those White folks. Careful has never been my strong suit. Now that I'm in theatre, I love the classes. I'm doing well and I feel like I fit. I've never fit anywhere else in my life. I was always kind of forcing it. How can I fit some place else…I'll be the only Black girl if I go to grad school. Hell, I'm from Detroit and I've spent the last five years at a Black College. What do I know about the mainstream?" I took a deep breath.

"No place on earth will be like FAM. Once we leave here, this will be over. There won't be any place like a Black college campus. We've been in a bubble. And it's about to burst for us." Z sank back in her chair. Something new entered the room on her words. For a moment

everything felt thin and ephemeral. I could feel it disappearing as we
spoke.

"I can't believe this is it. We'll all be scattered to the wind in a
month." I stared out of the window and watched three little girls playing
across the parking lot with their Barbie's. "Z, I need to ask you
something." I didn't turn from the window.

"Okay. This sounds serious."

"Why didn't you say something?" I still couldn't look back at
her. "Why didn't you do something that day over on Van Buren?"

"With Derrick and his friends?"

"Yes."

"I don't know. I didn't want to see any more, so I just left."

"But you didn't say anything to the guys. You didn't tell them to
leave. Not to watch. Why? Why didn't you stop them for me?" I
started to turn and look, but my body wasn't following the impetus.
Only my heart looked back.

"I don't know. I don't know why. I guess I thought you knew
they were…"

"You didn't think that. You knew I didn't know."

"Billie….."

"You let them do it. They're guys. They were just doing what
guys do, but you're supposed to be my girl. My best friend. You wanted
them to see me. You wanted me to be embarrassed. You thought that's
what I deserved. I've been over it and over it in my mind. You left me
there with the wolves. I guess I never said anything because in my mind
I thought I deserved it too. I thought that's what I get for bowing down

to Derrick over and over. That's what I get for being a slut. But you know what? I'm not a slut. Men go around and fuck who they want and nobody questions their self esteem. 'Oh, Derrick must have really low self esteem because he wants to fuck all those girls.' No, they just pat them on the back and say 'boys will be boys.' But if you're a girl, and you are sexual, everybody wants to know what's wrong with you.

"I have no intentions of sitting here waiting for some illusion of a Mr. Right. And, you know what else; I can never be my mother. I don't want to spend my life listening to a man belittle me and control me until there's barely a trace left of my real self. " My hands were shaking and sweat began to drip down my sides along my rib cage. The room regained something solid in the air. I looked over at Z and she stared back and me. Her eyes searched her mind and she began to cry too.

"You cry, I cry." She said and let her tears fall without wiping them. "You won't be like your mother. You could never be. We think of sex totally different. It's like power or something for you. For me it's different. Our mothers taught us to save it and how special it is. I need to make sure a guy deserves me before I give in. I can't let some guy just get away with it and leave me holding the bag. It's not that I'm ashamed; I just need it to be about love. You don't need love or something I guess." Z said.

"I need it. But I don't expect it from them. I expected it from you... from the girls. I just wanted the guys to respect me for wanting the same thing they wanted. Not punish me because they didn't have to trick me out of it." I told Z and exhaled.

"Billie, I'm sorry. I don't know why. I just don't know why."
She sighed. "I wasn't trying to hurt you." When Z put her arms around
me I collapsed on her shoulder and realized I didn't even care why
anymore. It didn't matter. We were both someplace different than that
day. Derrick wasn't even important anymore. He was just a sugar
substitute for Vaughn. And maybe even Vaughn didn't matter anymore.
The book was closing on that dark night. I could already smell the
morning.

"Z," I pulled up my head and wiped my nose on my shirt. "I
need a good drink and long laugh."

"I know, me too." Z breathed and sat back at the dinning room
table. "Well, there's Sean's party this weekend. That should be a good
way to end the year. He hired a DJ and he's setting up a bar. He's got
that big house him and his frat brothers rented. It should be fun." Z
smiled.

"Yeah. I can't wait. It should be fun. The last hoorah."

The weeks went by with the preparations for graduation
underway. My parents were coming, both of them. Dad hadn't been
down since they dropped me off at the dorms. I felt like I was walking
on the dry bottom of the newly parted Red Sea; everything that kept me
afloat had risen on either side of me and was being held up by an unseen
force. When I left this place, the water would splash back down behind
me and fill up the sea for the new crop of crossers. With the hanging
weight of the last goodbyes and the drag of an unknown future I headed
down Tennessee Street. I pulled up in front of Karma Tattoo and peaked

my head in the front door. I looked around for familiar faces. I saw a
few young girls thumbing through the photo albums. I was hoping Razz
still worked there. Then I smelled the scent of cigarettes and patchouli
faintly enter the room ahead of him. I smiled.

"Razz."

"Hey you. I remember you. Billie Simone, right?"

"Yeah. Good memory." I said smiling.

"I always remember custom tatts. How are you? You need me
again, getting some new work?" He leaned forward on the glass counter
top.

"Yup. I know what I want."

"I know you do. Come on back."

Razz led me to the back and we went to his chair. I told him
about those rows and rows of dead vines on crosses. I wanted to flip the
image of death and get an ankh with a single vine that wrapped around
my arm.

"It's the process of life. Growing and changing. I get it." Razz
said sketching.

"No color this time. Black." I explained.

He drew the image on my arm and then I held my breath as he
turned on the needle. The buzzing was a warning—all good things came
with pain. The tiny leaves burned when he went under my arm to
complete the band.

"A lot of people get armbands and go halfway around. They lift
their arms and you can see they chickened out. They can't take the pain
underneath. You're a soldier girl." Razz said comforting me as he

323

tattooed the soft, white, flesh under my arm. I let go and figured I may as well breathe; holding it in didn't make it hurt less. It didn't take long and I was newly scared. I told Razz that was it. I wouldn't be back, who knew when the next time I'd be in Tallahassee. He said,

"Well, you'll always have us in your heart and on your skin."

The party at Sean's finally came and the girls piled into my car and we headed out. Z, Cat and I sat excited about seeing everybody and closing out the year. We pulled onto the street and made our way to the house. It was a wet night in late March. The street was black and shining. The trees hung close the ground and the moist air made them glow in the street lights. I could hear the hum of Usher singing "Nice and Slow" when we got close to the house. The front door opened and a few girls came out and the sound increased and mixed with soft laughter. We stepped in their place in the door and went inside. We poured ourselves in the mix and found a place among the crowd.

Sitting on the arm of the sofa talking to a guy about poetry and how important it was to me, I had to stop mid-sentence. I looked across the room and saw the back of his neck through the crowd like the pupil of an eye. When the eye opened I saw more of him..... that stance. It was him. I got up and made my way to the kitchen where he stood. As I got closer I could hear his voice. It cut the air with sharp tones that indiscriminately cut the other sounds around him. I could smell that scent of something clean and wooden when I approached. My blood quickened and heat sent tingles through my face. I stood in front of him and watched him sip his drink and talk to his boys. He looked up and his eyes first assessed me like fresh meat, then remembered me like sweet meat. He smiled.

"C'mere Simone." I was in his arms and like glass shattering behind me I could feel everything else crashing. My heart beat. I could feel his skin on mine and, his body against mine.

"What are you doing here?" I said and pulled back to see his face..

"In town visiting. Hanging out. What's up with you?" He was inviting me. His tone went low.

"Just here with my girls." Just then Cat came into the kitchen and interrupted.

"Let me have your keys. I think I left my camera in the car. I want to take some pictures." I felt a nervous rush about her seeing Vaughn and Vaughn seeing her.

"Here." I fished my keys and passed them to her and she headed off.

"You look good." He ignored her completely and his eyes never left me. His focus charged the air; his not noticing Cat did as much as his noticing me. *We could slip out of here right now. We could just get my keys back and head out of here right now. We could just leave this place and find another place to exist for a moment. We could disappear behind a cloud and make our way up to the sky.* My mind raced. My hand slipped down onto his forearm and I felt the butter smooth skin and I could smell him, so close to his body. Clean.

"Thanks." I stood still.

DChristy Eves

And there I was faced with myself. Faced with everything that had led me down a path that led to a string of loveless encounters and scars that stayed. There I was facing his beauty and scent and all of the passion that intoxicated me and drew me like rain to the ground. He was tracing my body with his mind and specific moments played in his eyes. Their replay was as clear to me as if he'd set up a screening room in those dark eyes. He knew I wanted him too. *I could just lean in now and whisper in his ear, 'Don't you want to get out of here?' I wouldn't even have to speak, I could just let my eyes stay on his a second longer.* Then, something else surfaced. Just up from underneath, something else surfaced. I let my eyes drop. I felt myself turning to leave.

"It was good to see you." I heard myself say it. And I walked away. I put a switch in my sway and I walked away.

He watched me go.

CPSIA information can be obtained at www.ICGtesting.com
Printed in the USA
239952LV00001B/40/P